The Graveyard Shift

24/7 Demon Mart Book 1

by D.M. Guay

ISBN: 9781696398220

Cover by James at Goonwrite.com

This book is a work of fiction. Any similarity between the characters and situations within its pages and real places or persons, living or dead, is unintentional and coincidental.

Dear Nerd, Ray and Sid,
You better tell me this book is hilarious, or I will disown you.

CONTENTS

24/7 DEMON MART: THE GRAVEYARD SHIFT
A LOVECRAFTIAN HORROR COMEDY

I'll let you in on a little secret. When the gate to hell has been kicked wide open behind you, and you're suddenly fighting for your life, elbow-deep in the slimy lime-green gut of a one-eyed, bloodthirsty hell beast, you can't help but stop and ask yourself some questions. Like, how did I get here? Or, how did my life slide so far off the rails? And, how the hell did I get this job in the first place? Who was dumb enough to think I was qualified to battle a horde of monsters and stave off the apocalypse?

Oh, that's right. I remember now. Student loan debt. And, of course, the devil.

CHAPTER 1

Frozen sludge swirled around and around in the dispensers. Safety-cone orange. Neon lime green. Solo-cup red. No one loved slushies more than me, and they all looked so damned delicious.

The 24/7 Dairy Mart had one hundred thirty-seven flavors, more than any other convenience store. That's the only reason I regularly pedaled my busted-up Huffy the two miles from my postcard-perfect neighborhood to this sketchy, forgotten dirt bag corner of the suburbs.

The blinking neon mud-flap girl on the sign above Sinbad's Gentleman's Club and the creepy statues in the window of the Jesus Saves Discount Religious Supply store were enough to keep most respectable people away. This street was so seedy it couldn't even land a Starbucks. But as I stared down the sixty-foot row of slushy flavors, I was thankful for the ugly, forlorn parts of Columbus, Ohio, because that's where all the good stuff was.

Shoot. I better pick a flavor and fast. It was midnight already. I had to be online in thirty minutes, cutting up demons in Diablo 3 with my best friend, Big Dan. Tonight was my night. I was gonna beat that level

70 Nephalem Rift in under ten minutes this time. I could feel it. Those monsters better be quaking in their socks, because they were about to face the one and only Lloyd Wallace, aka AwesomeDemonButtKicker98.

I glanced at the smoking-hot chick guarding the door of the beer cave. And, okay, I admit it. I lied. The slushies weren't the *only* reason I came here. Her name was DeeDee. She worked the graveyard shift, ten at night until six in the morning, five nights a week. Yeah, I may have ridden my bike by here a few times just to figure out her schedule, but I'm totally not a stalker. I mean, I don't think I am. Anyway, if you were me you'd do it, too.

DeeDee was a dead ringer for Marilyn Monroe, if Marilyn's hair were dyed Manic Panic Shocking Blue and her slinky white dress were swapped out for black tights, combat boots, and a sterling-silver septum piercing with a diamond bead. DeeDee's skin was flawless and her curves stretched the seams of her cut-up Cure T-shirt so tight Robert Smith was blushing. Her lips were painted that dark burgundy red that looked like dried blood, and her black liquid eyeliner curled up to a sharp, deadly point at the edges of her brown eyes. Or blue eyes. Maybe they were green? It's not like I ever got to see them. DeeDee had never looked at me directly. Or at all, really. One day that would change. She was my soulmate. She just didn't know it yet.

I stared at her a good long minute, too long, imagining what it would be like to run my hands over Robert Smith's hair...uh, on the shirt, not on the real Robert Smith. I bet that would be pretty scratchy, not soft and curvy and... *Oh, boy...* Nope. My downstairs started to tingle if you get my drift. *Cut it out. Focus, Lloyd. slushies. Only twenty minutes until it's time to kick monster butt.*

I grabbed a Colossal Super Slurp cup—the one that's basically the size of a vertical punch bowl—and decided to get wild and crazy and blind random pick tonight's flavor. I closed my eyes and ran my fingers across the front of the machines. *Eeny meeny miny. This one.* I opened my eyes. *Yuck!* A big cockroach sat on the Perdition Peach nozzle, and the damned thing looked like it was staring right at me, peering into my soul. *Wait. Is it wearing a name tag?* I squinted. A tiny rectangle of white was stuck to its belly. I swore it said, "Hello, my name is Kevin."

Dude. Mom's right. I need to leave the basement more often, get some sunshine. My eyesight is going. The roach's antennae flipped back like cat ears as it looked me up and down. *Gross.* I flicked it to the floor. I swear it flipped me off before wriggling under the cabinet. *Blech. I can't stand bugs. They're so gross.* Now, where was I? Oh yes. slushy time! Not the peach though, because, ew, roach.

The Inferno flavor was right next to it. I'd never tried that one before. I stuck my cup under the spout and pulled the lever. A river of blazing orange blurped into my cup, sloshing and expanding until it erupted through the hole in the plastic dome lid like an angry volcano. Yeah. I knew I should stop pouring once it got to the part where the cup met the lid, but I never did. If I was gonna shell out $1.09 with tax, I had to get every penny's worth. I wasn't exactly rolling in dough.

I dunked the straw in and licked the slush off the outside of the cup before any of it could drip onto the floor. *Wowza.* Inferno, huh? It tasted like campfire smoke and brown bananas, in a weird but oddly satisfying way. It'd pair well with the pizza rolls Mom's got stashed in the freezer. Big Dan, Diablo 3, slushies and pizza rolls. The perfect Saturday all-nighter. I better step to it. Those demons weren't gonna slay themselves.

I fished all the lint and coins out of my pocket and stepped toward the register. Then I stopped cold. *Shit.* There was more lint in my hand than coins. I counted. One quarter. Nine pennies. Four nickels. Three dimes. One of them Canadian? *Double shit.* Eighty-four cents, only seventy-four American. I swore I had dug exactly a buck nine out from under the couch cushions before I rode over here. *Wait.* I'd heard a clink when I hit that monster pothole outside the Cash4Gold around the corner. My quarter must have flown out of my pocket.

Great. What do I do now? I couldn't put the slushy back in the machine, so I either had to pay for it or steal it. Or...go halfsies? I looked around. No one was near the register. DeeDee didn't notice me, just sat on the stool outside of the beer cave picking at her black fingernails, bored. I quick-scanned the store for Comb-over Carl, the middle-aged dude with the three hairs gelled over his bald spot. He usually worked the weekend graveyard shift with DeeDee. Hot dogs flopped lazily on the rollers. Pizza hardened in the warmer. The anemic fluorescent strip lights flickered, reflecting in the high-shine polish of the linoleum floor. No sign of Carl. Or anyone at all. The place never seemed to have any customers. I was always the only one.

All right. Decision made. I'd put my change on the counter and casually walk out the door. It wouldn't technically be stealing. I'd be paying for *most* of my drink. Then again, what kind of broke ass, can't-do-math loser would DeeDee think I was if I left eighty-four cents on the counter and skipped out? I'd have a better shot with her if I stole it. At least then I could deny deny deny if she ever asked.

I had no choice but to slurp and dash. I casually strutted toward the exit, clutching the Colossal Super Slurp to my chest.

"What the hell do you think you're doing, asshole?" DeeDee yelled. I heard a thud, like something heavy hit the floor.

Aw, man. Why did *she* have to catch me? Why couldn't it be Comb-over Carl? My heart thumped so hard it rattled my ribs as I turned to face the consequences. *Great. Just great.* I was going down for shoplifting to the tune of a dollar nine. I always imagined if I landed in jail, it'd be for something spectacular, like stealing a cop car, high on bath salts, wearing only the top half of a furry Panda costume, but with no underpants, like totally Porky Pigging it down there. Something memorable. But no. I was going down because I lost a quarter in a damn pothole. My tax dollars hard at work. Remind me to write a strongly worded letter to City Council after Mom made bail.

"Help me, stupid!" DeeDee grunted.

"What?" I turned around.

DeeDee was rummaging through a cabinet in the wall. Carl was on his knees in front of the beer cave with his eyes closed and fingers intertwined, praying. Huh. It took me a hot minute to realize DeeDee was yelling at Carl, not me. And she was acting really weird. Like *really really* weird. DeeDee began karate-kicking like a lady Bruce Lee, but her fists chopped at nothing and she round-housed thin air. Carl's face had gone white. He was drenched in sweat, screaming, "Oh Jesus, help me! Gaaaaahhhh!" and trying hard to keep the beer cave door closed. The door kept bucking open, like something was pushing on it hard, trying to get out. Except there was nothing there.

Okay, then. So, they're both either batshit crazy, or the door to the beer cave needed serious repairs. Either way, I could make a clean getaway. I swiveled to leave and made it two steps from the exit—*home free, suckas!*—when something hit me hard from behind, clipping my shoulder and knocking my precious Colossal Super Slurp right out of my hands. I swear time slowed down as I screamed "Nooooooo!" and watched my slushy hit the floor, bounce twice, then super blurp across the linoleum. As my Inferno formed an icy puddle on the floor, my dream of a perfect Saturday shattered. Mom's pizza rolls weren't gonna be the same without it.

But I didn't have time to cry, because my feet went total Fred Flintstone, slipping and sliding on the sugary goo. So did Comb-over Carl's. He clearly was the guy who'd hit me. We both fell. Carl landed on top of me and we were spinning in the melting syrupy slush, trying and failing to stand up and get away from each other. Then his feet kicked, and his shoe landed right in my nuts. I screamed. An unholy one, because you know, direct shot to the nuts.

"Sorry, man," Carl said, as he used the leverage he got from planting his foot in my junk to shoot straight up to the door.

His name tag spun on the floor, making slushy angels in my spilled Inferno. I picked it up and called after him. "Hey. You dropped your name tag."

He looked back at me. He was halfway out the door and his eyes were giant half-moons. He seemed totally spooked. "I quit. This place is cursed. See?" He pointed at something behind me, then pushed the door open so hard he knocked over my Huffy. One of the brake levers broke off and rolled away. *Aw, man. My bike!* Well, in his defense, the lever was duct-taped on.

Carl sprinted across the parking lot and disappeared into the inky black night. I'd never seen an old dude run so fast. I heard a *crack, crack, slurp* noise behind me, so I turned around to see what it was.

What. The. Fuck. Is. THAT!

Three spiky green tentacles, fat as tree trunks, dripping with slime, with thick barbs sticking out of the ends, hung out of the beer cave door, slapping at DeeDee, who jumped and dodged, narrowly missing each one. The tentacles thwapped the floor, crunching holes in the linoleum, slithering after DeeDee as if their sole purpose was to pound her into oblivion.

"God damn it," she cursed, dodging another slimy thwack, then shot what looked like a taser through the door into whatever was attached to those unholy appendages. The taser zurp zurped. The tentacles undulated. "Dude. You aren't getting through here. How many times do I have to tell you? No means no! Don't be gate rapey."

Whatever DeeDee had done didn't stop the slime fest for long. I nearly pissed my pants when the door opened and a single giant yellow...*what the hell is that? Oh shit. It's an eyeball!* emerged. *No. Way.* The tentacles had a face. *A face?* Well, no mouth, but an eye. That counted.

I sat, paralyzed on the outside, wet butt stuck to the floor by melting Inferno sugar glue, but absolutely losing my shit panicking on the inside. A sizzling *szzzzz szzzzz* sound snapped me out of it. *Ow! Ow! Ow!* I looked down. Carl's name tag was burning my fingers like they were raw burgers on a grill. Wisps of me-flavored smoke rose into the air, and I hot potatoed it back and forth between my hands, too dumb at the moment to just drop the damned thing. *What the fuck, Hello My Name is Carl!*

"Don't just sit there. Help me!" DeeDee's voice was strained. I looked up. She was talking *to* me and looking right at me, for the first time ever. WIN!

Except, the thing with tentacles had gotten her. She was all wrapped up. The tentacles squeezed her, and eyeball dude seemed happy, like a discarded pet python that had just caught its first meal in the Everglades. I stared at her. *Jesus.* Even with her veins popping out from struggling to breathe, she was so smoking hot. *I love you, DeeDee! Wait. I should help her. Yes. Nothing says "I love you" like a good saving.*

5

Now was my moment. "Hey, ugly. Let her go!"

The thing's one giant yellow eye focused in on me, and even though I couldn't see an eyebrow, I swear it furrowed because now it looked extra mad. *Great.*

Naturally, I panicked. Then I did something that was probably stupid but was the only thing I could think to do at the time. I threw Carl's smoldering name tag straight at its one giant eye like it was a ninja throwing star. I mean, I Chuck Norrised the hell out of that thing. The hard edge of plastic landed right in the middle of that one awful mean yellow eyeball, and it burned it (Him? Her? I wasn't looking under a tentacle to find out.) like it burned me. The creature hissed and screeched like an alien in a 1950s sci-fi movie. It let go of DeeDee, and it flailed around, knocking chips off racks and two-liter sodas off their pyramids. Tentacles thwapped. Tostitos and Fritos rained down like confetti.

DeeDee tucked and rolled and the thing trained its oozing, injured eyeball on me. The tentacles, slimy and oh so so so disgusting, slithered and snaked toward me. Then, it got worse. The rest of the thing emerged from the beer cave, breaking the door clean off the hinges. Oh, so many more tentacles.

Woah boy. I'm screwed. My stomach clenched and my mouth watered. Hot barf lapped at my tonsils. *Nope. No way. No barfing in front of DeeDee.* I swallowed that bile right on down as I watched the thing slide past a chest-high stack of Natural Light cases. It was a halo of lime-Jello green tentacles around that single yellow eye. The eye had a single red pupil, long not round, like a cat. And I was pretty sure it was mad. Like super mad. Yellow goop oozed over the "Carl" on the name tag still lodged in its eye. I'd injured it, and the thing was crawl-thrashing right at me, hellbent on revenge.

Okay. Okay. If it bleeds, I can kill it, right? I grabbed the closest thing to me and prepared to fight. Sadly, the closest thing was the long red slushy straw with the scoop spoon at one end. I gripped it like a knife. *Welp. This is it. I'm dead. Dear Baby Jesus, heat up the oven. I'm having pizza rolls in heaven tonight.*

Tentacle dude pulled himself closer to me, the barbs of his appendages punching holes in the linoleum, the tentacles slapping the edges of my melted puddle of Inferno. Just when the tip of the first slimy tentacle tusk lifted up, ready to spear me, a flash of blue arced through the air. Blue. Blue hair.

DeeDee jumped on its...*back?* It was hard to tell what bit because, you know, halo of tentacles. DeeDee lifted her arms and thrust a flaming sword right into the middle of its creepy red pupil. And when I say flaming sword, I literally mean a sword that was on FIRE. The creature popped like a pus-filled balloon. Gelatinous green chunks and putrid yellow sludge sprayed the floors and walls. And me. *Oh, Jesus. It smells like hot boiled garbage.* So naturally, I immediately projectile barfed right into that puddle of Inferno and guts.

CHAPTER 2

It was a quick barf, but bright orange because I had Cheetos for dinner. Hey. Don't judge me. Like you never have?

Anyway, I made the mistake of looking down at myself. I was soaked head-to-toe in upchuck, monster guts and slushy. Carl's name tag had somehow dislodged from that creature's eyes and landed in my lap. There was a piece of tentacle stuck in my shoelace. *Oh Jesus. Oh Jesus. Oh Jesus.*

I panicked and shook my shoe fast then faster trying to get the bit out without actually touching it. Finally, the chunk flipped off, skidding through the melting Inferno. Then I realized even my underpants were soaked through with this unholy soup. Talk about an epic case of swamp ass. All in front of the hottest girl in the Columbus, Ohio, metropolitan statistical area.

"I thought he was just really desperate, but he...curbed!" DeeDee sounded surprised or unsure, or maybe both.

I couldn't tell, because I was still assessing my underpants situation when she said it. *Holy shit. She just talked to me! I'm in! Wait. What does she mean "really desperate?"*

A teeny-tiny voice squeaked, "Isn't it obvious, kid?"

Wha? The slushy roach was next to me, waist-deep in guts. It eyeballed me, shook its head, then started...mopping? It stood with two of its six feet in the muck, using its other four arms to push around an impossibly tiny mop. I rubbed my eyes, deep and hard. *Roaches do not mop. Roaches do not speak. Big Dan must have slipped something into that weed we smoked this afternoon. I could have sworn I'd sobered up.*

"Tell yourself whatever you need to to get through the day," the tiny voice said again.

"This boy helped me send Bisozoth back," DeeDee said.

I looked up at her. Who was she calling a boy? I was a bonafide man. Of course, all I said out loud was "Biso-what?"

DeeDee stood in the muck, somehow still gorgeous despite a head-to-toe coating of green slime. She pointed at me but looked past me. Who was she talking to?

Suddenly, a firm hand touched my shoulder, and I rose off the floor, floating like a feather on a breeze, to standing. A warm, tingly sensation trickled through me. I felt relaxed, like I was getting a hot rock massage, not emerging from a pile of slushy, vomit and monster guts. A tall, impossibly handsome man stood next to me. He had pitch black hair, eyes dark and glassy like obsidian, and wore an expensive designer suit, even nicer than the ones that social-climbing rich kid / wannabe lawyer my girlfriend dumped me for used to wear.

"Young man. We have much to discuss." Mr. Impossibly Handsome ushered me to a nondescript white door tucked between two pyramids of stacked two-liter pop bottles. The door opened before us. I didn't see him touch the knob but after the mopping roach and the tentacle thing, I couldn't really trust my eyes. Because, you know, tentacle monsters couldn't possibly exist, and that boss battle DeeDee and I had back there? Couldn't have been real. Big Dan was gonna get an earful about his bunk crazy weed for sure.

The white door opened into a cramped hallway with boxes of Top Ramen and plastic-wrapped packs of toilet paper stacked floor-to-ceiling against both walls. The man led me down a narrow path through the boxes. As soon as we stepped past a pallet of microwave mac and cheese, the tiny pathway opened into a luxurious man-office worthy of Mr. Impossibly Handsome's designer suit. A fire roared in a giant stone fireplace behind a heavy dark wood desk. The floor was covered in wall-to-wall Persian rugs, and there was a huge chandelier hanging from a tall, vaulted ceiling. The room was lined with bookcases containing leather-bound sets of what looked like thousand-year-old encyclopedias and glass display boxes with fancy, weird stuff inside, like...what the hell was that? A monkey paw? And a curly weird goat horn? *Holy crap. Stop looking. Too Creepy. Eyes forward.*

"First, let's get you cleaned up, shall we?" Mr. Impossibly Handsome waved his hand in front of me. I expected him to toss me a towel or at the very least a wet wipe because that's what my Mom would have done, but he didn't. I got nothing. "That's better. Please, sit."

He slid into a red leather club chair behind the desk and motioned for me to sit in a similar chair on my side. I just stood there, blinking. I didn't know much, but I knew better than to sit on expensive furniture while covered in barf and melted slushy, and this guy's manspace was way fancier than anything in our beige, Target-chic tract house. "I, uh..."

"You won't ruin the furniture. See?" He pointed at my clothes as if he'd read my mind.

I looked down. I was squeaky clean. My "I'm With Stupid" T-shirt was wrinkled, but dry, and only had the stains it had on it when I'd walked in tonight. No slushy. No guts. No Cheetos barf. *How the hell? Oh, wait.* Big Dan's bunk weed. It was all a hallucination. For sure. Crap. That meant Mr. Impossibly Handsome was about to bust me for stealing the slushy.

"Now sit, please," he said.

I did as I was told, sinking into the plush leather chair. The calm, warm sensation was gone, replaced with absolute stone-cold dread. Mom was really gonna be on my case if he called the cops. Petty theft would be the gasoline on her already raging bonfire of "Lloyd, when are you going to get your life together?"

"We must discuss what transpired tonight," he said. His voice was deep, calm, with an accent I couldn't quite place but part posh, part aristocrat, part old European.

My palms began to sweat. *Here we go.* Going down for grand theft slushy. I sunk my hands into my pockets. I still had my eighty-four cents. *Stupid pothole.* Maybe I could give him what I had, and we could call it a deal.

"Now, be a good lad and hand me your file." Mr. Impossibly Handsome's eyes flickered bright red in the firelight. He extended his hand across the desk as if he expected me to put something in it. "Your file, please?"

"My...I don't..." *File? What? Did I look organized enough to keep a file on anything?*

He pointed at my shirt, and I suddenly felt something stiff and decidedly cardboard under the cotton. I reached under the hem and pulled out a green file folder packed with papers. I handed it to him on autopilot, because, uh, what the hell was it and how did it get there? I didn't even own a file folder, and if I did, I'd probably never get around to actually putting papers in it. I wasn't that organized.

"Yes. Perfect." He took it out of my hand. "Now, let's get started."

He put the green folder on his desk, opened it, and turned through the neat stack of papers, skimming each page, saying "hmm," and "I see," to himself. "Lloyd Lamb Wallace. Aged twenty-one. Your current domicile is your childhood bedroom on Hummingbird Court. How sweet. Oh. I see. You moved home because your former lover, Simone, changed the locks on your shared apartment one hundred eighty-seven days ago. Current romantic relationship: None."

"That's not true," I blurted out, horrified by the completely accurate stream of intimate truths he'd spouted about my life. "I'm dating a girl. I mean, online. I haven't met her in person yet, but..."

"I'm sorry. You aren't. Your file indicates that your online girlfriend, Caroline, is a catfish. Her real name is Bruce Hardin, and he's a sixty-year-old recently paroled felon who plans to scam you but hasn't yet realized you're broke," he said.

Crap. Seriously, Caroline. How could you do me wrong, girl?

"Which brings me to current employment: None. Savings, assets, and investments: eighty-four cents, only seventy-four in U.S. currency, all of it in your left pocket," he said. "Financial status. Oh my. More than ten thousand dollars in debt. Student loans, exterminators, late cable bills? Well, then."

His eyebrows rose. I squirmed. This had to be an epic joke. Or a hallucination. No human could know all of this about me. Yeah. That's it. It was a hallucination. Just like the tentacle monster and the mopping roach. *Oh, Jesus.* When was this high gonna wear off?

Mr. Impossibly Handsome flipped another page. "Let's see here. Completed education: High school. C student. Community college: Dropped out in the middle of your fourth semester. Time use: My, my." His perfectly tweezed eyebrows arched. "You average forty-seven hours each week of Xbox. And, thirteen hours each week masturbating, primarily in less than ten-minute intervals."

He shook his head and casually pointed at my crotch. "Be gentle down there, son. Don't hurt yourself."

My cheeks burned. Holy shit, this guy wasn't lying. He knew. And, hearing it all out loud, all summed up? My life was a dumpster fire.

"It seems you have a lot of time on your...hands." Mr. Impossibly Handsome smirked, and my face flushed. He dug back into my file. "Now let's see here. Sins. Sins. Sins. Where are the sins?"

He flipped through a few more pages, which presumably highlighted more embarrassing factoids of dubious, yet eerily accurate origin. He looked through all the papers again, then put his hands up in defeat. "It appears your sins are missing. I'm going to have to talk to Mr. Beale once again about the need for thorough accounting."

Sins? Mr. Beale? My stomach churned, and my heart beat hard against my chest. Yeah, I was pretty freaked out but too terrified to get up and leave.

Mr. Impossibly Handsome either didn't notice or didn't care. He leaned back in his red leather chair, crossed his legs, and tapped his long, manicured fingers on his knee. His face glowed orange in the firelight. He had a thick silver ring on his finger, with a weird design on it. A flat circle with one straight line down the middle, and some sort of snake-like thing crawling up and around it. I swear the snake thing was moving. "Well then, Lloyd Lamb Wallace. Since your file is incomplete, we'll have to do this the old-fashioned way." He locked eyes with me. His face flashed red for a split second in the firelight. "Tell me your sins."

My spine went stick straight and stiff. A heat rose inside me, and I had the acute feeling I no longer had control of my body. My mouth moved and words spilled out. "When I was ten, I put a booger in Lee Smeltzer's peanut butter and jelly sandwich when he wasn't looking. I never thought he'd eat it, but he did, and I didn't stop him because I was scared I'd get in trouble. My friends found out and started calling him Booger Eater. It stuck so hard people wrote that in his senior yearbook. He got really fat and got beat up a lot, and I always wondered if that booger sandwich sent him over the edge. He didn't deserve it. He was super nice, and he was so desperate for friends that his Mom would always give us as many Popsicles as we wanted if we went to his house. When he realized we only came over for Popsicles, not to hang out with him, he cried. He lives at the end of my street with his parents, and I run inside every time I see him in the yard because I still feel bad about the booger."

Oh Jesus. I was like a cursed ventriloquist's dummy, spewing embarrassing secrets.

Mr. Impossibly Handsome stared at me, waiting for more. My mouth, on autopilot, gave it to him. I tried to stop talking, but couldn't. My damn tongue kept on clucking and the words just kept on coming. And these weren't just any words. They were horribly embarrassing words from the deep, dark cavern of shame where I hid all the things that I never ever wanted another soul to know about me.

"And then this one time, Mom asked me to clean up the basement, and I told her I did, but I didn't really. I just pushed my Monster Burger bags under the sofa instead of throwing them away. A month later, the basement filled up with ants, I mean like tons and tons of ants, and my parents had to pay six-hundred dollars for an exterminator. The guy found the burger wrappers and leftover fries. My parents were so disappointed in me. They're always so disappointed in me. Waaaaaaaaa..."

Cue waterworks. Yes, I was crying. Ugly crying, snot and all.

"I didn't tell my parents I dropped out of school, either. I was so embarrassed that I couldn't hack community college, that I lied and told them I was still going. They had to pay all the tuition, because I missed the deadline to drop the classes. All I had to do was press two stupid buttons online, but I didn't because I'm so lazy. I slept all day and played video games instead."

Oh my God. Why am I telling a stranger all of this? This was worse than the file! I tried to zip my lips and run right out of there, but I couldn't. My body was frozen to the chair, and my mouth just wouldn't shut. I sniveled and watched as the last thin, gossamer thread of self respect broke free and floated away on the wind.

"And Simone, my ex? She'd yell at me for leaving the toilet seat up, and I told her I'd put it down next time, and I remembered to do it, I just didn't because I didn't care and I thought her butt falling in the water in the middle of the night was her problem and kinda funny. And I never cleaned the bathroom, even though when I had morning wood and tried to pee, I'd miss the bowl if I yawned. I'd get piss all over the floor and the wall. When Simone would get mad, I'd tell her cleaning up was women's work because I'd rather play video games than clean. Waaaaaaaaaa!"

Okay, full disclosure. I was epic-level blubbering here. Tears streamed down my cheeks. Snot clogged up my nostrils. Hey. Don't judge me. Real men cry when they mess their shit up really hard and are forced to fess up to a complete stranger. Remember, my life was a dumpster fire. Yeah well, I lit the match.

"I owe Simone, like, two thousand dollars," I sniffled. "I couldn't keep a job and never had any money, so she paid my half of the bills. She left me for some rich douche bag law student with a really clean apartment. Waaaaaaaaaa..."

The tears faucet was dialed up to eleven at this point. For realsies. Mr. Impossibly Handsome even produced a box of tissues and handed it to me. I wiped my nose and took a couple of deep breaths. My spine slackened. For a hot second, my body became my own again. Sniffle. Sniffle. *That's it, Lloyd. Pull yourself together.* "Why am I telling you all this?" I asked.

"I asked you to tell me your sins, so you're telling me about the choices you have made that cause you the most guilt and grief," he said. "Tell me more."

I went stiff again. *Shut up! Shut up! Shut up! Shut up!* But no. I blabbed like a cheap hand puppet. "I smoked weed today, and I tried to steal your slushy because I hit a pothole outside the Cash4Gold and a quarter fell out of my pocket so I didn't have enough to pay for it, and I didn't want DeeDee to know how broke and pathetic I am."

Mr. Impossibly Handsome perked up when I said DeeDee's name. "That's enough."

My mouth zipped shut.

"Tell me, young Mr. Wallace. Have you killed any people or animals?"

"No way! I'm not a monster," I said. There I go again, yapping. "Wait. Except for bugs. Mostly spiders. I hate spiders. They're terrifying."

"Any terrorist or gang affiliations?" he asked.

"Um, no...?" Weird question. Do terrorists steal slushies?

"Do you want to see the world, your government or civic institutions, or the people you disagree with politically, go down in flames? Or, do you troll people online?"

"Well, no. Not really."

"That'll be enough, young Mr. Wallace." He waved his hand. My mouth slammed shut again. "You certainly aren't what I expected. You're delightfully slim on sins. You have a pure heart. You're a breath of fresh air, actually."

"What about the slushy? And the masturbating? That's a sin, right?" I blurted it out before thinking. I was pretty emotionally raw at this point, and when you're in that state, things tend to come out.

"There's no sin there, young Mr. Wallace," he said. "Indulging a perfectly natural impulse alone, safely at home, while hurting no one else hardly counts as sin does it? Besides, every man does, and if he says he doesn't, he's a liar."

Mr. Impossibly Handsome winked at me.

Not a sin? Tell Pastor Woodruff over at the Holier Than Thou congregation. *The devil's hands go straight down your pants.* That's what he'd tell us at Vacation Bible School. Mom sent me there for a week every summer when I was a kid because it was free. Then again, you get what you pay for.

"Now, let's get right down to it, shall we?" The smile slid off of Mr. Impossibly Handsome's face, his fingers stopped casually tapping his knee, and he leaned forward. "You were brave and noble tonight. In the face of danger, you could have run, but you didn't. You rose to the occasion. As a humble thank you, we've refurbished your current mode of transportation."

He snapped his fingers and a shiny, perfect Huffy, the exact same make and model as mine, materialized against the bookcase that also housed the creepy glass case of maybe monkey paw. I was pretty sure that bike wasn't there when we walked in. "That's not my bike," I said. It couldn't possibly be. The one I rode over here was busted up, duct-taped together, and had lost a brake lever when Comb-over Carl made a run for it. This one was shiny, new, perfect. Mine was what, eight years old? I got it for my thirteenth birthday.

"I assure you, that is your bike. The clean-up crew has given it a tune-up as a thank you, and to repair the damage Carl caused on his way out," he said. "It's the least we could do to thank you for your assistance in sending Bisozoth home."

Biso what? It's that word DeeDee had said.

"Now, I have also brought you here to discuss Carl's abrupt departure. Or the consequences, at least. Now that we have dispensed with formalities, I can tell you I have a job opening. I look for a very particular set of qualities in an employee, and you, young Mr. Wallace, are exactly what I'm looking for," he said. "I'd like to offer you Carl's job. Graveyard shift, of course, but your file indicates you already keep nighttime hours. I provide generous hazard pay, some rather unusual but popular benefits and perks, as well as training in all the necessary arts. Would you like the job, young Mr. Wallace?"

"A...job?" I stammered. "I'm not going to jail for stealing your slushy?"

"Jail? Oh, heaven's no. The proprietors of all the fine establishments at this intersection work diligently to stay off the radar of human law enforcement and local ruling bodies," he said. "Now, where were we? Yes. You have proven worthy. It is also clear this job could solve many of your problems."

Phew. No jail. Stoked! But wait. Job? I stared at him for a minute. *Oh, man. A job?* I'd have to think about that. It'd seriously cut into my Xbox time. *Sucks.* Then again, maybe Mom would ease up on the cringey adulting lectures. *Bonus!* But I'd have to actually show up on time and work. Every boss I'd had to this point had made it clear I absolutely sucked at that. *Sucks.* A job also meant leaving the house and washing my clothes more regularly. *Double sucks.* On the upside, I'd have an excuse to be near DeeDee. *Bonus!*

"The job comes with free, all-you-can-drink slushies," Mr. Impossibly Handsome said. "Even on your days off."

"I'm in." Come on. We all have our price. Mine was free slushies. He should have led with that.

We shook on it, then he ushered me and my magically refurbed Huffy to the door. When I stepped back out into the store, the linoleum was sparkling and clean. No spilled Inferno slushy. No guts. No bashed in tiles from barbed tentacles. The chip rack was where it belonged, stocked, not a single bag out of place. DeeDee sat on her wooden stool outside of the beer cave, looking bored, picking at her black fingernails like it was any old normal night. Like nothing had happened. Because nothing had happened. *Boy.* Big Dan was really gonna get an earful about that weed. Then again, now that I had a job, I could afford to buy my own instead of smoking whatever sketchball stems and seeds he rummaged up.

Mr. Impossibly Handsome ushered me to the front door and handed me a fresh new Colossal Super Slurp cup filled with Inferno. I noticed he'd installed a cup holder on my bike. *Yes!*

"Welcome to the team, young Mr. Wallace," he said. "I only ask that you obey two rules above all: Do not let anyone else touch or wear your name tag. Also, the employee manual in your welcome pack is for authorized eyes only, do you understand? No unauthorized person is allowed to touch or see either of those items. Break those rules, and you'll be terminated immediately."

"Um, okay?" He hadn't handed me any welcome pack or name tags, so no problem.

"Now. Be here one hour and thirty minutes before sunset tomorrow. Ricky, the day manager, will begin your training. He prefers to leave before sundown, so don't be late," he said. "Oh dear, pardon my manners. My name is Asmodius Faust. I am the keeper of this gate, commander of legions, and your boss. I will appear when you truly need me, but bear in mind I am only available after dark."

He waved his hand in front of me like he was a cheap Vegas hypnotist. "Now be on your way. No Xbox tonight. Sleep long and well, for you'll need your wits about you tomorrow. You have much to learn."

Next thing I knew, I was standing outside in the parking lot alone beneath the flickering neon 24/7 Dairy Mart sign, Inferno in hand. I felt something thick and papery under my T-shirt. I reached in and pulled out a manila envelope with "Welcome, Lloyd Lamb Wallace." typed neatly in bold Gothic font on the front. I opened it up. Inside was a plastic name badge reading "Hello, my name is Lloyd" and an old, red leather-bound book. I fished out the name tag. My fingers tingled. The neon sign above me popped and hissed. I looked up. The curlicue neon letters no longer spelled out 24/7 Dairy Mart in cheerful blue, yellow and pink. The letters glowed blood red. They now read 24/7 Demon Mart.

CHAPTER 3

I slept like a dead man. Or, how I guessed a dead man would sleep, given I had no personal experience. A blinding beam of sunlight cut around the edges of my bedroom curtains, searing my eyeballs. *Man, brutal.* The red letters on my alarm clock read 4:48.

My teeth felt like they were wearing a wool sweater, thanks to the hardened coating of slushy sugar all over them. I could taste the Inferno remnants in my mouth. Note to self: Make more effort to brush teeth before passing out cold. Sweater teeth = super gross.

Last night was a blur. I vaguely remember fishing around the bottom of the cup for the last bit of slushy, then waking up. That was it. The sun lit up a slice of fat envelope on top of the clean-but-yet-to-be-put-away clothes Mom had left on my dresser. My new employee welcome pack. *Oh shit.* Cold fingers of dread tickled me all over. *Now I remember.* I got a job. I had to go to work. I had to get on a schedule. I actually had somewhere to be—on time. *Sucks so hard.* Six months of unemployed freedom, gone just like that. Poof.

My mind reeled. What time did that Faust guy say I had to be there? Oh yeah. He hadn't given me a time. He said an hour and a half before sundown, like I was supposed to magically know when that was. Ugh. It was already too much work just to figure out what time to show up. I fumbled around my bedside table until I found my phone, and as soon as the screen didn't light up, I remembered I hadn't paid the bill, the battery had gone dead and I didn't have the cash to replace it, and the screen was a giant spiderweb of cracks anyway. The stupid thing was as useful as a brick. I threw it onto a pile of dirty laundry on the floor.

Meh, I've got time for a nap. I rolled over and closed my eyes. But my mind zoomed straight to that mopping, talking roach and that beady yellow eyeball surrounded by tentacles. I sat straight up. That shit still seemed SO real. *You and your insane-o-weed, Big Dan. Jesus!* So much for that nap. I stumbled over to my desk and brushed the crumpled up Monster Burger wrappers off of my laptop. I powered it up. Okay.

Sunset time. *Shit. What's the date?* Don't judge. Let's see if you know what day it is after six months of nowhere to be. Okay, okay. Google "what's the date?" Type type, plunk plunk. Here we go. October 18. Sunset: 6:48 p.m. Minus an hour, minus another half. Count backwards on my fingers and...*voila.* I gotta be there at 5:18. *Okay.* Another glance at the clock. 5:01. *Shit.*

I tucked and rolled. Hard. Shoes on. Ready. *Wait.* I was still in last night's outfit. Should I change? Nah, too much hassle. Then again, DeeDee might notice. Girls always notice. Okay. I should probably change. I peeled off my clothes and threw them on the ever-growing floor pile. And yeah, I felt pretty bad about myself for a few seconds and sucked in my budding paunch when I caught sight of my abs in the door mirror. They were more like a flesh-colored party ball keg than a six-pack.

I scrambled around until I found my last two fresh socks, then dove into my dresser. Clean T-shirt, shorts, underpants (the feel of swamp ass was still tangible in my mind, real or not). Check. Ready to go. Except for the sweater teeth. I definitely couldn't dragon breath my way into DeeDee's heart. I was still brushing, mouth foaming and minty, when my feet hit the bottom of the stairs.

Mom called from the kitchen. "Where ya going, honey?" She stopped doing dishes long enough to shoot me a concerned smile. The worry/anger wrinkle between her eyebrows was twitching. "Are you okay? You slept the whole day."

"Gert a jorb," I said, pursing my lips to keep the toothpaste from splurping out. "Lade."

Her eyebrows shot up in surprise. "A job. How great!" She didn't even try to disguise her complete joy and relief. "Is *that* what you're wearing?"

I looked down. Army green cargo shorts. One white sock, one yellow one. "Female Body Inspector" T-shirt, perma-wrinkled, two stains of unknown origin. I shrugged. Good enough.

I dropped my toothbrush on the table next to the key bowl in the entryway and was on my Huffy pedaling for dear life less than a minute later. And yes, I do have a car, if you must know. But no, I can't drive it because I can't afford to pay the insurance or the thousand bucks to repair the dead battery, flat tire, and rusted-out brake lines, and no, my parents won't pay, I already asked. They said I needed to learn responsibility. I was an adult now and bailing me out wasn't gonna teach me anything. Blah blah blah.

Now, where was I? Oh yeah. Pedaling. Furiously. I spit out the last of my toothpaste at the stop sign at the intersection of Cemetery Road and Crossroads Crossing, the most rundown street in the burbs, where the 24/7 Dairy Mart, the Monster Burger, the Jesus Saves Religious Supply, the Cash4Gold, the Temptations Tavern, a weirdo pawnshop, and the Sinbad's Strip joint (where I'm sad to say I have never been because I'm too broke to tip), all reside. Yeah, I know, Crossroads Crossing. Stupid street name right? There are lots of those in the burbs in the Midwest. I passed Data Point Court on the way there. What kind of douche bag, polo-shirt wearing developer puts that street name on a city form with a straight face? I'll tell you: No guy with any respect at all for art, culture, or the people who have to drive by that stupid sign every damn day, that's for sure.

I pedaled to the parking lot faster than I ever had, in part because my newly refurbed Huffy just flew. Wheels go much faster when the rims and chain aren't rusty. Guess I didn't hallucinate those sweet sweet bike repairs. Still, I tried not to think too hard about it because that part of last night didn't make any more sense today than it did last night, and I couldn't blame the bike on Big Dan's weed.

The 24/7 Dairy Mart looked completely different in the daytime. For starters, there were other customers. The lot had a bunch of cars in it, and people were rushing in and out, most carrying bags of chips and twelve-packs of Lite beer or lottery tickets and slushies. Geesh. At night, this place was a graveyard. Abandoned.

I locked my bike to a post underneath the neon store sign. A chill ran through me, but I didn't quite know why. I examined the lot, the store, the sign, trying to pinpoint what was wrong, but came up zeros. Nothing was out of place. The store's wall of windows were plastered in yellow banners advertising "hot, fresh coffee," milk and eggs and chips, cigarette specials. The 24/7 Dairy Mart sign buzzed neon blue, yellow and pink, like always. The whiteboard section with the movable letters advertised "2 for $2 chili dogs," "Ice-cold beer at state minimum prices," and six-dollar packs of Pall Malls. Normal, corner store stuff. Nothing weird at all. All righty then.

I attempted but failed to smooth the wrinkles out of my T-shirt. Then, I stepped inside and stood there on the welcome mat, looking around like an idiot, as customers stomped past me on their way out. I didn't know what to do, which was why first days at jobs universally sucked. You didn't know where to go, who to see, what the routine was, what the manager looked like, who's cool and who's not. They didn't know you either, so you had no choice but to stand there like a wide-eyed dumbass waiting for someone else to make the first move. My stomach churned. Total reminder of why job hunting blew: You stick to it long enough, you'll actually get a new job.

"You lost, dahlin'?" The lady behind the register called to me.

She dropped change into the hand of a man in a tan tweed blazer, who quickly shuffled off with a box of mac 'n' cheese and a can of Vienna sausages. The world's saddest bachelor dinner.

The lady smacked some gum that was the same frosty pink as her lipstick. She raised an eyebrow, waiting for me to answer. She was what my friend Chico would call a Big Fine Honey. Five feet three, pushing two-fifty, most of it tits and booty. She had enough cushion on her belly to make her as soft and comforting as a full-body pillow in bed. Hey. Don't judge me. I'm using Chico terms. He's into that, and he's graphic. Plus, the hot pink tank top with "Sexy" written in rhinestones across the front showed off all the goods. A silver sequin scrunchie held back her bleach blonde ponytail. Her name tag read "Hello, my name is Junebug."

"Dahlin'?" Junebug said at me again, tapping her hot pink press-on nails on the counter. "You all right?"

"Oh...uh...sorry." I had to remind myself to look her in the eyes, not at her tits. "I'm Lloyd. The new guy."

She looked me up and down. "Ya made the cut, huh?" She blew a gum bubble and popped it between her frosty, glossed Wet 'n' Wild lips. She shook her head. "Never can tell by looking, that's for damn sure."

Junebug pointed at a tuft of greasy mouse-brown hair bobbing up and down in aisle two. "That's Ricky. He'll get ya started."

"Thanks," I said.

"Good luck, dahlin'. You'll need it." Junebug winked, then rung up a big biker in head-to-toe leather, who was buying a pile of beef jerky and chewing tobacco.

I shuffled over to aisle two. *Woah boy.* Where did I even start with Ricky? He was the exact opposite of the impeccably dressed, impossibly handsome Asmodius Faust. Ricky was a hot mess. He had greasy hair in a bowl cut, and brown-rimmed coke-bottle glasses in a frame they probably haven't made since 1972. The lenses were so thick his eyes were distorted. His shoulders were rounded to the point of barely existing. He was a porcine mound of a man, shaped like a long round potato and soft like a pillow all over. He didn't have a single defined muscle. Even his hands were pudgy. He wore blue plaid polyester pants pulled up way higher than his belly button. And worse, a white vinyl belt cinched him too tight right around the middle. He topped off the look with white, thick-soled orthopedic tennis shoes. Ricky needed some serious style lessons, and that was a sad commentary coming from a guy who only owned a drawer full of tasteless joke T-shirts (most with at least one salsa stain) and cargo shorts. One look and you just knew this guy lived with his purple-haired grandma, and she personally picked out all of his clothes.

Probably even laid them out for him the night before.

"Hey. I'm Lloyd. Mr. uh...Faust said you'd get me started," I said. "I'm new."

Ricky stopped stacking microwave bowls of Top Ramen on the shelf and looked at me wide-eyed. He white-knuckled one package in his hand, and from the shaking dry-noodle sound I could tell he was trembling. He looked absolutely terrified. A sweat-bead mustache formed on his top lip.

"You okay, man?" I asked.

"You're sure you want this job? Like, *sure* sure?" His voice cracked, going dog-pitch high.

"Uh, yeah. I guess. Why?" I shrugged. I needed cash. Plus, you know, free slushies. All. The. Time.

He tugged at his collar, buttoned up all the way, of course. "It's not too late to run," Ricky whispered. The sweat rings in the armpits of his short-sleeve yellow polyester dress shirt grew two sizes. "The graveyard shift is....*dangerous.*"

"I'm cool," I said. "It's all good."

What was the worst that could happen? Frat house beer run?

"It's your choice." Ricky nervously smoothed out the pleats of his plaid pants. Lord help him, those pants. "I can't stop you. That's the rule. So if you're *sure* sure follow me."

He aligned the bowl of ramen perfectly on the shelf, then I followed him to the white door between the pop bottle pyramids, the one that led to Faust's totally sweet man office. But once we stepped in, Ricky turned the other direction, left instead of right. We inched through a narrow tunnel between plastic tubs stacked high on each wall, labeled aspirin, cigarettes, condoms, personal care, automotive. Ricky's belly rubbed against the tubs as we inch-wormed through. We stopped at a purple door with a placard that said "Lounge. Employees only."

"Do you have your name tag?" Ricky asked.

Shit. It was on my dresser, in the envelope. "Uh. No. Sorry. Forgot."

Ricky huffed. "Where is it?"

"At home. No big deal. I'll bring it tomorrow."

He jabbed his index finger into my chest and locked eyes with me. His were distorted, blown up to doe-eye size by the curve of his impossibly thick lenses. "Never, ever leave your name tag or your employee manual unattended. Always bring them with you. Your life and the world depends on it. Do you understand?"

"Uh...sure man. Yeah." Wow. Over-dramatic much, Ricky? Clearly, this dude was too lazy to plink me out a new tag on the label maker.

"You can't work the graveyard shift without it." Ricky poked me as he talked, to emphasize his points. "You can't get into the lounge or communicate with Kevin without it. And, you can't *see* without it."

"I can see just fine," I said. Seriously, dude. I wasn't the one with two-inch-thick glasses.

"Yeah, sure. Keep telling yourself that." Ricky was super sweating now, beads of it nervously running over his pink cheeks. He closed his eyes and breathed deeply. "Okay. Okay. Stay Calm. Relax."

He wasn't talking to me. He was pep-talking himself. He ran his hands over his shirt and pants again. He moved a plastic tub. In the wall behind it was a rectangular green door, about the size of a microwave, with a keypad next to it. "What's your home address?" Ricky asked.

I told him, and he typed my address into the keypad as I spoke, along with "new employee welcome pack." He hit enter, tensed up and held his breath. The edges of the door lit up bright yellow, then the door hissed and popped open. Smoked wisped out. Inside, sat a half-opened manila envelope with my name typed on it. *Woah. Neat trick.* It looked exactly like the envelope at home on my dresser, but it couldn't be that one, just a really good copy. Don't ask me how he pulled this off, but I was impressed.

Ricky handed the envelope to me. "Now put on your name tag. And don't let this out of your sight ever again."

"Yeah. Sure, man." I fished out the name tag and put it on, mostly to shut Ricky up. No good ever came from riling up the high-strung rules lawyer on the first day of the job.

Ricky nodded, then pressed his own name tag against a black fob next to the purple door. It swung open.

Holee. Crap. Jackpot! Employee Lounge, my butt. The room was plush, like Vegas nightspot VIP room posh. (I mean, judging from the ones I'd seen on TV.) We're talking wall-to-wall red shag carpet. Black flocked wallpaper. Red velvet couches and booths. A giant crystal chandelier dripping with mood light. There was a wall of glass-front coolers stocked with any kind of beverage you could ever want. A zillion-inch TV was mounted on one wall, covering nearly the entire thing.

A guy in a big white chef's hat stood behind a counter with a built-in grill, like one of those made-to-order omelette stations at a fancy hotel breakfast buffet. Or, like, the guy working the steak-cutting booth at Golden Corral. "This is Chef." Ricky tugged hard at his shirt collar again, as if it shrunk a size and was choking him.

I waved at Chef and said, "Hiya."

"*Don't* make conversation." Ricky smacked my wave down, then squeezed my forearm so tight his fingernails left little half-moons in my skin. "Chef responds to food orders only. He'll make you whatever you want to eat on your break. And that's it. No conversation, got it?"

"You mean like a tuna melt? And potato salad? And macaroni salad?" My tummy rumbled as I said it. I did sleep all day. I hadn't eaten.

"Wow. That was really specific," Ricky said. "But, yeah, that. Or, anything else you could possibly want to eat."

"Uh, how much is that gonna set me back?" Gourmet meals I could not afford.

"It's all free. Drinks, food, everything in here," Ricky said.

I was so stoked I jumped up and down once or twice. Then, the hairs on my arms stood up, but not from excitement. "Dude, it's a bit cold in here. Can you dial up the thermostat?"

"No." Ricky snapped. "It's gotta stay cold to keep things...fresh."

All righty then. Who was I to question when the place was so deluxe?

Ricky wrung his hands and, despite the chill, his underarm sweat rings spread so far they basically drenched his entire shirt. "Don't be fooled by all of this. Never forget who you're working for. Everything has a price." His eyes darted back and forth as if he was letting me in on some huge secret. "Be alert. The graveyard shift guys don't last long. First Kevin, now Carl. You're the third new guy."

Ding. Chef hit a small metal bell. A tuna melt with a side of both potato and macaroni salads sat on a clean white plate on the counter in front of the grill. "Wow. Thanks!" I snatched the plate up. It was just the way I liked it. Tuna melt on rye with provolone. Bacon in the potato salad, little bits of mayo and green onion clinging to the macaroni. A-fucking-mazing. "You're the man, Chef!"

I put up a hand for a high five, but Chef ignored it. He stood still, swaying slightly behind the grill as if I weren't there. He didn't smile. He didn't react. He wore dark sunglasses inside. Maybe that was like a Stevie Wonder thing. Not my business. Chef did look a little green like he was coming down with something. "Uh, is that guy okay? He doesn't look so hot."

"Just don't touch him. Not ever. They say he's not contagious, but I don't believe them," Ricky said.

"Uh, okay?"

Ricky ushered me and my side dishes to a round, red booth in front of the massive TV. He sat me down in front of two papers neatly arranged side-by-side on the table.

"Read these and sign them. When you're finished, watch the employee orientation video. Then, put your personal items in your locker." Ricky pointed to a set of glossy black lockers tucked into a cubby next to the coolers. One had "Lloyd" written neatly on the front placard. "Then, go out on the floor with DeeDee. Everything else you need to know is in your employee manual. If you haven't read it all the way through, read it. ASAP. Memorize it, okay? It's life and death information."

Uh, yeah right. Keep telling yourself that, Ricky. We worked at a convenience store, not a hospital. Restocking beer and making change wasn't rocket science.

Ricky grabbed my arm again. "I'll ask you one last time: Are you sure you want to do this?" He was shaking all over now, jiggling like Jello. "Once you see the things you see here, you can't unsee them. And those things...they'll be able to see *you*. There's no going back."

"Relax. I'm cool."

"Godspeed then, Lloyd." Ricky let go of my arm. "I'll pray for you."

He looked at his watch, because, you know, he was that guy who still actually owned one, and not like a Rolex for status, a cheap one. It probably had a Mickey Mouse on it. "Dear baby Jesus." He crossed himself really quickly. "I lost track of the time. I gotta go. I have to be out of here by sunset, and I haven't restocked the tampons yet. Oh, and remember, you can use tampons to stop the bleeding in a big wound. Good luck, Lloyd. And remember, there's no shame in running away."

Which is exactly what he did right after he said that. Ricky was legit weird. Or just sad. I couldn't decide. Welp. Only one thing to do. I took a big bite out of the tuna melt, then challenged myself to see how much macaroni salad I could fit in my mouth at one time. I played that game with various foods until my plate was munched down to crumbs. I patted my belly. *Hellz yeah.* That was delicious. I could get used to this. *Yawn. Man, I'm spent.* Too many carbs always made me tired.

I hopped up and grabbed a soda out of the cooler. "Great sandwich there, Chef. Loved it." I looked at him, waited for a reply, but got nothing. He didn't respond at all, although I saw his greenish nose move in my general direction and start sniffing the air. I noticed he had some sort of collar around his neck. I could just see the top of it above the neckline of his crisp white chef's jacket. It looked like a dog collar. Chef must be punk rock. Although, it looked more like an electric fence collar than a studded leather one. Maybe he had a hot dominatrix at home who zapped him when he got out of line. "Whatever you're into, dude."

He just stood there, swaying, staring into space. I think? Who knew? Those sunglasses were super dark.

I shrugged and decided I couldn't put off the paperwork any longer. There were two sheets of paper on the table. A red gel pen sat between them. I wiped the crumbs off of them and got to work. The first was a short list of rules. The second was my income tax withholding form. *Blech. Forms.* I already felt overwhelmed. I shouldn't. I'd had so many jobs and filled out so many of these I should be a master at this. Okay, so I've had a lot of jobs. And so what if I can't keep 'em for long? Do you know how hard work sucks out there for a young man in America without a college degree, especially when all you can get is minimum wage? Even the baristas at Starbucks have Bachelor's degrees.

I filled out the tax form and signed it. Red seemed a weird ink color choice, but whatever. The IRS probably didn't care. Then the rules. Apparently, I had to initial each line, then sign at the bottom. Blah blah blah. Better tear this Band-Aid off quick. There was a free slushy waiting on the other side.

> I, Lloyd Lamb Wallace, agree to abide by the following rules in my duty as an employee of 24/7 DM, Inc., portal agent of Transmundane Gate 23, upholder of Celestial Order in Sector 17.

Huh. I'd heard of job title inflation, but this place took it to a whole other level. Skim. Skim. Skim. Okay, rules.

> 1. Never let anyone else touch or wear your name tag.

> 2. Never share, copy, or leave your employee manual unattended. It is for the eyes of current employees only. Violation of this rule could result in eternal darkness and unleashing of unspeakable terrors upon an unprepared world.

> 3. Doughnuts are to be consumed only in emergencies, and only when said emergency rates above level 23 as per the employee handbook "Emergency Rating Scale Index." Full doughnut impact is unpredictable and varies from entity to entity.

> 4. In the event of an armed robbery, secure your name tag. Give the offender

the money. Tell him or her to have a
nice day. Let the offender walk outside.
Do NOT call the police. Stay very still,
and justice will be served immediately.

5. Know the location, identification, and
best use of all 24/7 DM, Inc. provided
tools and weapons. Match the
appropriate weapon to the task at hand.
Fight smarter, not harder.

Soooooooo... Does anything about this list seem a little weird to
you? Did you fill out something like this for your job? I mean, maybe
this is standard wording now? I wasn't employable enough to be up on
this sort of thing.

6. Sexual relations between human
employees and unearthly travelers are
not expressly forbidden as long as both
parties consent without force or
enchantment, and employees are aware
that these relationships frequently have
unintended, sometimes fatal,
consequences.

Okay, then. Don't sleep with crazy customers. Didn't know that was
enough of a thing to warrant a mention.

Please be aware breaking the rules can
lead to immediate termination in addition
to plunging the world into eternal
darkness and infernal chaos. Please read
and commit to memory the guidelines
on portal/gate usage in your assigned
district. In exchange for competent
upholding of duties, you will be paid
$66.60 per hour. Payday is every Friday.

My jaw dropped. Sixty-six bucks an hour to stock beer and sell
lottery tickets? Dude. I was hoping for a buck or two over minimum
wage. *Sweeeeeeeet!*

Bonuses for excellent work include $13 per hour in additional pay for the shift where excellence occurred, plus perks and rewards management deems reasonably appropriate for level and quality of service and/or degree of crisis averted.

Medical treatment for any and all injuries sustained on company property will be provided free of charge by our on-staff practitioner. Training in all martial arts, including Choy Li Fut and Krav Maga, are encouraged and available free of charge to all current employees via Bubba's Yoked and Choked Kick Ass, Take Names training center at 1313 Cemetery Boulevard.

Dude. Why the hell would Ricky try to talk me OUT of this job? Free food, free slushies, fat paychecks, plus free gym membership and healthcare? Woot! I pumped my fist in the air. I'm so in I'm behind myself already. Okay. I just need to sign and initial this bitch and I'm done.

I clicked the silver tip of the red gel pen. *Ouch. Shit.* What the...? A bead of blood emerged from the tip of my thumb. I examined the pen a little closer. A tiny silver needle had shot out of the pen clicker. It had my blood on it, and it looked like it was sucking the blood into the pen. *Welp. That's probably not normal.* But oh well. I wasn't gonna let a little cut stand between me and some fat cash. I initialed all the little boxes. The red ink was darker, thicker than on the tax form. I could swear it looked like blood. *Nah. Couldn't be.* I signed my name at the bottom.

The orientation video started up on the massive, nearly wall-sized television right as I finished writing the "e" on Wallace. The impossibly handsome Faust appeared on the screen. He stood, designer duds head-to-toe, in front of the Beer Cave. "Welcome to the team, Lloyd."

Wow. Personalized. Nice touch.

"This is your introduction to essential job duties. Pay careful attention," he said. "Let's start here. This is no ordinary Beer Cave. It's what makes this store unlike any other."

Boom. The video ended. Okay. It didn't. It just ended for me, because I switched into nap mode almost immediately thanks to all those carbs.

Plus, you know, my brain being tired from having to show up for a job and talk to Ricky for twenty straight minutes. I snort-snored myself awake. The screen was black. My head was tipped back onto the plush booth, my mouth was open, and a trickle of drool had made it all the way down my cheek and dripped onto my shirt. And my pec was tingling where the name tag was pinned on my chest. (I say pec, but that implies muscles, which I'm sure are under there somewhere, but I ain't rockin' the definition like Thor, that's for sure.)

I stretched my arms and looked around for a clock. "Oh, shit," I yelped. "Dude. You scared me." Chef was a few feet away. Behind the counter, still, but at the part that was the absolute closest he could get to me. He loomed there silently, aggressively sniffing the air around me. "You can't sneak up on people like that."

Once again, he said nothing. He grunted, then he sniffed harder. So then I sniffed. What's got him all worked up? Gas leak or something? I didn't smell anything weird. *Hmmm. Oh well.*

The clock was right behind his chef's hat. 12:15. *Oh crap.* I must have seriously conked out. Time had zoomed. I stood up and tried again to smooth out some of the wrinkles in my shirt. (It didn't work.) I checked my breath. (Fishy. Note to self: Filch some mints off the candy rack.) All right. Go time. DeeDee was about to be wooed by my limitless charm and style. I glanced at my mismatched socks. Okay. Charm it is, then. Time to dial it up.

I adjusted my name tag. It was really warm, and I could feel the heat through my shirt. Stupid thing. I wondered if it might be made of some weird tainted Chinese plastic that had been recalled. Then the tag started pulling on my shirt. Or, more accurately, pulled away from my shirt? All I knew was that the darn thing was floating away from my chest, holding my shirt out. Then, it pulled me forward. *What...the...fu...*

I stumbled, trying to keep up. It led me out of the lounge, through the pathway between the plastic tubs, out into the store. It let up, dropping back to my chest as soon as I stepped between the pop-bottle pyramids.

"New guy!" DeeDee screamed. "Don't let him out!"

She pointed at a dude in a black trench coat and fedora moving quickly toward the exit, so fast and so smooth he looked like he was *slithering?*

"Don't just stand there, grab him!" DeeDee yelled. She was digging around in that cabinet again by the beer cave. "Whatever you do, don't let him out that door. He stays inside, no matter what. Got it?"

Uh... I'm not a bouncer, but okay. I jogged after him. "Hey. Mister. Stop right there."

Trench-coat dude ignored me and sped up. "Hey, man. I said stop."

I figured he'd stashed a couple of forties under his coat and was making a run for it. I decided to make a good show of stopping him in the interest of a good impression on my first day. I put my hand on his shoulder. His body writhed and coiled under my hand. He—and this is gonna sound crazy—began to stretch out like Plastic Man when I touched him, longer, higher, until he was nearly ten feet tall, towering above me. He twisted around to face me, and he wasn't a he at all. Men have faces. This thing was an it: A coil of black undulating scale-covered cables, twisting and slithering, with a fedora teetering on top of it all, like buttercream icing swirled on top of a turd.

Naturally, I screamed.

The trench coat fluttered open, revealing a row of yellow eyes, each with a mouth lined with fangs. The mouths opened and hissed at me, teeth bared. Jesus Christ, this dude was made of SNAKES!!

Oh, Jesus. Oh, Jesus. Oh, Jesus. I fell backward into the hot dog station, elbows first.

Sssssssssss. And no, that wasn't snake hissing. That was the sound of my skin melting on the hot dog rollers. *Ow! Ow! Ow!* That thing was HOT. And now, on top of two burned elbows, I had, oh, about thirty snake heads, fangs bared, prepping to bite me.

"Hold him off, new guy!" DeeDee yelled. "I need another minute."

"Hold him off? Are you kidding?" Uh, I didn't know what she expected me to do, so I panicked. I grabbed a handful of hot dogs and tucked and rolled behind the hot food station. The snake heads followed me. One lunged. I jammed a foot-long, super fat all-beef dog right into its throat. It ka-kacked, choking, and turned away. *Okay then. That worked.*

A second head struck, and I did the same. And that happened again, and again, and again, until the dozen or so hot dogs I'd grabbed off the warmer were all deep-throating snake heads. But the dude still had, like, twenty more heads. He was wriggling and shaking, knocking stuff over as it tried to upchuck the hot dogs. *Thwack.* It knocked the ketchup bottle off the food station, right onto the top of my head. *Boom.* The spork cubby clanged to the floor, sending sporks sliding in all directions across the linoleum. *Fwap.* Mustard fell open, tip down right on my shirt. *Man.* That was definitely gonna stain.

Another one of snake dude's heads came at me. *Shit. Shit. Shit!* I scooped up a couple of sporks, one in each hand, and stabbed the snake right in the eyes. It stopped, just short of biting me, and shook its head back and forth, blind, trying to dislodge the sporks. I grabbed the handles and wedged them in deeper, trying to spoon out some eyeball while I was at it. Man. Ten points for sporks, you are no longer the joke of the utensil world in my book.

"Uh, I could use a little help here." I called out. Where was DeeDee? We could use that flaming sword right about now. Plus, snake dude had already broken the handle off one of my sporks and shaken it loose. One eyeball dripped blood, the other had a white plastic handle poking out of it. His other faces didn't look happy.

"Got it!" DeeDee said.

The sound system crackled, and the muzak stopped. A second later, a song came on. A gruff, vaguely familiar white guy blues voice sang something about steel bars. The snakes reeled, like someone had poured acid on them, shaking and undulating at every word the guy sang. I had to admit I felt it, too. Blech. Easy listening.

The voice was familiar, like the songs my grandma used to play in the car when she drove me to preschool. I had a vision of a spectacular blond mullet. White mullet guy sang something about being a prisoner bound forever. I could picture the guy, but nope. The name wasn't coming to me.

One thing was clear, though. Snakes for heads *hated* that singer, like hate with a Capital H. At least I had hands and could cover my ears. He wasn't so lucky.

DeeDee jumped behind the angry, undulating snake thing, legs apart, knees bent, bracing herself. She held a plastic Michael Bolton CD case in her hand, opened it, and said something that sounded like "sarpa vallaka usetee dah-tee."

Duh! Michael Bolton. Spectacular mid-90s mullet guy! Yep. That's him. My grandma *loved* him. But seriously? A CD jewel case? Who the hell still had those anymore?

Wind kicked up inside the store. No. Not wind. A sucking, like a vacuum. The black tray of the Michael Bolton CD transformed into a swirling yellow cloud, like a vortex in Fortnite. Or a yellow cloud swirling down like a tornado in the middle. My hair fwap fwapped against my face, and I felt a strong force pulling me forward. The disoriented snakes uncoiled, one-by-one and peeled off of the single snake dude like string cheese. Each one detached, then got sucked right into the case. Each snake body spun and thrashed like a noodle being crunched up by the garbage disposal. The remaining rows of eyes and fangs turned to look at the CD and then wiggled toward me, trying to escape. But they didn't. They couldn't. One by one they disappeared into the middle of the swirl, powerless against the vortex and the rasping Top 40, white-boy blues of Michael Bolton. Except for one. A fat black thing big as a python, the core of the snake guy, managed to bite-grip the hot dog station then catapult himself up and over DeeDee. It was making a run for the door.

"Go get it!" DeeDee screamed, holding on white-knuckled to Michael Bolton's liner notes. "We need all the pieces or he'll reform somewhere else. We would have to start over."

Start over? Oh. Hell. No.

Before I could say "Nope, I'm out," which is what I should have done the minute that guy Plastic-Manned into a snake, I dove past DeeDee, blocked the front door and grabbed snake guy right as he was jumping for the push bar. It coiled up my arm and squeezed. Oh boy, did it squeeze.

It turned its yellow eyes on me. Then came the fangs. It lunged, ready to bite. I punched it in the nose. I mean, that's what you're supposed to do right? I'd watched plenty of Discovery Channel. No wait, that's what you do if a shark bites you. Doesn't matter, because it seemed to work. Its eyes crossed and its head lulled in dizzy circles. If we'd been in a cartoon, it probably would have had a halo of stars. Before it could recover, DeeDee had the CD right next to it, and it was getting sucked in. At least the butt half that wasn't coiled around my arm went in. Its beady yellow eyes were open again and staring right at me. It squeezed me so hard my hand felt like an over-inflated balloon.

"Peel it off you, new guy!" DeeDee yelled over the *swirrrrr* of the sucking vortex. "You sure as hell don't wanna go in there with it."

I punched it in the nose again, but it held tight. I felt around for anything even vaguely resembling a weapon, but the area around the welcome mat was pretty sparse. The snake squeezed tighter. *Think! Think! Wait a minute.* I sunk my hand into my pocket and emerged with a single pack of Taco Bell Diablo sauce. (Guess these pants weren't clean after all.) The fat, smug snake dude looked at me. I bit the corner off the pack, aimed, and squirted the sauce right into its two remaining eyes right as it moved to sink its fangs into my bicep. *Ha! Direct hit.* Smoke rose from its eyes. It screeched. It let go of me and immediately was sucked, hissing and smoking, right into the yellow cloud anus swirling inside DeeDee's Michael Bolton CD case.

DeeDee snapped the case shut the second snake guy was all the way in. The CD shook in her hands as if something was trying to punch its way out. But she held it tight, said those weird words again. "Sarpa vallaka usetee dah-tee."

The CD went still. She took a few deep breaths and opened the case. Black tray. Little teeth. No swirling cloud. Plain old jewel case. "Thank God," she said. "Now we can turn off that horrible music."

"What the fuck was that thing?" I was not proud of the high-pitched squeal that came out of my mouth.

"Great. Let me guess." DeeDee dug her fists into her curvalicious hips. "You didn't read your employee manual, did you?"

CHAPTER 4

Okay, so I'll be the first to admit I totally lost it as soon as the adrenaline wore off. As in, crawled behind the counter, curled up in a ball by the register, and tried to hide from the world while I told myself *Calm down. It's okay. No, no. This is fine. It's all fine. It's cool. Really. You've got this. You're not crazy. There's a reasonable explanation. There has to be. It's all good. Breathe. Breathe. Don't cry. Don't CRY!* On a loop, over and over, hoping I'd eventually believe it. That level of lost it.

I heard DeeDee shuffling around the store, turning off the Michael Bolton and flipping on the premixed Muzak selection. She whistled while she did it like nothing was wrong and she hadn't just sucked a dude made of snakes into a CD case. Now that I was listening closely, the Muzak sounded kinda like medieval chanting to a dance beat. Of course, it did. This place was insane.

I had no idea how DeeDee could be so cazh about this. I was freaking out. Who was I kidding? There was no use trying to talk myself out of my real feelings, which were more along the lines of *What. The. Fuck. Tentacle dude. Snake dude. It wasn't Big Dan's weed, was it? This shit's real!*

I had a dozen peach pits of ice-cold dread roiling around in my stomach. That was probably a normal feeling at the moment you realized the fabric that wrapped you up in a neat, tidy, totally makes rational sense reality had started to unravel. Because there was a dude made of snakes tugging at the seams. I hugged my knees tighter as if that would stop me from losing any more thread.

DeeDee stomped behind the counter, grabbed the collar of my T-shirt with two hands and yanked me up. "So what exactly did you think 'portal agent, Transmundane Gate Twenty Three, upholder of celestial order' meant when you signed the paper? Did you honestly think you were getting paid, what, eight times the minimum wage to stock beer and Fritos?"

Uh yeah, I did actually. And to eat free tuna melts. That made way more sense out here in the *real* world. But I didn't dare say that, because I could tell she didn't want to hear it. I was emotionally retarded, but not *that* emotionally retarded, so I just blank stared at her, and blinked a few times like a clueless dumbass. That was the smart move, trust me.

"I thought your eyes were wide open about this gig after Bisozoth." She tightened her grip on my shirt.

Man, she was beautiful. And strong. This bossy thing was working for me, too. *Oh, wait. What did she say?* I didn't remember, so I shrugged.

"Great. Just great." She shook her head. "All right. Listen up, new guy. Here's the deal. I do not have time for bullshit. I need a partner, do you understand? A real, equal partner, not another coward who's gonna turn tail and run away as soon as it gets scary. I will not waste my time training you if..."

She kept talking, but I didn't actually hear what she said. Her voice sounded a lot like how a list with bullet points would look on paper. All I saw were dark red lips moving. The sharp rise of her chest with every breath. The pillowy flesh beneath her Bauhaus T-shirt. OhmiGod she smelled like flowers. Not like old grandma potpourri either, like something exotic and tropical. *Oh, my God. DeeDee, I love you!*

So naturally, I did what every man does around a hot woman he wants to date. I just nodded and agreed with everything she said. I mean, let's be real here. I'd say yes to anything if it meant I had a shot with her. I'd stand on hot coals for an hour for a ten-second peek at her panties.

"So what's it gonna be, new guy?" She stared me down with piercing gray eyes lined in flawless, coal-black liner.

And...Busted. I had no idea what DeeDee was asking me. I searched her face for clues, but she was stone cold, intense. At that moment, the heat in my groin rose at the thought of being close to her and drowned out all rational thought. *Anything. Anything for DeeDee. Just say yes. Anything she wants, you give it to her.*

"Well? Are you in, or are you out?" She gripped my shirt tighter.

"I'm...in?"

"You don't sound sure. I don't have time for half-ass," she said. "I'll ask you one more time. Think carefully about your answer. Are you in? Or are you out?"

"I'm in. I'm in!"

"Okay then." She let go of my shirt and gently patted down the extra wrinkles she'd left on either side of my neck.

Crap. I hoped I hadn't agreed to something too crazy, like disposing of a body. *Man.* While I was trying to figure out what I'd said yes to, DeeDee was ruffling around under the counter. She emerged with a couple of brown paper napkins. "Here. For the mustard. Or your dripping cry snot. Your choice."

Cry snot? I touched my nose. Yep. Boogers. When I was rolled up behind the counter, hiding, I must have sniffled a little more on the outside than I'd realized. *Way to go, Lloyd. I'm sure she's hot for you now that you're drenched head-to-toe in boogers and condiments.* But hey, I could only go up from here, right?

I took the darned napkins, wiped my nose, then went to work on the pool of mustard on my T-shirt. My hands shook so much it was hard to do the wiping.

"So...let me guess." DeeDee crossed her arms and watched me. "You didn't realize what this job actually was before saying yes. You really did think you'd be stocking beer and refilling the slushies."

I nodded.

"Did you watch the orientation video?"

I nodded yes while thinking *nope.*

"You're lying."

I tried to look innocent, offended.

"If you'd watched it, then snake guy wouldn't have surprised you. So, you didn't watch it, did you?"

"No. I fell asleep." I couldn't get anything past this chick. Why try? "Sorry."

"Well, at least you're honest. Mostly." She rolled her eyes. "And, I've got to give you props. You helped me send Snakes and Bisozoth back. You're two for two."

"Bizo-who?"

"The green guy with one eye and tentacles?"

Ew. It had a name.

"That tells me you have at least a bit of natural talent, and despite screaming like a tween girl at a Taylor Swift concert, you did the job. Improvised a bit with the tools, but good instincts."

She looked me up and down. Between DeeDee and Junebug, I was getting used to being judged by my looks. "You're gonna have to lose this." She patted my gut. "The fitter you are, the easier the job can be. You don't look like much, but if Faust says you're worthy, you must have it where it counts." She shrugged.

My cheeks flushed red. Great. Snot. Mustard stains. A "you're fat" belly pat, and a "you don't look like much?" I had zero chance with this girl. I'd be lucky to even land in the friend zone.

"Anyway, I need a good partner. Someone who'll stick around," she said. "And someone who can convince Kevin to play something other than Dio."

"Who's Kevin?"

37

"The night manager. He's around here somewhere." She looked down and around at the floor, like she was afraid to step on something. "Oh well. You've already met Kevin."

"Um, I don't think so?" I ticked off the people in my brain. Impossibly Handsome. Junebug, Ricky, and Chef. That was it, so far.

"Anyway. I need to count on you, okay?" DeeDee said. "Are we on the same page?"

I nodded. *Yes, yes we are. Whatever page you're on is the one I want to be on.* Even though she was a ten who reminded me I was a two.

"Good, then I'll make you a deal. I'll go easy on you tonight. You can work the register, stay behind the counter, settle in. Familiarize yourself with the tools back here. Look, but don't touch, okay? Not until you read the instructions," she said. "I'll handle the gate traffic. In exchange, you have to promise me you'll read your employee manual, stat. Deal?"

She held out her pinkie, like a tween making a life promise. I looped mine through hers. "Deal," I said. But...what did she mean gate traffic?

"Great. Now get to work." She smiled and strode back to the wooden stool by the beer cave, where I'd seen her sit every night I'd ever come in for a slushy.

At some point, while I watched her delicious curves (and stellar personality, I'm not a total pig) walk away, a tall haggard guy with a silver mullet—balding on the top, but partying all the way down his back in thinning 80s hair metal waves—had walked in. He stood at the counter holding a giant pink box.

"Um...can I help you?" I asked.

"Wow. Another new kid, huh DeeDee?" He called over his shoulder. "Here we go again."

"Go easy on him," she called back.

"I'm Bob, the doughnut guy. Here."

He handed me the pink box. It had "Dolly's Divine Delicacies" written in gold leaf across the top. Row after row of fresh, glazed, frosted, sprinkled doughnut heaven stared back at me from behind the plastic window. No. They didn't stare. They *called* to me, whispering my name in seductive breaths, like a box of doughy sirens. *Yum. Mee.*

"Hey. You," Bob the Doughnut Guy snapped. "Don't even think about eating these. Store policy, remember? Paying customers *only*."

"Yeah. Sure. Of course. Duh," I said, but what I really meant was *I'm totally going to eat one of these things the second none of you are watching.* How could I not? Totes Delicious.

Bob the Doughnut Guy saw right through me. He grabbed the box out of my hand. "You know what? Why don't I take care of these?" He

38

plastered on a big, fake smile. "Since you're new, I'll show you how it's done."

He carried the box around the back of the counter, flipped the doughnut display case open and took out last night's empty trays. The trays were empty, sold out, except for an untouched row of glazed ones with pink frosting and rainbow sprinkles. They were untouched and flawless. He set the trays aside. He opened the pink box, lifted a fresh, full tray of doughnuts out of it and slid it into the case. Then he lifted another tray out of the box.

Wait. Was that thing like a clown car? The box was at most six inches tall, deep enough for one tray of doughnuts. But apparently not. Bob the Doughnut Guy pulled tray after tray right out of that box. Five in all, enough to fill the case with fresh fried and frosted deliciousness. He closed the display and was about to slap the pink box shut when he said, "Almost forgot. You guys have a special order tonight. Doc must be cooking up something big if he needs this bad boy."

He lifted a small pink box out of the bigger pink box and laid it on the counter. It contained a single doughnut, another glazed with pink frosting and rainbow sprinkles. *Lloyd, eat me and all your dreams will come true. Come on, I AM totes delicious,* it whispered. I reached for it.

Bob the Doughnut Guy smacked my hand away. "Never the pink ones, you understand? Never. Emergencies only! Besides, this is a special custom order. Extra potent. Not for you," he said. "Doc gets real crabby if he doesn't get his doughnut, and I wouldn't cross him if I were you."

"Okay! Okay!" I put my hands up and stepped back, but it was a ruse. I totally wanted to eat that doughnut. It looked even more delectable than the others. Just the smell of it made me feel...high?

"DeeDee, honey, keep an eye on this one." Bob the Doughnut Guy jabbed a thumb at me. "He's a little too interested in the doughnuts, ya feel me? And by the looks of him, he's got a taste for sweets."

"Will do," DeeDee said. "Hands off the doughnuts, new guy. Touch one, and I break your face."

Well, she certainly didn't mince words, did she?

Bob the Doughnut Guy put his giant hand on my shoulder. I hadn't realized he was that much taller than me until he was up close. He loomed over me. He was easily six-four, and was probably buff once, but he was now in his late fifties, and his long body had a big bubble belly right in the middle. He had the rough veneer of a lifelong working-class man who'd gone a bit grizzly because he'd seen some shit. "Good luck, son. You're gonna need it," he said. "Okay, then. Gotta go. I'll see you tomorrow night if you last that long."

With that, he waltzed right out the front door, taking the empty pink box with him. He peeled out of the parking lot in a pink truck with Dolly's Divine Delicacies written in gold sparkling letters across the side. Okay, then. Weird guy, but at least he wasn't a snake and didn't have tentacles, so that was good.

That's when I noticed a man jogging across the parking lot. At two in the morning. Wow. That was dedication. You really had to be into fitness to keep those kinds of hours. He ran right up and into the front door. DeeDee took one look at him, rolled her eyes, and went back to fingernail picking.

He had a lean, muscular body, an expensive tracksuit, and a slightly panicked look on his face. "Are they here? The doughnuts?" His voice was shaking. "Are they? Tell me, please."

"Um...yes?"

"Are they fresh? They have to be fresh," he said.

"Yeah." I got the distinct impression it was no accident he'd arrived right as the Dolly's truck was leaving. "Just delivered."

He sighed, relieved. "Oh, thank God. I *need* one. NOW!"

He jogged up to the counter, slid a waxed paper bag out of the holder clipped to the side of the doughnut case and carefully tonged a devil's food cake doughnut with chocolate icing into it. It took him a while to decide which of the chocolate ones to take. I heard him whispering, debating the value and quality of each one, even though they all looked identical to me. When he'd finished, he threw a crumpled five-dollar bill onto the counter and ran out the door.

"Don't you want your change?" I called after him, but he was out the door in a split second, sprinting across the parking lot faster than a man being chased by a lion. He stopped underneath the neon sign, ripped open the bag, and dug into that doughnut like a zombie eating a fresh brain. He held it with both hands, like a squirrel with a nut, and munched that doughnut down to crumbs in less than a minute. Then he ran across the road, past Sinbad's and off into the pitch-black night. The waxed baggie did somersaults in the parking lot, kicked up by the wind. "Dude!" I said. "Litter! Seriously?"

I put his crumpled up money in the register, and I won't lie. I glanced at those doughnuts at least a thousand times over the course of the next hour or so, thinking about that jogger. The expression on his face, dripping with need at the sight of them and euphoria as he ate them. Either these were the best damned doughnuts on the planet, or he had a serious sugar addiction. But I didn't eat one even though I really, really *really,* wanted to. Maybe in part because of the way that guy reacted to them, with crazed intensity.

It was hard, but I kept my hands off the sweets and did what DeeDee told me to: I settled in behind the counter. I'd say it wasn't so bad, but it kind of was. The stuff back here that DeeDee wanted me to "familiarize" myself with was a little odd.

There was a collection of crystals, gemstones and rocks. It looked like they'd been labeled at one point, but the ink had faded off all of the stickers. There was a very old, large black leather-bound book on a wooden stand. There was a whole shelf of jars filled with different flowers, leaves, and sticks. The names on the labels didn't mean anything to me—verbena, Five flavored Tea of F—like I knew what any of that was. There was some sort of taser, a fat purple gourd covered with dust, and a long trumpet thing with no buttons to press to make notes. Okay then. It was all tucked in back there, next to the extra cartons of cheap cigarettes, like it was standard corner-store stock.

The stuff behind the counter was super weird, no doubt about it, but there was one big thing that was more disturbing. It was subtle, so it took me a while to figure it out, but here it is: Apart from Bob the Doughnut Guy and the jogger, no one actually came *into* the store. That wouldn't be weird on its own, because this part of the burbs is ugly, run down, and doesn't have any chain stores. Suburb-dwelling Ohioans *love* chain stores, so this street wouldn't be much of a draw.

It was only weird because a lot of people were *leaving* the store. Dozens and dozens of people. A steady stream of perfectly ordinary-looking men and women came out of the beer cave. Each one stopped to talk to DeeDee and to show her something. I didn't know what. I didn't have a clear view from here. Then, every single one of them walked right out the front door. With no beer. No snacks. No nothing. Long story short: People came *out* of the beer cave, even though nobody ever went *in*.

Two cars did pull into the lot, though. But, both times, the drivers sat in their cars for a few minutes, then left without so much as stepping a single foot on the pavement. It's like there was an aura around this place that drove people away.

One truck did come into the lot and stay, though. The beer truck. The driver looked into the store nervously, then made the sign of the cross before he hopped out and ran to the back of the truck. I'd never seen anyone load a dolly as fast as that guy. He looked like he was competing for the world championship title for Fastest Beer Delivery. He stacked that dolly with cases and forties and had it wheeled through the front door in under five minutes Then he just left it all on the floor mat by the slushy station and split. Seriously. He dropped that dolly like it was hot, then ran like Usain Bolt back to his truck. He didn't ask me to check anything or sign anything. He just kicked it into gear and sped out of there so fast the tires actually squealed.

"Hey, new guy," DeeDee called across the store. "Looks like there's actually some beer for you to stock tonight. Lucky you."

Sigh. Fine. I mean, I couldn't complain. At least it wasn't another snake dude. I wheeled the dolly over to the beer cave. Man, how did that guy move so fast? This thing was heavy! I hated to admit it, but I huffed and puffed while wheeling it to the beer cave. DeeDee opened the door for me, and I was halfway through it when she put her hand on my arm. "Hey, new guy," she said. "Whatever you do, don't touch it. Don't even go near it. Promise?"

She looked genuinely concerned.

"Promise." I smiled at her and nearly melted when she smiled back. Of course, I didn't know what she was talking about. *Touch what? It's beer.*

I wheeled the dolly in, and the door closed behind me. The beer cave was a dim, large rectangle with stainless steel walls. It was so cold I could see my breath, and my body instantly broke out in goosebumps. The only light came from a single flickering fluorescent strip light running down the center of the ceiling, and the weak beams that filtered in through the glass-front, reach-in self-serve doors facing the storefront.

No one was in the cave but me. No mystery people. No snake guys. No tentacles. That made me feel a bit better, although I was still stumped about who those people were and how they got in here.

Beer stocking was self-explanatory, hard to screw up, so I kinda liked it. I slid forties into the slots behind the self-serve doors. The twelve and twenty-four packs were easy too because each beer brand had its own section. I'd just plunked down my first case when the cave suddenly lit up bright blue. I heard a *whirrrr whirrr* noise behind me. *Jesus fucking Christ. Snakes! Attack!*

I jumped, twisting around in mid-air, landing in a bad Elvis Kenpo Karate stance. Seriously. Just like a fat Elvis. My paunch jiggled, but without as much pizzazz. I didn't believe what I saw in front of me, so I blinked hard. *What. The. Fuck.* One wall of the beer cave was...*gone.* No, not gone, open, transformed into a swirling neon blue vortex of thick misty clouds, like a bigger bluer version of the thing inside the Michael Bolton CD case.

A black blob appeared in the middle, small and round like a bowling ball. Okay, it started out like a bowling ball but morphed and changed as if something was moving closer to me, through the mist, out of the mist. *Oh fuck. Here it comes.* It was the outline of a...man? A *human* man stepped out of the swirling vortex. I fell backward, toppling a stack of Pabst Blue Ribbon cases. I rubbed my eyes. *He can't be real.* I opened them. *Oh shit. He's real.*

The man standing before me was delightfully tentacle and snake-free, although he was outrageously tacky and reeked of Aqua Velva. *Dude.* That was my great grandpa's aftershave. Do they even still make that stuff?

The man pulled a comb out of his back pocket and ran it through his pomaded hair, sprucing up his black pompadour. He wore a powder blue polyester leisure suit—no joke. His shirt had a butterfly collar and was open nearly down to his belly button. *Dear Jesus, deliver me from 1972.*

He strutted toward me as if the Saturday Night Fever soundtrack was pulsing disco through his veins. I started to get up, but he put his hand on my chest to stop me. "Move aside, Champ," he said. He sniffed the air like a hound dog. "You smell that? Mmmm. Mmmmm. There are at least a dozen sad, lonely women at the Temptations Tavern tonight, and their panties aren't gonna take themselves off. Yeah. That's right, ladies. I'm coming."

He looked at me. "Well, son. It's time to make some lucky lady's fantasy a reality."

He readjusted his package (ahem, that one. Downstairs.) with one hand. "Let me show you how it's done. Watch the master work."

Then he scratched his ass and headed for the exit where DeeDee was waiting for him. "You're late, Morty," she said. "It's not like you to leave a bar full of lonely women waiting."

"Mmmm. Mmmm. Mmmmmm. You're looking good tonight, sweetheart. I've got a few minutes free if you're itching for a taste of real man." Morty sidled up to DeeDee and leaned in real close to talk to her, one arm on the wall, the other curling a strand of her blue hair. "Whadaya say?"

I wanted to keep staring at this man, Morty. I mean his moves were so disco porn, he was hard not to watch. But the blue, the swirling whatever, that stood where the wall used to be, I felt it...calling to me? Voices whispered, sweet and soft, even sweeter than Dolly's doughnuts.

I looked back at DeeDee. She wasn't watching. The voices. They were so close, right on the other side of the swirl. I couldn't resist. One look couldn't hurt. The whispers were too tempting, the mist too beautiful. I crawled closer, my knees freezing on the cold steel floor, entranced by the blue. The colors were so vibrant, so thick, they looked like the splurps of color in the opening credits of Barbarella. Neon. Teal, cerulean and navy blues moved in a circle like a slow, gentle hurricane. I had to touch them, see if they felt as amazing as they looked.

"Aw, Morty. Always such a charmer," DeeDee said behind me. Her voice sounded far away. "You know the rules. Besides, you know I don't

43

mix work with pleasure."

"Rules. Ha. More like guidelines, sweetheart. But, suit yourself." Morty shrugged. "Someday you'll get a whiff of what you're missing. When you're ready, I won't let you down."

There were whispers in the mist. I had to know what they were saying. *I'm almost there, voices. Wait for me.*

"Got your papers?" DeeDee said to Morty. I heard rustling. "All right. Have fun tonight. Be back by dawn. No afternoon delight like last time, okay? You know your face doesn't stick as well in the daylight."

"Or does it?" Morty blew her a kiss and whisked out of the beer cave. "Maybe my real face is even better."

I was so close to the swirling beautiful blue. I reached out to it. The mist twirled faster. *I'm coming. Don't leave.* The mist lapped at the tips of my fingers.

Smack. Suddenly, I was butt-sliding backward across the freezing metal floor. My back hit a wall of beer. A case crunched open, raining cans down on top of my head. "Ow!"

DeeDee stood between me and the beautiful swirling blue, which was shrinking, undulating, swirling smaller and smaller behind her, until it completely disappeared, leaving only an ordinary steel wall where it once stood.

"No!" I shrieked. My soul felt like it was sinking. I was so close. I was dizzy, a little disoriented, the ghosts of those secret whispers still in my head.

"I totally get it." She pulled me up off the floor. "It put me under its spell the first time I saw it, too. It's beautiful, isn't it? And the voices. You want to know what they're saying, don't you? And who's saying them."

I nodded.

"Okay. But don't. Not ever. Do you understand? Put it out of your mind. The voices, all of it, is bad news. There's nothing good in there for you and me. It's not for us, for humans, for mortals, okay? This is for other things, other creatures. We're not equipped for whatever is on the other side. We can't survive over there. Do you understand?"

I shook off the haze. "Wait. What? Mortals? Other creatures? But the wall. The tacky guy..."

I'd like to say I pieced this together like Tetris, but no. I didn't.

DeeDee walked me over to the cold steel wall and touched it gently with her fingertips. "Welcome to Transmundane Gate Twenty Three, Celestial Sector Seventeen," DeeDee said. "The blue swirl? That, new guy, is the portal."

"The portal to where?"

44

"Do you want the long, nuanced answer or the short, easy-to-understand answer?"

"The easy one," I said. Duh. Always choosing the easy way was kinda my thing.

"That's the gate to hell," she said. "Welcome to celestial homeland security. We're the border patrol between hell and earth."

CHAPTER 5

I didn't sleep at all that night. Okay, technically day, since my shift ended when the sun came up, and no it wasn't the blinding bright sunlight burning through the curtain cracks that was keeping me awake.

I rolled over and checked the clock. *Gah.* Ten a.m. I was exhausted but too wound up to sleep. My mind reeled. The blue swirl. The Michael Bolton CD. The snake guy. A gateway to hell in a beer cave in Columbus, Ohio? The single yellow eyeball surrounded by barbed tentacles. It couldn't possibly be real, but it sure felt real.

I pinched myself a zillion times. I tossed and turned. At one point, I smacked my own face, hard, convinced I was actually asleep and all of this had been an insane crazy-go-nuts dream. But no. I was awake. Like, awake awake, not in a dream where I just thought I was awake. Which meant I was either clinically insane, or I had to come to grips with the fact that there was a portal to actual hell in the back of the beer cave at the 24/7 Dairy Mart. Or was it the 24/7 Demon Mart? The memory of the glowing red neon sign rolled over me. If the portal was real, the sign must be, too.

Okay. Okay. Suppose I believed this was all real. If the beer cave was a portal to hell, what did that make Faust? Was he the devil? Like, *the devil* devil? Lord of hell, fallen angel, source of evil in the world yada yada all that Bible crap? *Holy shit, I didn't eat an apple there did I? Think. Think. Chef. Tuna, yes. Apple, no.* And if I worked for the devil, did that mean I had a soul and that he now owned that soul? *OhmiGod.* If hell was real, was it all lake of fire and eternal torment a la Dante's Inferno? And wouldn't this mean heaven was real, too? And if it was, was sin an actual thing I needed to start worrying about? Was Saint Peter up there at the Pearly Gates, keeping tabs on us all like a creepy Santa Claus?

What if Pastor Woodruff wasn't a nut job? So. Much. Masturbating. I'd jerked it so much I could be doomed to eternal hellfire on that charge alone. Add in lying to Simone and my parents, plus Lee's booger sandwich.

Jesus. I'm fucked. Shit. Wait. Was that using the Lord's name in vain? That's a sin, too, right?

I'll be frank. My brain was not set up for this much analysis. So. Much. Reeling. I couldn't even keep that whole assassination of Arch Duke what's-his-name / start of World War One stuff straight in history class, and that was laid out in a neat little timeline. (Look. There was a reason I was a community college dropout.) I was not qualified to tackle this level of ambiguity or existential crisis. I hadn't even taken Philosophy 101 yet.

But the money, Lloyd. You NEED the money! Sixty-six bucks an hour. At thirty-five hours a week, count on fingers, carry the one, holy crap, that was north of two grand a paycheck. I couldn't make more than minimum wage anywhere else. I couldn't even finish an associate's degree. I had no skills. I couldn't plumb, weld or wire. Minimum wage was it for me, and that would get me max three hundred bucks a week. Before taxes. I was in debt. I worked for the devil. I was doomed.

Can't deal. I pulled my sheet up tight around my head. *Ew.* What's that smell? Armpits and feet. *Gross.* Note to self: Wash sheets ASAP.

I tossed and turned, trying to put it out of my mind. I could talk myself out of believing in devils and hell gates, but I couldn't talk myself out of debt. It was there whether I believed it or not. Stupid money. It always got me into trouble, because I didn't actually have any of it. I owed Simone two grand in back rent. Plus, the unpaid cable bills from our apartment, all in my name, and all sent to collections. I needed a thousand bucks to fix my car, plus however much to insure it. I had four grand in student loans with payments set to start any day now because I wasn't in school anymore. Then there was the six hundred bucks my parents paid for the exterminator. Plus, if I were a decent son, I'd pay them the twenty-five hundred bucks for the semester of community college I blew by "forgetting" to drop out. I did some more math on my fingers. Six plus five, carry the one. Plus two, plus...*Crap.* Whatever. I was no math whiz, but any idiot could see I had ten grand in debt, easy.

I was in a hole so deep I couldn't see the sun. That wasn't even counting money to get my own apartment or buy food. My brokeness sat like a two-ton boulder of adulting-is-too-hard on my chest. I'd have to work forever just to break even. *It's official: Lloyd, you are a loser, and you're massively up a creek of shit so high it's beyond flood stage.*

But Faust already knew that, didn't he? He'd said I had ten grand in debt before I'd even added it all up. That's how the devil got you, wasn't it? With money. Because you're desperate. Riches now for damnation later. *Man.* I was easy pickings.

Come on, God! I don't deserve this! It wasn't me. It was the system.

Hear me out. Jobs didn't pay squat, so you went into debt for an education for the promise of a good job. If you messed up and didn't make it, you were even more screwed than if you'd never tried at all. Everyone in the world was fighting for a chance at a Kardashian life, but most of us fail. I had failed. And now here I was. I went down in flames, and the devil scooped me up. I should have turned tail and run the second I saw that yellow eye pop out of the beer cave.

All right. Decision made. Work for the devil? Nope. I can't. I quit. I'm not the best guy who ever walked the earth, but I'm not bad enough to burn in a pit of fire for all eternity. No job was worth that. I'd find another way to make ten grand. Can you legally sell a kidney? I didn't need two, did I?

Apparently, deciding to quit was all I needed to do to fall asleep. I zonked out hard. Sure, I had a vivid dream about the mist swirling. In my version, the voices belonged to a handful of super-duper hot chicks with horns who wanted to do me. I'm gonna stop there because it got pretty graphic, and I had to do a five-finger sin on myself for a hot second when I woke up. The chicks in my dream were sexy. I had no choice. Morning wood would have been all-day wood, ya feel me? But I swear, that was *the* last time.

When that was finished, I vowed right then and there that I was gonna be a model citizen. Heaven, here I come. I was gonna find a job that wouldn't imperil my immortal soul. Work hard. Finish college. Keep my hands out of my pants. (Hardest part, frankly.) Go to church on Sundays. (Snooze, but pretty sure that was required.) I was going full polo-shirt and khakis, respectable-haircut, shark-white Joel-Osteen-teeth Christian. The "Hell is Real" billboard on the highway between here and Cincinnati? *Yeah. I feel you dude. I get it.* I was gonna rock the fuck out of the Ten Commandments, starting right now. Except that I just said fuck. Was cursing a sin? If so, sorry God. Honest mistake.

I crawled out of bed. The clock said it was nearly eight at night. My red leather-bound employee manual sat on my nightstand. *Nope. Nope. Nope.* I dropped it into my trash can, then covered it with the dozen or so Monster Burger wrappers I suddenly felt compelled to clean off of my desk. Cleanliness and Godliness, and all.

Crap. If I was gonna make it into heaven, I better wash the stink off of my sheets. I yanked them off the bed by the corners, gathering it all up into a dirty ball to carry down to the washer. I immediately tripped over a pile of filthy laundry on the floor, landing face-first on the rug. I had crumbs stuck to my face when I peeled myself up. Clearly, cleaning was gonna be the second hardest part of making it as a Christian, behind not touching myself. Dude. No wonder so many evangelicals were angry all the time. It was hard work vacuuming up floor crumbs and washing clothes after a maximum of two wearings. I'd seen those Christian Mommy Blogs. Their houses were spotless. Maybe they thought Jesus might drop in any second. Was that how the Rapture worked? Ugh. This new leaf I'd turned over already kinda sucked. So. Much. Work.

But, if the alternative was eternal torment...All right. Decision made. Step one. Quit job. Then, clean room and do laundry. Tomorrow: Sell some plasma, apply for a job at Monster Burger, research black market kidney prices. Flipping burgers and dipping fry baskets would keep Mom happy while I sought my riches via a Mexican organ transplant racket, right? I stumbled down the stairs, dirty sheet ball in arms, swelling with the confidence that came with having a plan.

Mmmm. A delicious honey-barbecue-scented cloud wafted down the hallway. My tummy rumbled.

The laundry room was a cubby in the main hall leading between the front door and the kitchen. There was only enough space to jam a washer and dryer, and all Mom's other cleaning tools that I had never touched once in the twenty years we'd lived here. I pushed the Swiffer out of the way and put the sheets in the top-loader, poured in the detergent, and turned it on. The machine filled with water and started vibrating. I accidentally brushed against it when I yawned, so you know how this story was about to go. The vibrations sent my mind and my nether region right back to those misty dream sirens. Yep. New wood.

"Good evening, honey." My Mom stepped in and wrapped her arms around me, hugging me from behind.

My hands moved lightning fast to cover my crotch, by instinct. There were some things moms didn't need to see and hard-ons were number one on the list.

"How was your first day—um, night—at your new job? Come into the kitchen and tell me all about it. I want details!" Her voice was sing-song happy. She spun me around and as soon as we were facing each other, she said: "Are you all right?"

I adjusted my pants. "Yeah. Fine. Do you need something? I gotta vacuum my room."

Her jaw dropped for a split second, and she mouthed "vacuum?" When the shock wore off, she said, "Well, honey, I like this new industrious employed you. It suits you."

Oh, man. That wasn't good. Cue painful Mom lecture about quitting after one shift.

"Tell you what," she said. "The vacuum can wait. Come eat dinner. I made your favorite. Pulled pork and cheesy potatoes!"

She pinched my cheek, smiled, then cheek-yanked me into the

kitchen. Dad sat at the table itching to dig into his plate, but resisting because Mom clearly had told him not to touch a thing until we were all ready. I saw the pain in his smile/grimace. *Dude. I feel ya.* A mound of pulled pork slathered in barbecue sauce blooped out of his overstuffed burger bun. His plate was piled high with canned green beans and a steaming yellow mountain of sliced potatoes, smothered in melted American cheese and onions. It smelled so so good. This was five-star Ohio Mom cuisine.

"Go on, make a plate," Mom said.

I did. She did. We all sat at the table together. Which is what families are supposed to do, but it was weird because we weren't *that* family. We rarely ate together or even at the same time, except on holidays. Or when my sister was home from college, rubbing it in my face that she was actually going to get a degree. With honors. Stupid sister.

I took a bite of my pulled pork sandwich. So sweet, so salty, so delicious. "Mmmm." I groaned. I couldn't help it.

"Oh, sweetie, I'm glad you like it. I made it just for you," Mom said. "To celebrate."

My gut sunk into my shoe. "Celuhbrade wha...?" My mouth was stuffed full, okay?

"Your new job, silly," she said. "We're very proud of you."

Shit. How was I gonna tell her I quit? I had a minute to think while I chewed a giant wad of sweet barbecued meat.

"Yep. Real proud, Lloyd," Dad said. A blob of barbecue sauce sat on his chin. "Frankly, we were worried you'd never get back out there. You haven't had a job since Simone left—"

Mom kicked him under the table and shot him a death stare at the mention of Simone's name. Dude. They were so melodramatic. It's not like I couldn't keep a job. It hadn't been *that* long. I'd had plenty of gigs. Like the Subway on campus. Okay, so they fired me because I couldn't remember which meat stack went on which sandwich. I mean cold cut combo vs BMT? Next time you're in a Subway, look at the menu and see if you can keep all the damn sandwiches straight.

Then, I had that hipster coffee shop gig. Okay. Bad example. I was canned after a single shift because my clothes weren't hip enough. Who can afford sweet duds on nine bucks an hour? Well, maybe it was because I put real milk, real sugar, and full-powered espresso in that one Lululemon MILF's sugar-free soy latte, double half-caf, no whip. She freaked. I was fired. I guess the boss didn't like it when I asked her, "Why drink coffee at all if that's what you order?"

But come on, that wasn't that long ago. Hmm. Okay, maybe it was. Simone dumped me that very same night. So yeah, it'd been a while since

I'd had a job. But I wasn't so hopeless that this merited Mom making us all sit down to eat together.

"Well, sweetie?" Mom asked.

Crap. I'd done it again. Mom and Dad had been talking to me, but I was spacing out. "Well, what?" I asked.

"Your new job. What is it?"

"Oh, you know, the 24/7 Demon, uh, Dairy Mart. The place with all the slushies?"

"Great. That's just great." She kept a big smile plastered hard on her face, even though I knew deep down she was thinking that her son, the college dropout, worked at a corner store while all his high school friends were getting their degrees and working office jobs with benefits. Yep, I knew how to make a mom proud. "So what's it like? What sorts of things do you do there?"

Fight snake monsters that spring from the depths of hell. "Stock beer, doughnuts. That kinda thing."

"And your boss. Does he seem nice?"

Sure. If you think the devil is nice. Ugh. I had to just rip the Band-Aid off already and tell her I was quitting "Uh, I guess, but, I'm qu—"

"I nearly forgot, call Grandma after dinner. I already told her the news. She wants details."

Oh, man. There was no going back now. She'd brought Grandma into this. My stomach twisted up in stress knots and suddenly my appetite disappeared.

"The ladies at book club want to know everything, too!" She was so excited she clapped her hands.

Dear Lord, help me. She'd told her book club. That was like writing it in concrete. It was out there forever.

"Oh, and I nearly forgot. You definitely want to be a clean plater tonight. There's an ice cream cake in the refrigerator. Cookies and cream. Your favorite!"

CHAPTER 6

It was the ice cream cake that did me in. If I burned in hell, it was straight up my Mom's fault. Because yes. I showed up for work tonight, even though I planned to quit. *Because Mom bought a fucking ice cream cake.* She only busted those out for super special occasions, like birthdays and graduations. We'd sunk to the point where my getting this job apparently ranked that high on her chart of life milestones. If I quit now, I'd poop directly on the small buzz she was getting from her very low expectations of me.

It wasn't quite eleven, and I was standing behind the counter. I scooped the last puddle of cherry slushy out of my Colossal Super Slurp cup as I stared at the neon sign through the window. It was definitely not the same sign customers saw. I was damn sure about that. The blue and pink neon I *used* to see wasn't there. Instead, the letters glowed red, spelling out 24/7 Demon Mart. The movable letters that normally announced hot dog and beer specials said "Gate 23, this way." The neon arrow pointed directly into the store. "Open from witching to dawn. Hours and standard gate rules strictly enforced. Please have your documentation in order."

Welp. There you have it. Dairy Mart was officially Demon Mart. And, thanks to Mom's special dinner/ice cream cake/called Grandma guiltfest, my soul had been gift-wrapped and delivered straight to the devil. Yep. No way around it. An ice cream cake had doomed me to hell forever.

Fine. Whatever. I know you're thinking it, and I couldn't quit, all right? I absolutely couldn't, because if I did, I'd stomp on Mom's happiness. And worse, she'd give me The Look. You know the one. The Look that said abject disappointment and broken dreams. The Look that said all she wanted was to be proud of you. Just. One. Time. The Look that said "Please do something right so I can say nice things about you at book club. All the other ladies gush about how awesome their overachieving kids are, so why can't you give me One. Nice. Thing. to say about you?"

Gah. All people with mothers—no matter how old they are—are powerless against that. It wasn't just me. So I showed up tonight. I'd spent the last hour terrified, doing whatever DeeDee told me to, but jumping at the smallest noise or shadow for fear another nefarious hell beast was about to attack. And all this while trying to figure out how I could quit and still make my Mom proud.

I nearly had it worked out. I'd work here, but not one second longer than I had to. I figured at sixty-six bucks an hour, I'd need to work full time for about a month and a half to pay back all the money I owed. I could be debt-free by Thanksgiving. The student loans, the exterminator, Simone, all of it. That would impress Mom and show Simone I wasn't a deadbeat. I'd have a clean slate. I could get a safer job somewhere else. *Gulp.* If I survived until then. These hell monsters, they couldn't *kill* us, could they?

I hadn't quite worked out how to save my soul. I didn't know if it was already too late. Honestly, I had to throw my hands up at this one, because I didn't know how any of this heaven stuff worked. My family wasn't exactly churchy. Mom only sent me to Vacation Bible School because it was free. Well, and because I nearly burned the house down one time when she left me home alone so she could go get groceries. Long story. So yeah. I figured it was a safe bet to start at Christian 101 and full-on obey some commandments. I'd have to work on the Jesus-approved clothes, though. I looked down at my "I'm the Worst" T-shirt. It was the only clean one left in the drawer.

Jesus, is it hot in here? A thin film of sweat covered me. My heart was beating so fast I felt like I'd actually jogged. I'm guessing because I'd only ever jogged from my bedroom to the fridge. *Oh, wait.* This feeling wasn't exercise, it was full-on fear. Because I was butt clenched-tighter-than-a-pickle-jar-lid scared, wondering how many snake and tentacle dudes I'd have to fight before my debt was repaid. The ice-cold slippery slope to doom grew steeper by the second.

"New man, you have my payment." A deep voice boomed in my ear. "Give it to me quickly."

I jumped. *Jesus!* The voice belonged to a tall, very ripped black man standing at the register. *His payment? Give it to me? Wait.* Was I being robbed, but eloquently? It was hard to tell. He didn't have a gun or anything. He just stood there, silent, serious, with his muscled, Schwarzenegger-in-Predator-sized arms crossed. Seriously. He was so buff, his arms looked like tree trunks made of meat. He wore black head to toe and looked like he'd never smiled once in his whole life. Yep, a robber in the perfect all-black slip-into-the-shadows-like-a-ninja outfit.

"Make haste. I need my payment now, or there will be hell to pay."
He had an accent, something vaguely Caribbean. "I cannot be away for
long. Give me what I came for. Now, if you please."

Welp. Here it is. My first robbery. I pressed 'No Sale' on the register
and the drawer slid open. The man eyed me, puzzled. Or angry. I couldn't
tell. All I knew was his eyebrows furrowed so hard he went from two
down to one.

"What are you doing, new man?" he asked.

DeeDee ran up to me and slammed the register drawer shut with my
fingers still in it. *Ow!* I screamed, pulled my fingers out, and sucked on
the tips. I didn't know why that made them hurt less. It just did.

"Forgive him, Doc. He's new. Very new," she said to the man. "I've
got it here. Made just for you, as usual. I hid it from him, because I was
afraid he'd eat it."

She reached below the counter and pulled out a small pink box with
Dolly's Divine Delicacies embossed in gold across the top. It contained a
single glazed doughnut with pink frosting and rainbow sprinkles. The
box was tied shut with a gold ribbon. It was Bob the Doughnut Guy's
special order.

The man's eyes lit up when he saw it, like a little kid on Christmas
morning. Wow. This dude seriously loved a pink doughnut. We're talking
Barbie pink, too. Only a real man would be caught dead eating *that* in
public. But Mr. Meat Muscle Ninja Arms here could eat a giant cream
puff and no one would dare question his masculinity.

"Thank you, Ms. DeeDee." He took the box. "Godspeed."

The large black man left, completely disappearing into the shadows
the second he stepped off the curb. See, I was right! Ninja!

DeeDee put her hands on her hips. "Why did you open the register?
Did you think he was robbing you?"

Uh oh. I could tell I was in trouble.

"Let me guess. A black guy comes in here, so he must be a robber,"
she said. "Are you a racist shit bag?"

Oh, my God. No! No! No! Oh man. I'm not that guy. I swear. "But...
I...He said...I didn't know—" The more I talked the worst I sounded.
Great. I was one smartphone video away from becoming the next Permit
Patty.

She glared at me. "I'll let it slide one time only because you're new.
But if you are a racist, cut it out. We live in Ohio. We're the Union, the
North. We won the Civil War, freed the slaves and all that, so fucking act
like it."

"Okay. Okay!"

"Good," she said. "Now that we're straight. That's Doc. He manages the Go Away charm on the store. We pay him in doughnuts."

"The...what?"

"The Go Away charm. It flips on at midnight every night."

I waited for her to elaborate because normal people usually throw in some details without prompting when they drop a WTF bomb that big, but she didn't. "He owns the pawnshop across the street. He's a regular."

"Uh. Okay." I knew the place. It didn't have a name. It was a two-story brick building directly across the street from here. It had huge glass display windows full of used stuff and a light-up sign that only said 'Pawn'. I didn't think it had an actual name. "I've never been in there. I'll have to go check it out sometime."

She grabbed my arm and squeezed. "Don't do that. Don't ever buy anything from there. Never. Never ever. Got it?"

"Why not? Overpriced?"

"Let's just say you never get what you're expecting," she said.

So, was she saying the big guy was a rip-off artist? Her expression was hard to read. "So why do we give him the doughnuts again?"

"I don't know." She shrugged. "That's always been the deal. I guess he likes them."

I glanced at the doughnut case. Empty. All crumbs. Except for another completely untouched row of pink-frosted ones. "They do look delicious. Maybe I'll try one."

DeeDee stepped between me and the case. "Nope. No doughnuts for us. That's the deal."

"Why not? What's so bad about eating a doughnut?"

"They make you fat," she said. "Did you restock all the cigarette racks?"

"Um. Yeah." Visions of doughnuts dancing in my head turned to the sad reality of Pyramids, Eagle 20s, and off-brand cheap smokes. They sat on carousel racks on the counter, like candy for all the broke-ass people who still smoked and hadn't yet realized vaping was the new hotness.

"Great. Oh, and you should start reading that tonight." She pointed at the giant black book on the wood stand.

Read? Not really my thing. Headache pending just thinking about it.

"Remember that TV slogan? The more you know? It definitely applies here, new guy." She smiled at me, and for a split second my knees got a little noodly.

At least DeeDee was talking to me. Maybe this job wasn't all bad. Of course, she couldn't be any more beautiful. The diamond on her septum piercing glittered under the fluorescent lights. Her outfit, as usual, was all black and showed off her curves in a badass, goth Tomb Raider way. I was debating either falling at her feet and telling her I loved her or asking her if our souls were really doomed to hell when the door opened and in walked Caroline Ford Vanderbilt.

Fuck. If guts could actually sink into shoes, mine would be piled high in my Pumas. Caroline Ford Vanderbilt was the richest lady in our suburb, or at least she wanted everyone to think she was. She was so upper crust that one last name wasn't good enough. Oh no, she and her two snooty children introduced themselves as Ford Vanderbilt, not just Vanderbilt. She was the mother of Madison Ford Vanderbilt (See? She'd given her daughter a third snooty last name as a first name!), the insufferable valedictorian of my high school graduating class. The girl that drove a BMW, but referred to it as "this old thing" and had her name on every damned trophy in the display case by the principal's office. If you think money doesn't buy opportunity, show me one instance where Mean Girl Madison Ford Vanderbilt had to bootstrap for anything.

"Why, I don't believe my eyes. Is that you Lloyd Wallace?" Caroline feigned surprise. Her voice was sing-song high. "I heard a little rumor you were working here. That's so wonderful. I had heard you got yourself a little job. Bless your sweet little heart."

Jesus, Mom's book club hens had a well-rooted grapevine. Caroline's auburn bob brushed the collar of her black fur coat, which was an odd contrast to the crisp white tennis skirt and polo she wore underneath. It was a look that screamed Great Gatsby. Caroline Ford Vanderbilt had mastered the fake sweet smile, and she was pouring it over me like corn syrup. Her mauve lips curled up tight at the ends, showing just enough shark-white teeth to remind you how hard she could bite.

She rounded the corner. "Why Lloyd, don't you look *healthy,*" she eyed me, shoes to hair then down again. *Chomp.*

"I think she just called you fat," DeeDee whispered.

I tried to get her to shut up by swatting her under the counter so Caroline didn't see, but DeeDee didn't take the hint. I forced a polite smile so hard it hurt. "How are you, Mrs. Vanderbilt?"

"That's Mrs. Ford Vanderbilt," she corrected.

DeeDee dug her fingers into my forearm and squeezed so hard I could almost feel her eyes roll.

"What a delightful surprise to see you, Lloyd. I popped in to get some..." she looked around, frowning at the low status of her surroundings. "Dish soap. Yes. Dish soap. I was on my way home from the Country Club. Did you know our family have been members since 1903? Gracious. Can you imagine? Anyhoo, I had just finished a doubles tennis match and a much-needed cocktail hour with the top-rated neurosurgeon in the city and his wife—you wouldn't know them—when the maid called to say we needed dish soap. Naturally, I didn't want to send her home. She simply has to wash up. This was the only place that wasn't out of the way, although I admit I rarely visit this part of town."

She looked around again, barely disguising her disgust. I didn't have to be a mind reader to know she was lying. She only came here because I worked here. She came for details, so she could embellish the gossip she was going to spread about me. Poor Mom. She was in for it now. Her loser son, the hot topic of the day.

"Oh goodness, look at the time." She glanced at her watch. A gold thing, with some sort of diamond crust around the face, all real, most likely. "I have to get home tout de suite. The maid can't possibly risk falling behind. We're having a party this weekend. Madison will be home for the first time since she started Yale Law last month. I'm sure you heard. Madison aced her LSATs. Harvard and Yale were practically fist fighting over her. Well, we decided to go with Yale, because why settle for second best? Oh, dear sweet, Lloyd. I see you haven't changed a bit. How's your mother holding up? She's so brave. I've heard it's so hard to have a special-needs child."

Oh. My. God. Did she just call me "special needs?" DeeDee's fingernails dug even deeper into my arm. Caroline shook her head and gave me her most faux-sincere pity eyes.

"Wow," DeeDee whispered. "She's actually shit-talking about you in *front* of your face."

"What's that, dear?" Caroline pursed her Botoxed lips and raised an eyebrow at DeeDee.

"The dish soap is in aisle five," DeeDee said in a voice as sweet and thick as buttercream icing.

"Thank you...Miss?" Caroline evaluated DeeDee, but with a blank expression. She looked like a computer with an error code like she didn't exactly know how to categorize DeeDee or where she fit in the pecking order. Caroline didn't care enough to figure it out and pranced off like a show horse, her tennis skirt swishing under the hem of her fur jacket.

"That lady is a piece of work." DeeDee then pinched my cheeks and started talking to me in an imitation mommy voice. "I didn't know you were special needs. Aw, my sweet little retard. Don't worry. I'll take care of you."

I blushed. Hard. Partly from the humiliation of Caroline, partly because DeeDee was being super nice to me. Caroline's barbs were almost worth it. Almost. Or not. The moment didn't last. DeeDee and I couldn't help but watch Caroline's dyed-auburn hair bobbing up and down in the cleaner aisle, dreading the fresh insults she'd bring with her when she came back to the register.

Suddenly a bright green light flashed on the shelf by my foot. A tiny swirling green cloud appeared there. I jumped backward and shrieked. "Jesus, what is that?"

What manner of monster was gonna step through this swirling hole?

"What's your problem?" DeeDee asked, legit unconcerned.

I watched a tiny black shape emerge from the lime cloud. *Okay. Okay. At least it's small.* Maybe I could squash it, step on it. Then again, a small monster might be worse. What if it crawled down my throat and ripped outta me like an alien chest-burster? *Oh. Hell. No.* I wasn't about to die here. I was gonna live to see another Thanksgiving.

A pair of thin long tentacles emerged from the vortex, then a flat, round head. *Oh, Jesus. Please don't let it be a bug. I hate bugs!* Two thin legs with little spiky hairs all up and down them poked out, then two more matching legs, then two more, all attached to a flat, long brown roach body. It was a roach. A roach from hell.

I practically parkour jumped over the counter. *Bug spray. Bug spray. Where is the fucking bug spray?* Oh yeah. Aisle five. Household cleaners and random hardware, because you totally need that when you're buying beer and lotto tickets. I sprinted to the end of aisle five. Thankfully Caroline Ford Vanderbilt had her back to me and didn't notice. I grabbed a can of Kill 'Em Dead off the shelf and ran back to the counter. The filthy hell roach was now casually perched on the microphone for the store-wide intercom system. I popped the cap off the bug spray and aimed. The roach looked me right in the eyes and lifted its front two legs like it was...surrendering? *Wait.* Roaches aren't capable of surrender. They're insects. They don't have higher brain function. They're too stupid.

My index finger was in position, ready to press down on the nozzle when I heard a tiny, high-pitched voice. "Really, dude? Who are you calling stupid?"

"What the hell do you think you're doing?" DeeDee asked. "Put the can down right now."

"Roach..." was all I could squeak out. Roach out of yet another vortex to the other world. Just like the beer cave, just like the Michael Bolton CD. What, could these portals just open up anywhere? Doesn't matter now, okay it does, but the takeaway was "devil roach," I said. "From hell."

DeeDee and the roach laughed. Laughed! But when I fixed my Kill 'Em Dead on the roach again, DeeDee ninja hurdled the counter and kicked the bug spray out of my hand all in one smooth move, crouching fucking tiger style. *Jesus.* "What did you do that for?" I squealed. "He's a hell roach. He's gotta go!"

"He is not a hell roach. That's Kevin. He works here," she said. "He's the night manager, remember? He's in charge."

I looked at Kevin. Kevin looked at me. *Shit.* He had a tiny white name tag on his little bug chest. Thorax? Chest. *Whatever, I don't know.* Then it dawned on me. He was the roach on the slushy machine the night that green tentacle dude thwapped out of the beer cave. The roach who flipped me the bird. *Oh shit.* I hated bugs, and now I had one for a manager.

Kevin the roach pressed one leg down on the button that turned on the intercom and stretched his tiny mouth up to the microphone. The speakers crackled, as his tiny, high-pitched voice announced. "May I have your attention, DeeDee and mentally-challenged new guy. There's a Grade Two Possession in aisle five."

CHAPTER 7

Grade Two Possession? I didn't know what that meant, but I did know it couldn't be good.

DeeDee and I looked at each other, eyes wide, then slowly turned toward aisle five. Naturally, I was scared shitless, and it didn't help that DeeDee looked nervous, too. Ms. Calm, Cool, and Cazh in the face of a halo of tentacles and a bundle of snakes in a fedora looked rattled, so yeah. If something could actually ruffle *her* feathers, I had a God-given right to be terrified.

She grabbed my shirt and pulled me close to her. "Here's the plan." She whispered in my ear. Her breath was hot, and it tickled all my sensitive ear bits. I won't lie. Even in the face of death by grisly hell beast, my reptile brain sent a signal straight downstairs. *Half chub pending. Crap. Cut it out, Lloyd! Pay attention. This is life or death here!*

"We're gonna tiptoe over there as quietly as we can and check it out. Okay?" Her voice was so low I suspected pods of whales a thousand miles away in the Atlantic could hear it. "All right. Let's go."

We inched across the walkway, closer and closer, stepping so lightly and so quietly the linoleum floor could have been made of cotton balls. We made it to the end cap, hidden from the view of the aisle five peril by a rack of first-world survival necessities such as unicorn-shaped cell phone chargers and Hammer All Night boner pills. DeeDee held tight to my arm. My heart rate was, oh, about zillion beats per minute at this point.

"Okay. On three." DeeDee whispered.

"What on three?" I squealed.

"Shhh. Jesus. Quiet! On three, we take a peek to see what's there. Then we come up with a plan."

"Don't you already have a plan? You always have a plan. You're in charge of the plan. You've worked here longer. You're supposed to know what to do!" *Okay. Seriously freaking out here.*

"Dude. Relax," she said. "Step one: See what we're dealing with.

Step two: Make a plan. Got it? Now let's do this. Three. Two. One."

We ever so slowly stuck our heads out around the end cap and looked straight down aisle five.

Huh. Caroline Ford Vanderbilt had her back to us. She swayed ever so slightly. Which wouldn't have been weird on its own, but her bare, spray-tanned legs had turned gray-blue and the veins were bulging and black. She was also hunched over like Quasimodo, leaning to one side, and her knees were knocking together. Thing was, she usually stood up stick straight. Perfect posture. She and Mean Girl Madison would never be caught dead hunching. Neither one of them would sit or stand in any way that could give off even the faintest hint, however fleeting, of a muffin top. Plus, the higher their noses were, the easier it was to look down them at other people.

A bottle of dish soap lay on the floor, open and leaking peachy pink fluid across the aisle, puddling around one of Caroline's shiny gold designer tennis shoes.

"Um...Does this seem off to you?" DeeDee asked.

Before I could answer, Caroline Ford Vanderbilt jumped three feet straight up in the air and did a one-eighty turn. She thudded down, designer shoes shoulder-width apart, squatting like a NFL linebacker getting ready to plow down a quarterback.

Caroline Ford Vanderbilt smiled. Her bright white veneers had turned into crooked, rotten yellow-black corn kernel teeth like she had suddenly acquired the worst case of hillbilly trench mouth on the planet. Like, a test case in the dental school textbook level bad. Her cheekbones were extra bony, poking out of her face, pulling her skin in odd, painful angles. Frankly, I didn't know a face could move that much after so much Botox, possessed or not, but what did I know? She had deep purple bruises around her eyes, and those eyes were completely covered in an opaque milky white film. Staring at us. And, as if that wasn't bad enough, she then levitated four feet off the floor, dangling in mid-air like she was on wires filming a B-grade Kung Fu movie.

"Yep," DeeDee said. "That's off."

Kevin's tiny roach voice sounded via intercom again. "Correction. Grade THREE possession in aisle five. Grade three, people. Grade three. Hold on to your butts."

The possessed Caroline stared at us with her milky white eyes and cackled. "Hee hee hee hee hee."

Oh, great. Demon Caroline had a villain laugh. It sounded like a high-pitched toddler squeal combined with an Andre the Giant baritone, both at the same time. You know, just to add more octaves of creepy.

"Hey. Look. I've got tits." Demon Caroline put her hands on her breasts and squeezed. "This is awesome."

Green liquid leaked out of the corners of her mouth as she spoke.

"This conversation's starting off a little weird," DeeDee whispered. "Okay then. Rules: No head injuries. Whatever you do, DO NOT get knocked out, you hear me? And, just to be safe, see that gross green drool? Don't get any of that or any other goo or fluids that thing might emit inside you, like through a cut or in your eyes or mouth. You got that?"

Demon Caroline, hovering in the air, had pulled up her own tennis skirt to look at the panties underneath. "I'm gonna take this for a test drive later," she said.

Well, this possession was getting a little awkward. "You're sure about all this?" I asked DeeDee.

"Well, no, but I've seen Evil Dead 2, like, seventy times so those seem like solid guidelines. I'm just gonna roll with that until I figure out something better."

"What?" My heart was in my throat at this point, and I was so tense I probably wouldn't be able to poop for at least a month. "You based your plan off a fucking movie?"

"Well, yeah. Look at her. She screams Deadite to me." DeeDee shrugged. *Shrugged!* "Don't give me that look. Do you have a better idea?"

"But... You...You're the expert. You're supposed to be training me!"

"Uh, okay Mr. Demanding. We've never had a possession before, so we're gonna have to wing it," she said.

Wing it? Aw, hell no!

"Oh, and by the way, we can't go full Ash Williams and kill her. We have to remove the entity possessing her *without* killing Caroline. Store policy. DE-possession, not dismemberment, you feel me?"

Store policy? We had a fucking store policy for this?

"What do you mean, DE-possess?" My courage, barely there to begin with, was getting spindlier by the second.

"Look. This thing is using your pal Caroline Fancy-Pants Rockefeller like a big meat puppet. We have to get it out without killing her," DeeDee said. "That means no shots to the head. No strangling. No breaking its neck with a baseball bat or cutting it to bits with a chainsaw. Just don't kill it, or else Caroline will die too, like dead dead, got it? We can't kill the real Caroline, even though she sucks and kind of deserves it."

Grade three Caroline floated there, smiling and hee heeing at us. *Listening.* Honestly, her real smile was just as menacing as her demon smile. Suddenly, Demon Caroline's arms reached out. Her hands were curled up, veiny and blue, and now bearing three-inch, curved brown claws on every swollen-knuckled finger. Small consolation: Real Caroline would be horrified by the state of her manicure.

"The Angels of Divine Eventuality shall rise again. We shall take what we are owed. We shall have our revenge!" Demon Caroline announced in her multiple-layers of creepy voice. "We shall ravage the most beautiful of women and lounge on piles of gold. The world is ours!"

"Oh great," DeeDee said. "This one's got a fucking speech."

Demon Caroline pointed at me. "You. Basement-dwelling fat man. You are one of us. Join me. Bow to your master. Open the gate. The Angels of Divine Eventuality must be freed."

"What do we do?" I was legit shaking in my socks right now.

"Well, no matter what, *don't* give her what she wants. Keep her inside the store and away from the gate. Got it?" DeeDee patted me on the shoulder. "Distract her. I'll be right back."

With that, DeeDee pushed me into aisle five and...ran away. *Fuck! Fuck! Fuck!*

I stumbled right into the puddle of peach dish soap, slipped and then fell flat on my ass in front of the floating Demon Caroline, who watched me with ghoulish milky eyes. A noxious green cloud floated around her. I looked up at her, she looked down at me, and I would like to say I was a hero and totally knocked that demon right outta Caroline with one punch like a boss. But I didn't. I froze, like the chicken shit I really am deep down inside.

She dropped on top of me in a split second. Her clammy monster hands went right around my throat. Her rotten smile pulled back tighter than her facelift. "Recognize that I am your leader, and obey, you lowly worm. Obey! Or I will roast you on a spit like the fat pig you are! Open the gate, and I will reward you with a buffet of lustful women!"

"No?" I said, maybe not as firmly as I should have.

She cackled like an evil clown at a haunted carnival, then pounded my head against the linoleum. Again. Then another couple of times. And again. Again, while she screamed "Obey!" over and over. "Embrace your destiny!"

Ow. Ow. Ow! Please stop! But nope. She didn't stop. Did I mention she was choking me, and I could barely breathe? Oh, and now she was talking about which of my internal organs she was gonna eat first if I didn't open the gate. Liver fricassee anyone? Yeah. This was so awesome. *Dammit, Mom. Why ice cream cake?*

"Open the gate, worm," Demon Caroline demanded again. "You cannot deny your destiny. You cannot deny who you are!"

"No." I had to push the word through a currently-being-crushed-by-creepy-bone-hands windpipe.

Stop. Don't even go there. Of course, I tried to peel her gnarly claws off of my throat, but you and I both know that shit never works, not even in the movies. So she kept on pounding my head against the floor as I lingered on the cusp of asphyxiation. Terrified. Yep. This was it. I was gonna die here. *I'm looking at you, Mom. Ice cream cake? Really?*

DeeDee was nowhere around. She'd hung me out to dry. My skull-cracking headache was nearly eclipsed by my hurt feelings. Nearly.

Ow. Ow. Ow. Demon Caroline didn't let up. Choke. Choke. Pound. Pound. Choke. Pound. Pound. Choke. She mixed up the routine, loving every second of it, cackling and laughing and calling me a worm. "Join me," she bellowed, "And we will claim what is rightfully ours! We will purge the earth in blood and fire."

Woah boy. Whirlybirds. Getting dizzy. I clawed at her, trying to push her away. *Don't get knocked unconscious. Don't get knocked unconscious. Do something. You can do this. You've played, like, a hundred hours of Street Fighter. You've got moves. Save yourself, dumbass. Fight! Fight!*

It was clear DeeDee wasn't coming back anytime soon, so I did something I hadn't done since I was eleven. I rocked back and forth a couple of times to gain some leverage. Demon Caroline rocked right along on top of me. *Come on, abs. You can do it. Yes!* Awkwardly, and with a bit of struggle, I somersaulted. Now *she* was on the floor, and I was on top of her. *Ha. Take that!*

I punched her in the nose. She looked confused by the sudden turn of events. So I kept on punching her, my fists flying, Dee Jay Air Slasher style (at least in my head), landing one hit after another on her distorted, disgusting face, cutting my knuckles on her cheekbones.

Ha! This is what you get for calling me "special needs!" I found this incredibly satisfying until I realized the noises she was making were chuckles, not ouches. She thought this whole thing was hilarious.

"Ha. ha. Hee. Hee. Hee. Ha ha ha haha Ha ha ha haha." She never once stopped cackling. She still had a chokehold on me, but my medium fatness—the pudge real life Caroline had so graciously pointed out—was keeping her contained, in the store, away from the beer cave, as per DeeDee's instructions. Sure, Demon Caroline wiggled and bucked under me like a mechanical bull at a seedy cowboy bar, but I was just chubby enough that she couldn't throw me off.

"Guys. A...little...help...here." I gasped, not quite as loudly or elaborately as I'd hoped, but you try getting a word in edgewise while a demon's strangling you *and* hell cackling.

I punched Demon Caroline again and heard a disgusting, deep crack. *Crack. Pop. Crack. Slllp. Jesus.* It sounded like raw meat getting pulled off a bone. Woah boy. Had I accidentally killed real Caroline? Like, punched out an eyeball or something? I looked at her face. She flashed a fetid smile, and then something hit me hard on the back of the head. *Ow. Really?* I fell to the floor. Then, I made the mistake of looking back to see what hit me.

Oh God. So. Gross. I clenched my teeth and held back the hot vomit lapping at my tonsils. Caroline's femur was poking out through the skin, bleeding. Her leg was full on out of her hip socket, and her shin was bent in half right in the middle. Her leg looked like a bloody meat "C." She'd busted and dislocated her own leg so she could hit me with it, cackling like it was hilarious the whole time. *So. Gross. Gonna barf.*

But I didn't. Nope. Not this time. I ran instead. Demon Caroline had a gimpy leg, so how fast could she go? Probably not very. This was my chance. I turned tail and...nope. I wasn't even out of aisle five before Demon Caroline jumped on my back and wrapped her crusty arms around me. My legs moved, running, but I wasn't going forward because the floor was a Slip 'N Slide of spilled dish soap. I fell forehead first into a shelf. *Yeouch. That hurt. So bad.* Half-sized bottles of Drano and bleach plink plunked down on her back and my head. I saw a couple of stars but willed myself to stay awake. *Don't get knocked out. Don't get knocked out!*

"Hee. Hee. Hee. Hee. Hee. Hee." Cackling. So much cackling. *Shut up already!* "Open the gate, slave! Or I'll fuck your mother. Just as soon as I'm finished with your hot coworker."

Oh. Hell. No. This bitch did not just bring my Mom into this. Or DeeDee. It didn't matter that Demon Caroline didn't actually have a penis with which to fuck my Mom or DeeDee. There were some lines you absolutely did not cross, and that was one of them. My fight instinct recharged. I swatted at Demon Caroline but had trouble landing any hits. She was square on my back, and my arms just didn't bend like that. She pulled my hair. At one point, I'm pretty sure she ate some of it. She clawed at my face and tried to choke me out with her clammy elbow.

"Open the gate!" she demanded. "Free the Angels of Divine Eventuality."

"No!" I squeaked.

DeeDee jumped in front of us and started shooting something out of a yellow, marked-down-to-two-dollars Super Soaker water gun I swear she'd filched out of the summer clearance bucket in the candy aisle. She squirted Demon Caroline right in the face while yelling, "Take that, bitch! Hiya!"

Yes, she really said "Hiya." I rolled to the side so DeeDee could get a better shot. *'Bout damn time, DeeDee.*

DeeDee pumped and pumped the neon yellow gun. Whatever shot out was clear, like water, and some of it splashed on me, but didn't hurt or smell like chemicals, so who knew what was in there.

Demon Caroline let go of me and limped toward DeeDee. Her broken gimpy leg dragged behind her like she was a zombie. Let's be clear, here: I mean a slow, Romero-style classic zombie, not one of those stupid super-speed bullshit ones that run like Jesse Fucking Owens even with busted-up legs.

I crawled away, embracing my inner coward, thrilled to not be choking. I only looked back to see if anything was following me. DeeDee squirted and pumped liquid all over Demon Caroline until her Super Soaker ran dry. Demon Caroline—mystery liquid splashing on her face and all over her mink coat—commanded DeeDee to open the gate.

The stream shooting from DeeDee's Super Soaker suddenly petered out. Out of ammo. Demon Caroline was, overall, unfazed by the attack, but mildly annoyed DeeDee had gotten her expensive fur jacket all wet. *Huh.* Guess there was a bit of Real Caroline left in there after all.

"I was sure that was gonna work. Guess it isn't Catholic. Hey, Kevin," DeeDee shouted as Demon Caroline floated up off the floor, busted bloody leg now dangling with one foot facing backward. "Put holy water on the shopping list!"

Kevin said, "Already did." Over the intercom.

"New guy," DeeDee called to me. "Distract her while I come up with Plan B."

"You don't have a Plan B?" My voice was shaking, even though I was rage yelling.

"I said I was working on it, geesh," DeeDee said. "Cut me some slack."

"I absolutely will not cut you some slack." I was really mad now. "Hello. Demon hag! Anyone?"

Demon Caroline lunged at DeeDee, but of course, DeeDee rolled out of the way and bolted away like the Flash, leaving me hanging out to dry. Again.

"Who are you calling a hag?" Demon Caroline turned her attention back to me. *Great.* She three-octave screeched. "Open the gate. Now!"

"No." *Sigh.* I slumped in defeat. This was gonna suck. Hard. The things a man had to endure to pay off student loans.

Demon Caroline was on me in a split second. This time, she stayed afloat. I guess she realized floating was faster than limping. She had a death grip on my hair and used my follicles to pull me down aisle five toward the glass reach-in beer doors. I couldn't really slow down or resist because the floor was coated in dish soap. And Jesus, my poor scalp. Getting dragged by your hair hurt, like nine out of ten on the pain scale.

She dragged me down the aisle. I tried to peel her hands off, but she had a Superman grip. I grabbed at the shelves, using whatever I could get hold of as a weapon. I shoved a pine tree car freshener into her mouth. She spat it out. I poked her in the ear with an oil funnel. She punched me in the face. I squirted her face with dish soap. No response. A four-pack of mini Charmin rolls to the cheek? Nope. Nothing. Too soft.

"Open the gate, parasite," she snarled.

"No."

"You cannot deny me. I will rip you limb from limb until you submit!"

"No." I'll be honest. It was getting harder and harder to say no. I mean limb from limb? That didn't sound fun.

I had just grabbed a toilet plunger off the shelf and was about to poke Demon Caroline with the wood end when DeeDee popped out of aisle four with a bright red rectangle in her hand. It looked like some sort of taser. Sure enough, DeeDee hit a button and two prongs shot off of it and landed right on Demon Caroline.

"DeeDee, don't!" I screamed.

Look, I'm not the smartest dude, but I've watched enough reality cop shows to know that if you're touching someone who's getting tasered, the electricity will zap right into you, too. And Demon Caroline had a pretty good grip on me.

DeeDee looked at me like I was a Grade A moron and hit the button anyway. *Welp, here it comes. Please, God. Don't let me lose so much control that I poop myself.* I'd heard it could happen. I braced for it, but I didn't get a shock. The lines lit up and wiggled, sure, but not with electricity. It made some sort of low humming noise. It was voices. Low, steady, voices, repeating words over and over in a monastic monotone kinda like the Muzak only without the catchy dance beat. I couldn't make out any of the words, but they definitely weren't English.

Demon Caroline stopped moving. Yeah, she still had a death grip on me, but she held still, her monster knuckles knotted in my hair. She was listening to the voices, too.

"Ha. Take that, bitch!" DeeDee said.

Phew. DeeDee was doing it. *Finally!*

"That music's not very catchy," Demon Caroline said. "What is that, Justin Bieber?"

Demon Caroline shrugged and dragged me out of aisle five.

"Kevin!" DeeDee backed up, fiddling with the taser. "What's this thing set on?"

"Aramaic," Kevin said over the intercom. "Try Sumerian."

"What number is that?"

"Thirty seven," Kevin announced.

I tried to buy DeeDee more time. I clocked Demon Caroline upside the head with the plunger handle. She demon eye-rolled me, grabbed the handle and tried to wrestle the plunger out of my hands, but I death-gripped that thing.

"Open the gate, worm," she demanded.

"Come on guys, a little help here!" I yelled.

"I'm working on it!" DeeDee said. "Kevin. Sumerian isn't working. Any other ideas?"

"Try Palaic. Number eighty-three," Kevin announced.

"You sure?" DeeDee asked, fiddling with the controls. The lines powered up again, this time wiggling and glowing red.

"Why don't you ask her how old she is, where she's from, and what the dominant human religion was last time she was banished? That's the only way to be sure," Kevin said.

Wow, that roach sure was a sarcastic dickhead.

Whatever settings DeeDee tried didn't seem to work. Demon Caroline decided she'd had enough and plucked the taser wires off of her and smacked DeeDee up in an arc through the air, sending her sliding flat on her butt down the candy aisle. She dragged me, head bumping every single door handle, down the front of the reach-in coolers toward the beer cave entrance. *Ouch. Like, seriously. Ouch.*

Judging by this show of skills, if the hot goth chick and the dickhead cockroach were the only things standing between hell and earth it was pretty amazing the world as we know it hadn't already been consumed in a blaze of fire.

Demon Caroline had forgotten about my toilet plunger, which I clung to for dear life. Between face thwacks on cold steel door handles, I did manage to get Demon Caroline to turn around so I could stick the red plunger end directly over her face. I plunged it up and down like she was a toilet. No, it didn't really hurt her or stop her, but if I imagined it was Real Caroline, it was immensely satisfying emotionally.

And that's when I heard the click of a fake camera aperture opening and closing behind me. Demon Caroline and I both stopped. *Click. Click.* DeeDee had her Smartphone out and had snapped pics of us.

"Are you kidding me right now?" That might have been the most legitimate question I'd ever asked in my life.

"You'll thank me later." DeeDee then produced a canister of kosher salt. She opened it and threw handfuls of it at Demon Caroline, who in return just stared at DeeDee like she was stupid. DeeDee harrumphed like she really expected Demon Caroline to burst into flames or something when the salt granules hit her.

"HELP ME!" I screamed. Seriously. All that stood between Demon Caroline and hell on earth was a toilet plunger.

"Kevin's working on it," DeeDee said. "Plan D, Kevin. Stat!"

Demon Caroline said, "Open the gate."

"I can't," I said. "I don't know how."

Might as well be honest at this point. Maybe she'd cut me a break.

"Useless asshole!"

But she didn't let go. No slack for me.

"Then I shall sacrifice you on the altar of destiny. Your death will show the world what happens when you cross me. You will be slain like the fat piglet you are!"

Yep. You can say "I told you so" now. I should have quit when I had the chance. I could have been playing X-box right now. But no. Mom bought an ice cream cake.

Before I knew what hit me, I was flying through the air. My face and body abruptly thwumped into a reach-in cooler door, chinking it into a spiderweb of crunched glass. She'd thrown me two rows over. I slid down the glass and when I tried to get up and run, my head spun and I fell backward right into the shelf of bread and burger buns in aisle two. All the plastic-wrapped bread bags fell on top of me like flimsy gluten armor as I lay there on the linoleum in agonizing pain.

Demon Caroline floated above me, scowling. "Time to die, asshole."

She dropped right on top of me, mouth open, and moved to bite my throat with her yellow rotten teeth. I didn't have time to think, but I had to do something. So I jammed the eight-pack of burger buns I already had in my hands right into her mouth. She bit right into the bag and chewed. "Mmmm. Is this Bunny Bread?" she asked. "They make the best rolls."

She swallowed half the buns, plus most of the plastic wrap around them, before she came at me again. She lunged to bite my throat out, then suddenly stopped, hovering a couple of inches over my face. Her milky white eyes got really wide. An unholy gurgle erupted in her gut.

Fffffffrrrrrrrttttt.

Yes. You heard that right. She massive wet-farted, a painting-her-undies-brown level wet fart.

"What...what's happening?" Her creepy toddler/Andre the Giant combo voice asked. "This body. Something's wrong with it. It's. It's...*defective.*"

She looked me right in the eyes and projectile vomited all over my face.

"Close your eyes and keep your mouth shut!" I heard DeeDee

scream. "Don't get any of it inside you!"

Uh, duh. I had already squinched everything tight. But you try zipping your lips *and* mouth *and* not breathing while some unholy creature dumps thirty gallons of hot festering vomit all over you. It's not easy. The vomit felt like hot chunky beef stew, liquid but thick and slimy with lots of unidentifiable bits in it. The vomit shower went on for a minute or two then suddenly stopped. Demon Caroline moaned in agony. Suddenly, her weight lifted off of me. I wiped my face on my sleeve and dared open my eyes.

Demon Caroline appeared to be glued to the ceiling right above me. The floor—and I—were covered in a green slimy liquid that actually reminded me of lime Jello, the kind with the little carrot shreds in it that my Great Grandma used to make.

Ffffffrrrrrrttttt. Ffffffrrrrrrttttt. Demon Caroline groaned and wet-farted like an elderly white man who'd just eaten a ghost-pepper burrito. Throw in a half gallon or so of snotty green vomit squirts in between skid-mark farts, and you've got a pretty accurate idea of the situation. The place smelled like a hundred horses with intestinal issues had just taken a dump in the candy aisle.

Moaning in pain from her ceiling perch, Demon Caroline blurped out. "Fools. Your gate cannot contain us forever."

Ffffffrrrrrrttttt.

Oof. It was hard to make a compelling speech with gas like that.

"We will be free. We will take what the world owes us," Demon Caroline continued. "Rivers shall run red with blood. We shall meet again!"

"Melodramatic much?" DeeDee said.

Ffffffrrrrrrttttt.

And with that one last sloppy wet fart, a shimmering silvery pool that looked like the mercury out of a broken thermometer appeared on the ceiling around her. Demon Caroline convulsed and twitched. She closed her eyes and the undulating mercury puddle absorbed into the ceiling tile. Demon Caroline fell to the floor with a dull, meaty thud. A strange wind gusted around the store, then dissipated into nothing.

A sound, like the long, drawn-out *reoowr* of dueling cats sprang from Caroline. DeeDee immediately went into Karate stance. I grabbed my vomit-soaked plunger and prepared to strike. Caroline lifted her head and glanced around, in shock. *Oh. Snap.* Caroline Ford Vanderbilt was normal plain-vanilla, real-life Caroline again, only every inch of her was coated in green Jello with carrot shreds vomit. And let's not forget her horrifically broken leg, which didn't go away once the demon had filtered out of her.

Kwack. Kwack. Kwack.

Caroline heaved, tongue darting in and out of her mouth, shoulders pumping like a cat getting ready to hack up a hairball. *Kwack. Kwack.*

A string of spit leaked out of her collagen-injected lips. Caroline dipped her once perfectly French-manicured fingers into her mouth and pulled out something long, see-through and shiny. She pulled and pulled, and it kept coming, like cheap scarves out of a magician's fist. *Oh, man.* As soon as I saw the bunny face, I knew it was the plastic bag the buns had come in. Caroline examined it, horrified, then she hacked up a chewed corner of burger bun and spit it on the floor. In retrospect, it was that burger bun—not the broken leg or the vomit-soaked mink jacket—that broke the spirit of Caroline Ford Vanderbilt.

"Oh...no. no..no...no. No no no no. Is that, no. No, it can't be. Is that ...*bread?*" She said 'bread' like most people would say poison. She shrieked. "You two low-class, under-achieving, white-trash delinquent losers fed me *CARBS*?!?!"

Welp, the polish had certainly worn off, but there was no doubt Demon Caroline had reverted back to the equally horrible in completely different ways Caroline Ford Vanderbilt.

"Huh. I think you actually depossessed her with a burger bun." DeeDee walked up next to me and assessed the situation. "That makes a weird kind of sense now that I think about it. Atkins. Paleo. Keto. Women like her haven't eaten carbs since 2001. Guess her body couldn't handle it, and it pushed that critter right out of her."

DeeDee put her hand up, waiting for me to high five her, and said "Hail to the carbs, baby!"

CHAPTER 8

Caroline nearly landed a punch on a paramedic's nose when he said he needed to cut the shiny gold tennis shoe off of her shattered, rapidly-swelling foot. (The foot that was on backward fifteen minutes ago. Dude. Trust me. You can't unsee that.) "Noooooo!! Don't touch my SHOE!" She wailed. "It's Prada!"

He cut it off anyway, and Caroline sobbed. "That shoe cost more than you make in a week, you unwashed, mouth-breathing animal!"

She seemed more upset about her shoe than her compound fractures. She clutched its gold-toned, sawn-in-half remains to her chest and moaned.

The paramedics were unfazed by her insults and had her strapped to the gurney, leg in a temporary brace, ready to be wheeled out into the waiting ambulance a couple of minutes later. Her genteel, high-class veneer had completely melted away by this point, revealing the rabid viper underneath. Caroline spat venom and insults non-stop. At the paramedics. At DeeDee, who asked Caroline to smile as she snapped pics of her screaming, throwing air punches at paramedics while soaked in green slime, mascara cry-streaking down her face. And, especially at me, because it was somehow *my* fault her gossip recon mission had gone horribly awry.

"You and your trailer trash mother will never live this down, Lloyd Wallace," she hissed as they wheeled her past me. "You and your family are nothing, losers, and you will always be nothing. I will destroy you! You'll pay for this. I will ruin you if it's the last thing I do!"

Uh, why waste your time, Caroline? I thought it was pretty clear I was already ruined. I was ten thousand dollars in debt, lived at home, had no degree, no girlfriend and I worked for the devil. The only place I had to go was up.

Demon Mart? Well, that was a different story. Faust better have good insurance or a zillion dollars in the bank, because Caroline was definitely the type to sue. It wouldn't take her long to calculate how she could turn this incident into ten more Prada whatsits in her walk-in closet and another Benz in her garage.

"Bye bye, Caroline. Come back and see us again. It was an absolute delight to have you!" DeeDee waved goodbye to Caroline. As soon as the front door shut and the ambulance flipped on the siren and drove away, she turned to me. "Karma is real. That woman is proof. The way she walked in here talking shit? She was asking for trouble. But, man. I gotta give you props. The things you accomplish around here with food products are genuinely impressive. I mean, carbs? Genius!"

She patted me on the shoulder and suddenly a red hot rage built up inside me. My body shook uncontrollably. I felt like a volcano about to blow.

"Are you okay, new guy?"

Okay? OKAY!? I was covered in green demon vomit. My face was throbbing. Even my hair hurt! I was one hundred percent not okay. And DeeDee, the most beautiful woman I had ever seen, who was supposed to be training me to handle all this supernatural literally straight outta hell bullshit, had left me alone to tangle with a Jello-barfing demon. And she couldn't even remember my name. *She didn't know my name!* "My...name...is...LLOYD!"

My voice echoed around the store. I didn't know I could scream so loud and long. My stress volcano fully erupted in screaming rage lava.

"Woah there. Calm down. It's okay," she said in her best soft, soothing "holy crap, I better back off" voice. "Are you all right there...new...um...Lloyd?"

I just stood there shaking, too rattled to make words.

"No time for therapy and feelings circles, people. The gate opens in fifteen minutes, and we've got an unscheduled level two decontamination to get through. Get moving," Dickhead Roach Kevin's tiny voice announced over the intercom. "But first, let us celebrate this victory with rock n roll."

Kevin held a tiny pink—holy crap, was that a Zune?—up to the microphone and hit play. Heavy metal music pounded through the intercom.

"Kevin. Seriously, dude. We talked about this." DeeDee screamed over the music. "Play something else!"

A rock bravado rolled over the guitar, some guy singing about the devil never being a maker. And heaven and hell?

"Give in to the magic that is Ronnie James Dio, DeeDee," Kevin announced. "He's the one true master of rock. You kids don't know shit about real music. Listen and learn. Rock on forever, Ronnie."

Kevin was air guitaring with four of his six legs at this point.

"I want you to know I have tried so so hard to convince him to play something—anything—else," DeeDee said to me. "But Kevin was a metalhead before...Well, before. He picks Dio every single time, and he's got seniority so I can't stop him. Plus, you know, he's a roach. I try to give him some wins because that's gotta suck."

"Take the new guy to the green room," Kevin said over the intercom. "I don't think he's got the emotional fortitude to meet the cleaning crew just yet."

Emotional fortitude? My fists balled so hard I thought my knuckles would split open. *I'll...show...you...fortitude.* Said the guy about to punch the shit out of a talking roach. *Oh, God. Is this how it happens? Is this how people go bat-shit crazy?* Was I on the slippery slope to the nuthouse? Yes. Yes, I was. I could feel my heels sliding off the ledge, to a soundtrack of heavy metal guitar solo.

"You heard the roach," DeeDee said under her breath. "Come on."

She led me into the storeroom/hallway, and this time we didn't turn toward the employee lounge or Faust's luxury man cave. There was a green door in front of us as soon as we stepped in, right there between the tubs of tampons and the pallets of Top Ramen. I didn't remember seeing it before, but I wasn't Mr. Observant.

"Go on in. Take a shower. Wash *everything*, but especially your...uh...face." She grimaced and reached out to touch my throbbing head, but pulled back before she actually made contact. Yeah. It was bad. I didn't have to look to know it. I could feel my skin tightening, stretching as the tissue under it puffed. Remember that part where Demon Caroline used my face to shatter a glass cooler door? I'm assuming that left a mark. "Look. Just let the water run over your face," DeeDee said. "You'll know when to stop because it won't hurt anymore, okay? Don't question, just do it. Promise?"

She sounded tender and genuinely concerned for me. "I know this is a lot to take in, but you're doing great. It's not always like this. Most nights it's fine. Calm. It's just been unusually crazy around here lately. If you stick with it, it'll get easier. I promise," she said. "Anyway, everything you need is in there. I'll get you some clean clothes."

DeeDee gently pushed me through the door. Literally *through* the door. It didn't open, but I didn't hit wood. I just kind of stepped through it like fog. *Ugh.* This place was too weird, but I had no choice but to roll with it at this point. On the upside, the room I stepped into was the poshest bathroom I had ever seen. It looked like something that should be in the penthouse of the fanciest hotel on planet earth. A stack of fluffy perfectly rolled white hotel towels sat on the counter. The room was twice the size of my living room, all white marble, glossy and sparkling, with a floor-to-ceiling mirror behind the sinks.

That's when I saw the disgusting lime-green monster, face swollen and covered in black blood, standing in there with me. *Jesus. Not again!* I jumped and put my fists up, ready to punch. So did the monster. That's when I realized it was my own reflection in the mirror. The monster was me. Holy crap, I looked terrible. Not that I was a romance novel cover model on a good day, but wow. Demon Caroline really did a number on me. My clothes were saturated with barf, to the point where they looked dyed green. My face was all gashed up, crusted in blood, and one eye was nearly swollen shut, puffy and raw.

Yep. Quitting. I'm outta here. Decision made. I'd rather be hounded by collections agencies than nearly die via horrific supernatural creature every night. How had DeeDee lasted so long? *Shit.* How was I gonna break the news to Mom? You know what? I'd just have to tell her the truth. Well, no. Not the truth. I'd have to leave out the monsters. Anyway, screw the plan. I'm out. *After* the shower. They owed me some clean. And some serious dry cleaning. And a medal of honor or whatever the demon-slaying equivalent would be.

When I stepped in, the shower was already running, the perfect temperature, steaming up the mirror. DeeDee was right. Boy did that water feel good. I know it sounds crazy, because water's water, but it was sooo steamy, hot but not too hot, and gentle, like standing in the warmest, softest summer rain. *Perfect.* There weren't any knobs or anything in the shower, but I didn't care. Sometimes the water smelled citrusy. Sometimes flowery, like that relaxation bubble bath my Mom used, like, constantly, probably because my life choices stressed her out.

I stood there, letting the water cascade over me for a long time. Once, I looked down and there were soapy suds on me, even though there weren't any mini shampoos or so much as a bar of soap in the shower. But I didn't mind. The Jello slime pooled around my feet and washed down the drain. And not only did my body feel good, but my mood was like cotton ball clouds, absolutely floating, content and fuzzy like a zenned out Tibetan Monk. I had no idea how long I'd been in the shower. I just knew the longer I stood in the water, the better I felt.

The shower shut off automatically, oddly at about the same time I decided I was finished. When I stepped out, there was a stack of clean clothes neatly folded on the vanity. *Huh.* Upon further inspection, I realized they were *my* clothes. From home. My red "Education is Important, but Beer is Importanter" T-shirt with the honey mustard stain was paired with clean socks, one with a cartoon banana print, and one orange, but balled together fresh out of the dryer. The salmon-pink dad shorts my Mom had bought me on clearance at Kohl's were there, too. *Crap.* I hated those. I only wore them when I had absolutely nothing else.

The clothes were totally, no doubt about it, mine. From *home*. I tried hard not to think about how they ended up here.

There was a note in curly handwriting next to the stack of clean clothes. "Lloyd. Your wardrobe screams 'idiot frat guy.' Please buy some clothes that won't melt out my eyeballs when I look at you. Love, DeeDee."

Hey. I liked my clothes. Except for the shorts. But in my elevated, super-relaxed lavender body wash mood, I was focused solely on the fact that she remembered my name and the "Love, DeeDee" portion of the note. I wondered, for a hot second, if she'd go on a date with me if I one day saved her from some giant Cthulhu. No chick could deny a bonafide knight in shining armor, right?

Wait. What am I thinking? Nope. Double nope. Quitting. No monster fight was worth it. Then again, we were talking about DeeDee here. She was a perfect ten. Too bad I was a two. Okay, I was a physical six who could maybe hit seven if I dropped a couple of pounds, but debt and living with my Mom made me a two. And there weren't gonna be any epic monster battles. I couldn't do this. I had to quit.

I put on my clothes, and when a comb magically appeared on the vanity, I took that as a sign I needed to brush my hair. I wiped the steam off the mirror and dropped the comb in shock. *No way.* The cuts. The bruises. The swelling. It was all gone. My face was fine, as if Demon Caroline had never used me as a battering ram. And now that I thought about it, my epic skull-crushed-on-the-linoleum headache was gone, too. I glanced at the shower. *Dude. What was in that water? This place is unbelievable.*

I had to give Faust credit. The employee lounge with the personal chef and infinite food? The posh magic-healing five-star automated shower? He gave you all the tools you needed to treat yo'self. I could get used to this.

Oh no, you won't. Don't even think about it. Faust is THE Devil. *I think?* Didn't matter. He was close enough. This place was insane. The night manager was a talking cockroach. Caroline Ford Vanderbilt went full Exorcist in aisle five. I fought a snake dude with some hot dogs and a Michael Bolton CD. No shower could erase that face beating I got tonight. Okay, it could actually erase the damage, but not the memory. It wasn't gonna get easier or safer. It could only go down from here.

You're quitting, Lloyd.

But I need the money.

No. There had to be another way to make ten thousand dollars.

I contemplated the most gentle way to French exit this job. (I wasn't gonna Comb-over Carl and run screaming. I wanted to at least leave quietly and with some dignity.)

When I stepped back out front, clean and dry, I was shocked by the state of things. The store was spotless. No green barf. No broken glass cooler door. Not a single item on a single shelf out of place. *Man.* That cleaning crew was on top of their game!

DeeDee sat on a stool at the beer cave entrance picking her black-painted fingernails, like this had been any boring, normal night. My head spun. How did she deal?

Well, it doesn't matter. This is not my problem anymore. I'm out. I turned to leave, and my plan fell apart. The impossibly handsome Mr. Faust stood outside the front door talking to a tall, smoking hot brunette with two platinum blonde streaks in her hair that made her look like a sexy skunk. He smiled, she smoldered, both of them laying on the charm. A moment later, she sauntered off across the parking lot and Faust stepped inside.

"There you are, young Mr. Wallace." He put his strong, impeccably manicured man hand firmly on my shoulder. He was dressed head to toe in a black designer suit. Even the shirt and tie were black. He smelled expensive, like crisp new money fresh off the press at the U.S. Mint. "You did excellent work tonight. Excellent. Dee Dee and Kevin informed me of your bravery, singular focus, and innovative use of food products in not one but two instances of gate breach. You're certainly the right man for the job. Bringing you on board was an excellent decision."

I just stood there, stunned. No boss had ever said so many nice things about me. Come to think of it, no boss had ever said *any* nice things to or about me. Not once. So...it was probably best not to tell this guy I was gonna quit. He was too smooth, too convincing. And, you know, probably the devil.

"Good news. I was just informed the entity that entered Caroline was a doomed soul and not a denizen of our gate. She was temporarily inhabited by a Mr. Homer Wiley of Plain City, the self-proclaimed leader of the Angels of Divine Eventuality."

"The what?" Was that a bad Swedish death metal band?

"They were an aspiring, but already failing, doomsday cult that formed in a subreddit two weeks ago. They met once, in person, earlier this evening in a conference room at the Sleep Rite Motel on Highway 37. Naturally, it ended in disaster. You'll read about them in the news tomorrow, I'm sure," Faust said. "Mortals are fascinating creatures. Such imagination. I digress. Where were we? Oh, yes. The absolutely stunning Ms. Destiny informed me..."

"Who?" I was not following any of this. Were you?

"Destiny's the reaper for Doomed Souls Gate thirty-seven. She frequently graces the stage at Sinbad's as well. Lovely woman. Absolutely radiant."

Wait. There was another gate? At the strip joint across the street? And the sexy skunk was a stripper and in charge? Brain...not...computing. My dick did tingle, though, because dude, I was only a man.

"She informed me that Mr. Wiley intended to release the twelve late members of his cult to seek revenge on the world. He was angry that his afterlife predictions were incorrect. The others had already been ushered through the proper gate, but he escaped right before crossover. Of course, he wouldn't be able to use our gate, but if he had stumbled upon the correct one, we could have had twelve more possessions. The owners of those stolen bodies would have surely perished. Not everyone would be as willing to stop a possessed individual non-fatally, as you did this evening. Your proper handling of the situation saved up to thirteen human lives tonight."

I just stood there, blinking, while he pelted me with words I didn't understand. Thirteen *human* lives? Me? Saving lives? Sexy stripper? Doomed Souls gate? My brain hurt.

"I am genuinely impressed. You've done a great job, especially for someone so new and fresh," he said. "That is why I did a quick soul search. The reward for your excellent performance needed to be personal, meaningful. Here. This is for you. I believe it's exactly what you need."

Faust handed me a thick, blood-red envelope, and said, "You have a bright future here, young Mr. Wallace. Keep up the good work."

He bid goodnight to DeeDee, and waltzed through the storeroom door, leaving me standing there with a fat envelope in my hand. My heart thumped hard against my ribs as I carefully opened it. Really slowly, because come on. Anything could be in there. The envelope could open up into another dimension, or a man-eating centipede could crawl out.

Phew. Nope. No swirly vortex cloud. No dickhead talking bugs with bad attitudes. It was a slip of paper, a little bigger than a personal check. It was yellow on the ends, purple in the middle with a green bar across the top that said "United States Postal Service Postal Money Order." It was made out to Jennifer Wallace for $677.85. The memo line said, "Mom. I wanted to repay you for the exterminator because I love you. Sorry about the ants. It won't happen again. Love, Lloyd."

CHAPTER 9

Eeeeeoooooooowch! The big black dude in the white lab coat couldn't have pushed the needle into my vein any harder. He wasn't gentle, and I got the vibe he probably wasn't trained in any sort of nursing or medical field either. I mean, registered nurses didn't wear cheap jet-black sunglasses when they drew blood, did they?

He wasn't subtle either. He'd grunted and called me "big boy" when I weighed in, muttering something about how I needed to lose twenty pounds, before saying "fatties like you are ruining us."

Rich, coming from a guy who had his own budding spare tire growing around his middle.

I guess I should have expected as much. The plasma center was sketchy, nothing like the clean, sterile, sunny office filled with smiling people portrayed in their website photos. There were about forty narrow yellow recliners jammed into one big windowless "donation" room. Anemic fluorescent strip lights flickered cold and white overhead. About half of the seats were filled, and the crowd skewed heavily toward vagrants, broke college kids, and haggard working-class roofer guys. There was one hard-as-nails, seen-some-shit grandma with an epic permed mullet sprinkled in for good measure. They sat in their chairs, tubes of blood leading from their arms into a tiny centrifuge which spun and hummed and whirred, then sent the leftovers right on back into where they had come out. Gruff, white-coated techs paced the room with clipboards, putting needles in arms and pulling them out. Every single one of them wore dark sunglasses. Inside a windowless room. That was totally weird, right?

Welp. I had officially hit rock bottom. If this place were a soap opera, they'd call it the Broke and the Desperate. The web sites made plasma donation look all hospital sterile and professional, but let's face it. These places didn't exactly thrive in nice neighborhoods where people had steady, good-paying jobs. And trust me, I'd checked out a few. Blood 'R' Us was the nicest of them, and that wasn't saying much.

I sat in that chair for the next ninety excruciating minutes, my blood getting sucked out, spun then put back in. Every second of it was a reminder of how many rocks I was hitting as life dragged me face-first across the river bed of my personal rock bottom.

I gave Mom the money order for the exterminator as soon as I got home from work this morning. I didn't plan it that way, but I stepped in around seven a.m., and Mom was awake, getting ready for work, standing in her robe, comatose by the coffee machine waiting for the pot to finish brewing. I swear she'd just lie under the drip with her mouth open if there were a way to pull that off without second-degree burns. She wasn't a morning person.

Still, the money order lit her up like a million-watt stadium bulb had flipped on inside her. She literally cried when she saw it. Cried. Like, real tears, and enough of them to totally streak down her cheeks. And worse, she had that tight sad/happy "I'm so touched" smile she gets when she's hyper-emotional. She hugged me so tight my head nearly popped off and told me, "I'm so proud of you, Lloyd. This new job is really turning your life around."

Fuck. Once again, I embraced my inner chicken shit. At that moment, there was no way I could tell her I had to quit, and I finally understood what my grandpa had meant when he always said, "You can't win for losing."

I'd have to have another job lined up before I quit. For Mom's sake. And some money in the bank. Okay, in my sock drawer. I couldn't open a checking account because my last one had been overdrawn ninety percent of the time. So here I was, spending my day selling plasma and applying for other jobs. Safer jobs. Jobs without demon vomit and talking roaches and devil bosses.

I'd filled out so many applications today that my fingertips ached from typing. McDonald's. Popeye's. Wendy's. Pappy's Good Times bar (although the vibe was more 'Where alcoholics go to die" than party palace.) The Ponderosa Steakhouse Buffet *and* the Golden Corral. (Dude. So many buffets. The Midwest needs to step away from the all-you-can-eat chicken drummies, if you know what I mean. Seriously. Step away.) Target. (I could stock the hell out of some socks and diapers.) Speedway (Maybe I could parlay my two nights at Demon Mart into experience?) Jiffy Lube. (I lied and said I knew how to change oil. How hard could it be? That's what YouTube is for.) I walked right on past Starbucks. Know thyself: I couldn't deal with the half-caf no-whip coffee shop crowd. Plus, most of their baristas had bachelor's degrees. That didn't feel good. I couldn't even compete for entry-level.

Surely, though, some offer would roll in soon. I just had to wait.

Maybe I could turn this plasma thing into a decent side hustle in the meantime. I flipped through the brochure. Fifty bucks for the first four donations, then thirty bucks a pop if you donate twice a week. Wait, the rates actually went *down*? *Crap.* I looked at the dude who'd stabbed in the needle. He looked back at me and grinned, an extra toothy grin. My stomach churned. I didn't think I could put up with Mr. Stabby for thirty bucks a pop. Ugh. Okay, new plan. More applications. Tons more.

I grabbed the newspaper out from under the trashy celebrity magazines on the chipped-up side table next to me. I didn't even know they still printed news on paper anymore. I stopped cold before I made it to the want ads. There, on the front page, was this headline:

Cult Leader poisons self, 13 others, in Motel Tragedy

Plain City resident Homer Wiley was found dead along with thirteen others in a conference room at the Sleep Rite Motel on rural route 37 last night. Police said in a statement the victims appeared to have died from poisoning, but they are awaiting the official coroner's report. A police source, who spoke anonymously because he is not authorized to comment, said they believe the poison was consumed orally and was hidden in the sherbet punch.

All the dead had met via an online internet forum dedicated to recruiting new cult members. Wiley was the self-proclaimed leader of the Angels of Divine Eventuality cult, who said those who timed their death with the peak of the Leonid meteor shower would be absolved of earthly troubles, and their spirits would travel on the tail of the Tempel-Tuttle comet, which passes by the earth once every 33 years, to a new Eden in the Alpha Centauri solar system. Wiley, in the forum, claimed "New Eden is populated by large-breasted nymphomaniacs and had free, all-you-can-eat taco trucks on every corner."

Eighty-seven-year-old Phyllis Dinkle was also found dead at the scene. She was not a member of the online cult. Relatives say she was a long-time church volunteer who had mistaken the cult gathering for a church committee meeting on restocking the local food bank. That meeting was being held in the conference room across the hall. Dinkle appears to have consumed the punch, unaware that it was poisoned.

NASA officials, when asked about the cult, seemed confused, saying the peak of the Leonid meteor shower was at least a month away and the Tempel-Tuttle comet wouldn't pass by the earth until 2031. They encouraged other burgeoning cult leaders to check the accuracy of their calculations before following through on such extreme plans.

Most of the victims were single men over thirty who either lived alone in squalor or with their aging parents. The men were all college dropouts who appeared to have few meaningful relationships or social connections. None had steady employment. Wiley's aging mother said he had more than fifty thousand dollars in outstanding student loan debt and late-payment fees from his failed attempt at an associate's degree. She said he never recovered after his fiance dumped him at age twenty one, and that she wished he'd cleaned his room before passing.

Gulp. Oh, my God. Faust called it, and the big picture hit me like three thousand boulders smack on the top of my head. I could be this dude someday if I didn't turn my life around. I was on the fast-track to forty-year-old Internet cult killer who'd disappointed his Mom so many times she didn't even seem sad that he'd died, only that he'd left unfinished chores. I vowed right then and there that I would pay off my debt ASAP and turn my life around with a capital A.

Mr. Stabby came to release me from my IV soon after. He shuffled me off to a gum-smacking lady cashier with an epic yellow beehive and powder-blue cat-eye glasses. She sat in a tiny cube surrounded by caged, bullet-proof glass. The thing was like a bunker. I couldn't tell if they were trying to keep me out or her in. Anyway, I had decided to use the fifty bucks cash to pay down the late cable bill that had gone to collections. *Take that, Homer. I'm getting my life together. I'm not gonna be you!*

My dreams were dashed when the cashier said, "We don't pay cash, chubs," and handed me a prepaid Visa along with a slip of paper outlining the three zillion fees I'd have to pay to use it. My heart sank. A prepaid card? I needed money. Actual money. Not some stupid gift card!

I stumbled outside, light-headed from the gallon of juice they'd sucked out of me, and checked my receipt again, trying to figure out if there was a way to get cash off the card when I noticed something. It hit me like a combat boot straight to the nuts. They'd only paid me forty bucks, not fifty, because I was too fat to qualify for top tier rates. The lady had written "Drop fifteen and we'll pay you fifty next time, Chubs." She'd drawn a tiny cartoon pig next to it and had written "Oink! Oink!" right there on the receipt.

"Gaaaaaaaaaaaaaaahhhhhhhhhhhhhhhh!" I screamed and ripped apart the pig, paper shreds raining down over me like the world's saddest ticker-tape parade. I sucked so bad I couldn't even sell blood the right way! Plasma didn't pay. Nothing paid. Except for the 24/7 Demon Mart. That paid. And, if I didn't get paid, I might kill a bunch of Internet losers then end up trapped inside a social-climbing bitch like Caroline Ford Vanderbilt. Hell couldn't possibly be worse than that.

CHAPTER 10

So I went back to work at the 24/7 Demon Mart. Stupid? Probably. Fatal? Hopefully not. But what choice did I have?

None of the places where I'd applied had called me back yet. Not a single one. Zip. Zilch. Zero. And, I was beyond forty job applications by this point. I needed money. Plus, Mom was happy. *Dude.* Do you know the magic of a happy Mom? She'd scrubbed and organized my bedroom *and* washed and folded every last bit of laundry for me while I was getting my blood sucked and spun by Mr. Stabby. Happy Mom equaled easy street.

But the last straw was the collection agency. They'd called twice today. On the landline. I deleted the messages before my parents heard them and prayed the jerks wouldn't call back. Mom also casually let it drop that Simone had texted her asking if I had the money I owed her. So. Humiliating. The debt noose was tightening around my neck, so I had no choice but to revert to my original plan: Work at 24/7 Demon Mart until another job came along or I paid off my debts, whichever came first. And, try to save my soul while I was at it. I was not gonna be the next Homer Wiley. No. Way.

So here I was, cowering behind the counter, reminding myself that every hour was another sixty-six bucks, pretending to be all casual, but nearly jumping out of my socks in terror every time I heard a noise, every time someone stepped into the store, and especially every time someone (or were they some *things*?) came out of the beer cave. And there had been a steady stream of them tonight.

I tried to ignore them, but couldn't. I examined each and every one, hair to shoes. The weird part? They looked like totally normal people. No tentacles. No snakes. No red skin, cloven hoofs, or horns. But I knew they weren't people. At least, not human people.

The giant black book behind the counter had taught me that much. I'd been flipping through it to kill time. The book was hand-drawn, super-duper old, with elaborate text and illustrations, like the kind medieval monks would spend years copying way back in the Dark Ages. Most of the illustrations were of creatures that looked human, but on closer inspection had something odd about them, like big pointy ears, wings, claws, pointy razor teeth, feathered bird legs, blue skin or four arms. Their names were written in embellished cursive across the top of the page, and there were instructions? Well, something, written in weird old languages next to each creature. DeeDee had told me to flip through this book, but it wasn't making me feel better about working here.

After a particularly boring section on magical properties of minerals and crystals (Seriously, spare me hippies!), was an illustration of nightmare creatures. A thing with a thousand eyes and a dozen octopus arms: *Drauger, the summoner.* A big scary spider with a double set of fangs: *Neophilus, the clearer.* I hated spiders. Just looking at the picture gave me chills. There was an icy blue centipede with two rows of claw-tipped arms running down its belly. *Bubura, the opener.* And, a guy with green barbed tentacles and a single yellow eye. *Bizosoth, the herald.*

That guy. He was real, which meant these other guys must be, too. *Woah boy.* They looked like something straight outta that crap Call of Cthulhu game I got out of the clearance bin at GameStop last summer, all extra eyeballs and slime. There was some sort of green compass underneath them. They stood, one at each cardinal direction, facing a red circle containing a big-mouthed fish guy with fangs: *Lagopex, the devourer.*

Suddenly, a swirling lime green vortex opened right by my shoe. "Aaaaaaaaaaaaahhhh!"

Yeah. Of course, I went full toddler, screaming loudly and nearly pooping my pants. So would you! By instinct, I lifted my foot to squash whatever came out.

"Sorry I'm late." Kevin emerged from the swirl and looked up at me. "Wait. Were you actually gonna step on me? Don't even think about it, punk. I'll come back as a T-Rex and eat your dumb ass. Don't think I won't."

Kevin scuttled across the floor, shaking his head. A crimson red hand, big, five times as long and wide as mine, with long black nails, followed Kevin out of the vortex.

"Nooooooooo!" I screamed again and stomped on the hand. Again. Then a couple more times. But the hand didn't go back in. "Kevin. Help!"

He looked back and sighed heavily. "That's just my asshole roommate looking for a handout. That douche needs to get off the sofa and find his own job. Give him a slushy, or he'll never leave."

"A slushy?"

"You aren't the only one getting fat on free drinks around here," Kevin said. "Get him a Colossal Limbo Lemon Lime, or he'll bother us all night."

I lifted my foot off the clawed red hand, which was out of the vortex, all the way up to the elbow, and flipping me the bird.

"Well, I can't carry a drink that big, so get moving, noob!" Kevin snapped his leg bristles at me.

"Fine." I rounded the counter and made the darned slushy.

Jerk. You'd think a cockroach would make more effort to be likable, so you wouldn't *want* to kill him. But no. Kevin was a total dick. He deserved to be on the bottom of someone's shoe. A few minutes later, I stepped behind the counter and sat the slushy on the floor close to the red hand, which was now impatiently tapping its black demon nails against the linoleum. "Uh, here's your slushy, dude," I yelled at the hand. (No way I was gonna touch it or hand it to him directly. Nope.)

The red hand shot me a thumbs up, grabbed the Limbo Lemon Lime Colossal Super Slurp, then the hand and drink went back into the vortex. It closed and totally disappeared. *Phew.*

"Are you the new boy, dear?" A short, plump white-haired lady stood at the register. That wouldn't have been weird except it was after midnight, which meant we'd reached the time when most normal people pulled into the lot, then pulled right back out because their guts, rightly so, told them to run. My guess was it was pawnshop dude's Go Away charm.

I was scared to death of her. She had to be some awful creature, even though she looked like a sweet Midwest Great Grandma, the kind of lady who should be knitting at the retirement home or in bed by nine p.m. She had that short, white permed hair helmet old ladies have, and she wore a royal blue sweatshirt with embroidered kittens playing with a ball of yarn on the front.

I waited for her to unzip her grandma suit to reveal a horrific beast within. She just kept on smiling and said, "You look like a sweet young man. I'm Henrietta Getley. I own the store around the corner."

Henrietta pulled a red cardboard box out of her flower-print quilted purse. "Jesus Saves Discount Religious Supplies" was written in white block letters across the top. "Here's your order. I'm sorry it took so long, dear, but these are special, straight from Rome. Go on. Open it up and make sure it's all there."

I did. The box contained two rows of little white plastic bottles with silver crosses printed on each one. "Holy water. Two dozen two-ounce bottles, blessed by the big man himself." She winked and mouthed "The Pope."

"I heard about what you did, dear," she said. "Very brave. Sending that awful man where he belonged and saving that woman."

She grabbed my hands and held them in both of hers. Her hands felt like dry, toasted English muffins made of bone. "Very brave, dear."

Suddenly, she squeezed super tight, like she had the grip strength of Dwayne Johnson. The sweet smile melted off her face. She began to quake, head to toe. Her eyes went wide and round like quarters. My intestines knotted up. She seemed to be looking through my skin into my soul.

Welp. Here we go. Raging hell beast pending. I tried to pull away, but she had me in a death grip. This old lady was Hulk strong.

"The answers you seek are right in front of you," she said in a tranced-out monotone. "Be watchful. Desperate love will breach the gate. In darkness, three rocks might save you, but true defeat will be sweet."

And just like that, her eyes went back to normal, and she let go of my hand. "Oh, my." She pulled an embroidered handkerchief out of her purse and patted up the tiny beads of sweat that had formed on her forehead. "Did I have one of my little episodes?"

"Um...Are you all right?" I played it calm, even though my heart was in my throat. Episode? Sure, if she meant going full-on Zoltar machine.

"Oof. Pardon me." She said it like she was excusing herself after a burp. "I'm getting old, dear. Eighty-two last Thursday. My mind isn't what it used to be. Now, let me see here. Oh, yes. I have something for you. It arrived today."

"For me?"

She pulled one of those black Magic 8-Ball toys out of her purse and handed it to me.

"Wow, thanks!" I was legit excited. I hadn't had one since I was eleven. (It died in a tragic game of "let's see how hard you have to throw it off Big Dan's roof to break it.") What a weird, sweet old lady, with a purse full of awesome kids' toys. She was definitely somebody's meemaw.

"Oops. How could I forget? I believe this belongs to you, too." Henrietta slid a red leather-bound book out of her purse. *Geesh.* Was that bag bottomless? *Wait. No way.* It was my employee manual. The one I'd dumped in the garbage can in my room, and ergo Mom had put on the curb on garbage collection day. How did she get that?

"Have a good night, dear." She waddled out the door, and cut across the lot toward the Monster Burger, completely unfazed by the pitch-black shadows undulating around her and the glowing red neon sign pointing straight to hell.

I heard a watery rattle. The Magic 8-Ball was nearly vibrating off the counter. I caught it right before it dropped off the edge. I shook it by instinct, without really thinking of a question. Okay, yeah, I knew that wasn't how it worked, but everybody knew the darned things were bogus anyway. I flipped it. The white triangle floated up out of red liquid. Wait.

Wasn't it usually blue?

It said "A. I'm not bogus. B. I can't answer if you don't have a question. C. Why are you dressed like that?"

What the hell? Magic 8-Balls didn't talk like this. I shook it again. The triangle emerged.

"Seriously. We covered this. No question, no answer. Got it?"

Fine. I'll play along. *Am I gonna burn in hell?*

"Probably."

So I'm damned because of this stupid job.

"That's a statement, not a question. Clearly, you're an idiot who has not yet mastered the English language, so I'll let this one slide. No. You are not damned, not yet."

Wait. So you're saying I will be soon?

"Only if you royally fuck up."

Wait, what?

"You heard of those things called Commandments? Follow 5, 6, 8, and 21 through 25 for sure, and you'll be fine."

Uh, I was pretty sure there were only ten commandments.

The triangle turned. "Oh, really? You're an expert now?"

Prove it. Where's the list?

"You haven't read the employee manual yet, have you?" It said. "How are you still alive?"

Good question.

"I know."

Who are you?

"I'm your guardian angel."

Are you kidding me?

"Sadly, no. I've been assigned to help you through your (failing) transition to adulthood. From the looks of you, we'll be together for a long time. Seriously, where do you even buy a shirt that ugly? We're gonna have to go shopping if I'm gonna be seen in public with you."

This had to be a joke. What kind of angel hung out in a Magic 8-Ball? The triangle turned.

"The kind who doesn't like to commute, okay? I work from home. I'm not sitting in traffic for you, dude."

The red liquid bubbled and churned, and the triangle turned itself, landing flat. Again. "Okay. Let's get this shit show moving. Like Henrietta said, the answers you seek are right in front of you."

Huh? It bubbled and turned again. This time, there were no words, only an arrow pointing away from me.

I looked up. DeeDee stood on the other side of the counter, her glitter blue fingernails tap tapped on the glass counter that housed the lottery tickets. She was beautiful, in a strategically scissored Sisters of Mercy T-shirt. I could tell she'd re-dyed her hair because the blue was extra deep. She'd added a hint of silver glitter to her eyes tonight. "What are you doing?" she asked. "What's that?"

She pointed at the eight ball.

It vibrated in my hand. The triangle read "DON'T tell her about me. I'm your guardian angel, not hers. I'm not getting paid enough to work two people at once."

"Oh, uh, it's nothing. A toy." I nervously smiled and held it behind my back.

"Did Henrietta give you that?" One of DeeDee's meticulously tweezed eyebrows shot up.

"Um yeah, why?"

"A toy, huh?" she smirked. "Yeah, right. Tell yourself whatever you need to to get through the day. Anyway, you remember that note I wrote about your stupid T-shirts? These clothes are worse. Even Mormons have more style than you."

Okay. So yeah. I'd gone full church camp counselor with the wardrobe. Remember the save my soul part of the plan? I'd unearthed my one pair of respectable khaki pants. It'd been a while since I'd worn them, and they were a size (all right, two sizes) too small and squinched my middle so tight I had a man muffin top. Not a good look, but you had to make some sacrifices to avoid hellfire. And the only polo shirt I could find was a foamy sherbet orange color. Pastor Woodruff and the VBS people were always talking about how righteous they were and how much God loved them, and they all dressed like this. For all I knew, this was heaven's dress code.

She crossed her arms and raised an eyebrow. "So, why are you dressed like that? It doesn't seem very...*you*."

"I... I'm trying to be a good person."

"So what exactly do you think it means to be a good person?"

Uh, I don't know. Obviously. Duh! But I was too chicken to say that out loud, so I shrugged.

"I'm pretty sure dad-khakis and pastel polo shirts aren't it," she said.

The eight ball shook violently in my hand. I looked at it. "She's right. Lose the outfit. You're dressed like a pedophile. Oh, and remember that whole 'the answers you seek are right in front of you' thing?"

The triangle turned, and this time two arrows pointed right at DeeDee.

Geesh. I get the hint! DeeDee must be the answer, well, *have* the answers. To a question that isn't quite coming to mind.

"I feel a gate check coming," DeeDee said. "Why don't you come with me. See how it's done. You can't hide behind the counter forever."

Oh yes, I can. I glanced, terrified, at the beer cave.

"Kevin's obviously got it covered back here," she said.

We both looked at Kevin, who was balanced on the magazine rack with his head poking into a small hole in the plastic modesty wrap of a Hustler magazine.

"Come on. Don't be scared. I'll protect you." She squeezed my hand and smiled at me. I melted, putty in her skeleton-ring-clad fingers.

I followed her to the beer cave door. A moment later, the guy from the other night stepped out. The one that had emerged from the swirling blue cloud wearing the leisure suit? Yeah, him. This time he was in full country singer gear like he'd just stepped off a rodeo bull. He had stiff, dark blue Wranglers, cowboy boots, a black shirt with embroidered roses across the shoulders, and a black Stetson hat.

"All dressed up, Morty?" DeeDee asked him.

"You know it." He stood a little taller and adjusted his bolo tie. "Meeting a hot-to-trot married heifer with a *very* strong desire to ride a cowboy, if you get my drift. You showing the young buck how it's done?"

"I sure am, cowboy," DeeDee said. "You know the drill. Papers please."

He took out a small black book that looked like a passport. She opened it. There was elaborate writing on the page, similar in style to the illuminated book behind the counter. DeeDee used a tiny device to scan it. A yellow light flashed on the passport, a green light on the scanner lit up. "See?" she said. "Green means go, approved for entry. Red means stop. It's that simple."

"Go get 'em, tiger," she said to Morty.

"Sure thing, honey pie. You let me know when you're ready to ride." He winked at DeeDee, and for a hot minute, his eyes glowed bright red.

I froze in sheer terror. He strutted out the door, tipping his hat and flashing a shit-eating grin at us both through the window. *Woah, Boy.* Red eyes. Swirling vortex. Nope. In over my head. "I can't do it," I said.

"Can't do what?"

"Work here."

"Yeah, right." She laughed at me. Laughed!

"I'm serious. This isn't funny. Dude made of snakes. Cowboy with laser eyeballs. Green tentacle guy. Demon Caroline?"

"Okay, technically Caroline wasn't a demon, just a jerk with a half-ass online cult. That's why the taser and holy water didn't work. Besides, problem solved. It's over. What's the big deal?"

Gah! This chick! "How can you be so cazh about burning in hell?"

"Who's burning in hell?"

"We are! Faust...He's...we work for the devil!"

She laughed, a deep loud belly laugh.

"This isn't funny." My gut was squeezed tight with frustration knots.

"Faust isn't the devil," she said. "He's *a* devil, not *the* devil. Big difference."

My brain was about to explode. "Big difference?" I squealed. "Hello? Burning in hell?"

"We're not burning in hell. Well, I'm not. You're probably not either, unless there's something you want to confess there, tiger. Hold that thought." DeeDee turned back to the beer cave.

The Magic 8-Ball shook in my hand. "You're like defcon dweeb right now," it said. "Chillax. She's right. Remember, you aren't damned. Not yet."

Why do you keep saying not yet?

"Because you're kind of a fuck up. Never say never."

I shook the ball so hard the cube rattled against the plastic. *Shut up. You shut up. You don't know anything.*

"Dude. Hot chicks, twelve o'clock," eight ball guardian angel said.

I looked up. Four of the most smoking-hot women I had ever seen in my life walked out of the beer cave. One fiery redhead, two sorority-sister blondes, and a kinda witchy in a hot "The Craft" kind of way brunette. All had flawless smooth skin and perky, toned everything. They looked like nudie mag pin-ups who'd come to life, torn right off the centerfold page. And...they had no beer. Which could only mean one thing. *Great. Hot demons. Straight from hell.*

DeeDee started scanning passports. "You ladies out for fun or are you working tonight?"

"Working. You should try it sometime. You'd make a killing," the redhead said. She then turned to me, running her hand around the collar of my polo shirt. "Who is this tasty little morsel? Aw. His shirt's orange like candy. He's like a pudgy, sexy circus peanut. I could just eat him up."

I started tingling all over, but particularly in my downtown area, if you get my drift. *Gulp. Stop it, Mr. Penis. These are demons. Don't even think about it.* But her body was so close. Like so so close and radiating heat all over me. Hell heat. *Too late. Full-on wood.*

"Go easy on him," DeeDee said as she scanned the brunette's passport. "He's the new guy."

"Tell me, new guy," the redhead said, curling a bit of my hair around her blood-red fingernail. "What's your secret fantasy?"

She looked me in the eyes, and I watched as her red hair turned royal blue. The curves of her body morphed, and in less than a minute, she'd turned into a dead ringer for DeeDee. "Oooh la la!" The new demon DeeDee said. "Looks like you have a secret admirer, D."

"Cut it out," real DeeDee said to her.

In an instant, the curvy redhead had returned. She blew me a kiss, then all four of the flawless vixens sashayed right out the front door, across the parking lot, and into the Sinbad's strip club. *Oh shit. They're hot demon strippers. Welp, that boner's gonna hang around a while.*

"Well, now I know how you really feel about me," DeeDee said, once again too cazh and completely unruffled.

My cheeks went hot. Okay, so she saw that. *Play it cool.* "They're not people, are they?"

"Of course not. Duh."

"What are they?" I braced myself.

"Succubus," she said. "You know, sexy demons. They, like, shrivel up if they don't have sex or something. It's like food for them. They eat sex like you eat Monster Burgers."

Gulp. "And Morty? What's he?"

"Same thing," DeeDee said. "But I think the boy ones are called incubus? I'd have to look it up. It doesn't really matter."

Oh yes, it does matter. Demons! "That's it. I can't. I quit."

I started toward the door, and DeeDee ninja-rolled in front of me, blocking the way. "Stop right there. You said you'd stick around. You promised."

I stood there, totally blank. *Shit.* Had I done it again? Promised a woman something when I wasn't paying attention?

"Why are you so scared? They're harmless," she said.

"Harmless? Harmless!! How can you say a demon from hell is harmless?"

"You haven't read your employee manual yet, have you?" She put her fists on her hips.

"It's like a hundred pages. Who has the attention span to read that?"

"Um, most normal people?"

Great. Now she's calling me stupid.

"And it's actually only about ten pages," she said. "There's room in the back to take notes about your experiences, you know, for posterity and to help those who come after you, blah blah blah."

"Don't care." I took another step and DeeDee pressed her body, arms out, across the front door.

"Wait five more minutes." She looked out through the glass. So did I. The parking lot was dark and empty.

"What? Why?"

"Because I don't see your replacement," she said. "Which makes me think you're not a hundred percent sure you want to quit."

My replacement? "I just quit, like, five seconds ago. How could there be a replacement?"

"If you were serious, there'd be a replacement." She looked out again. "Nope. No one's coming, so more of you wants to stay than wants to go."

"What are you talking about?" This place made me feel like I was going nuts. All. The. Time.

"When Carl decided to quit, you were here," she said. "When Junebug decided to move to day shift? I was here. Junebug was here the night Kevin, well...poor Kevin."

"So what? People come here. It's a convenience store for God's sake. People come here to buy beer and Slim Jims and Combos. I came in for a slushy."

"Yeah. Sure. You just happened to come for a slushy at the exact moment Bizosoth made an escape and Carl quit? Come on. You don't get it, do you? People don't come here for no reason, not when the Go Away charm is on. They have to either be drawn here, part of the otherworldly community, or super desperate. We were drawn here for the job, at the precise moment we were needed."

"You're nuts." Hot, but nuts. I made for the door again.

"You are not leaving." DeeDee spread her arms wider across the glass and dug in her heels.

"Oh, yes. I am."

Eight ball angel shook in my hands. *What? What now?*

"She's not lying," it said.

No way. This was all bullshit.

"Don't make me come down there," it said. "You have a job to do. Just do it."

Jesus. I can't believe I'm having this conversation with a floating triangle.

"Technically it's an icosahedron, and you're not talking to *it*, you're talking to *me*, your guardian angel. I just move this shit around in the fluid."

Gah! Dick!

"Watch your mouth. I do have feelings, you know."

I threw the Magic 8-Ball on the floor and grabbed the door handle. DeeDee held tight.

"Listen. When you asked me about the big blue hole in the beer cave, you said you wanted the short, easy answer, so I told you it was the gate to hell. And that's technically true. But it's not what you think."

"If demons come out of it, then it's hell. Hell is hell!"

"Yes, but no. We let the harmless things out and keep the bad ones in."

"Hello. Demons? They're *all* bad."

"Nothing is black and white. There are degrees, rules. We only let out the creatures that can take human form, respect free will, don't plan to kill people or start plagues. Any being that wants to take over or destroy the world, or bring the old gods back. They're shit out of luck. They can't come out."

"And that magically makes it okay?" I asked.

"Look. Before the gate system, anything that wanted to could cross over to earth anytime, anywhere and do as it pleased. Famines. Plagues. Whole cities and cultures destroyed. Have you heard of Pompeii? The Titanic? Krakatoa? The San Francisco earthquake? The London and Chicago fires? Monsters used to run slipshod over the world, and there wasn't a damned thing we could do to stop them. Now we have gates to contain the worst of them. And those gates need people to enforce the rules. Good people like us. Faust hired you because you were pure of heart, didn't he?"

How did she know?

"Yeah. That's what I thought," she said. "Me, too."

Angel eight ball rolled around on the floor and landed window side up. "She's totes right. You'd know this if you'd read your employee manual. Wait. Do you know how to read?"

"I'm talking to you, aren't I?" I screamed. *Man, Angels are dicks.*

"Good point," angel eight ball said. "And who are you calling a dick?"

"You are talking to me, aren't you?" DeeDee glanced at the eight ball.

"Yeah. Uh, sorry," I said. "None of this is making me feel any better."

"It should," she said. "What other job will you ever have that matters as much as this one? Face it. You're a loser, Lloyd. A reject. And so was I when I started here. But now? We protect the world. We keep bad guys from wrecking the place. You heard Faust. You saved a dozen people's lives when you fed Demon Caroline that burger bun. How could you say no?"

"Because Faust is the devil!"

"*A* devil, not *the* devil. Big difference," she said.

"I disagree," I said.

"Okay, then chew on this: Devils are angels. Devils just do God's important, but dirty work. Like, oh, keeping the biblical plagues and the hungry gods in check. They're an essential gear in the grand machine of the universe. But they need humans. Good, pure of heart humans, to help them keep the balance. You have been given a rare gift: The chance to do something that actually matters in this giant, messed-up world. So what do you want to be, Lloyd? Do you want to be a zero or do you want to be a hero?"

CHAPTER 11

Of course, I picked hero. Duh. Had any man in the history of the whole world ever once chosen zero when there was a smoking hot chick on the line? Yeah, no. I didn't think so. And, so far, surprisingly, I didn't regret it.

DeeDee had stirred something in me. A resolve, a new perspective. Feeling like my life mattered? Like I was important? Honestly, that was a new feeling for me. I had never once in my entire life felt that. It helped a lot that my next two shifts were relatively quiet. No tentacle guys. No subreddit cult-possessed Caroline Ford Vanderbilts.

When there weren't any weird hell beasts to fight, 24/7 Demon Mart actually had a predictable rhythm. Kevin arrived via green swirling vortex around eleven every night. Bob the Doughnut Guy delivered a fresh batch of doughnuts every night, and the weird guy in the track suit always jogged to the store and bought one as soon as Bob's truck left the lot. Honestly, that guy looked buffer every time I saw him. I had no idea how he stayed so fit eating so many chocolate doughnuts.

Three times a week, Pawnshop Doc came in to pick up a single large, special-order pink-frosted glazed doughnut with rainbow sprinkles packaged in its own separate box.

Regular human customers would come in and buy beer and beef jerky. Lots of beef jerky (Dude. So. Much. Beef jerky. Why??) pretty steadily until midnight. At midnight, Kevin pressed a purple button behind the counter to flip on the "Go Away' charm. It worked, well, like a charm. The second it flipped on, people filed out of the store, paying for their lotto tickets, beer and chips as quickly as possible. All of the people brave enough to pull into the lot after midnight immediately pulled right back out, without so much as stepping a single foot out of the car.

"It keeps 'em out of the line of fire," Kevin said as he flipped the button. "Of course, they can still technically come in, but only if they're super motivated, super desperate, have been summoned here. Or, if they're super stupid."

He looked at me with his shiny black roach eyes, and made it pretty clear he thought I'd managed to get in because I was stupid.

Every night, Kevin took over the stereo from one to two a.m., so he could play the heavy metal album of his choice over the Muzak, which literally was ancient magical chants looped over dance beats. It flipped on at the same time as the Go Away charm, and supposedly helped reduce gate breaches. Words with magical powers actually existed and bad demons hated dance beats. Who knew.

Kevin's albums, on the other hand, only involved the magical incantations of Ronnie James Dio. Rainbow, Black Sabbath, Dio, Heaven & Hell. Jesus. Every Dio band. Why did I know this? I'd never even heard of Dio before last week. Oh yes, because Kevin presented his DJ hour as a public service to DeeDee and I, opining "so you young kids can learn what real music sounds like. None of that Auto-Tune bullshit."

At one a.m., he pressed play on his busted up pink Zune. (Where the hell did he even get that?) The synth guitar intro to "Rainbow in the Dark" filled the store for the third time this week. Kevin had somehow used a set of speakers and copper wire to jerry-rig his Zune to the store intercom system, creating a slipshod surround sound system.

"Dude," I said. "Can we listen to something else?" This song was slowly burning into my brain.

"No," Kevin said. "If you can't handle the rock, go take a break."

I shrugged. Fine with me. I grabbed a Gehenna Grape slushy. (I swear I'd drunk half my body weight in iced sugar this week alone.) and headed for the Employee Lounge.

Chef was in his usual spot, standing behind the grill swaying slightly, wearing super dark tinted sunglasses, that kinda reminded me of the ones the Bloods R Us techs wore. "Hey man."

He grunted. I ordered two medium-rare ribeyes and slid into the big round red plush booth. The eight ball was sitting on the table. *God damn!*

The eight ball rolled. "Don't bring Him into this."

"Fuck off already!" I shook the ball really hard and slammed it down on the table. Gah. This angel! He was the worst. I'd tried to ditch him several times, but the stupid ball just kept reappearing. No matter where I left it, it always ended up right next to me. And he wanted to chat all hours, day or night.

"I'm your guardian angel. I can't do my job if I'm not with you."

"Fine. But did you really need to binge-watch all of Ash Vs Evil Dead season three when I was trying to sleep today?"

"Hey. We can't get that show up here. I had no choice. Why are you complaining? Bruce Campbell is a national treasure."

"He can be a national treasure when I'm awake. You're a shit roommate. You know that?"

"Says the guy who leaves dirty, poop-streaked underpants all over the floor."

You shut up! I shook him. Too hard. *I do not!*

"Oh yes you do."

Ding. Chef's bell. *Yay steaks!*

I left jerk angel eight ball on the table and got up to collect my dinner. Behold, on a large plate in front of Chef were two perfectly-cooked steaks with a gigantic baked potato drowning in sour cream *and* a giant sweet potato covered in butter and brown sugar. I hadn't ordered them, but I totally wanted them. "How did you know?"

Chef groaned. And swayed. And aggressively sniffed the air all around him.

I sniffed, too. Hmmm. Only the smell of steaks. He must have super sonic smell. He was always sniffing something, but I only ever smelled food. I shrugged. "Man of few words. I get it. But thanks."

I slid back into the booth, mood a thousand miles high, and dug in. Oh my God. Best steak I'd ever had. Buttery, with just a little bit of blood dribbling down my chin as I shoveled it in.

"Take it easy there, fatty," eight ball said. "Ditch the sides and the drink. You eat too many carbs. That's why you're fat."

I tried to ignore him, but he rolled into my arm so hard I dropped my fork. Yep. Guardian angel eight ball was officially ruining my dinner.

"Keep it up and that little pouch of yours will go full gut."

Gah. Shut up! But he didn't.

"Look. I have a job to do. I can't save your ass if you're too fat and out of shape to run from danger."

I kept eating, trying to ignore the damned ball as it rolled around, throwing shade all over me. The triangle would flatten, and I'd look away. *Nope. Not interested in your opinion.* So of course it bumped the fork out of my hand again, and I saw "You know a free gym membership comes with this job, right?"

Then he hit my arm again and said, "Did you see Zombieland? Rule No. 1: Cardio. Sage advice."

Halfway through my second steak, a fat envelope with "Lloyd's weekly pay" written on the front magically materialized on the table. I opened it, and my heart skipped. A wad of cash was inside. I counted it. Twenty five hundred bucks. For one week? I counted it three more times. I couldn't believe it. This was like, Silicon Valley money, not Columbus, Ohio, corner store community-college dropout money. *Woot!* I definitely pumped my fist up and down a few times.

The movement must have caught Chef's attention because he

stepped closer to me, still silently sniffing. I sniffed my arm pit. Was it me he kept sniffing? I smelled like Old Spice. Oh well.

Who cared? Time to celebrate. Finally, sticking around was paying off. This batch of cash was gonna loosen the debt noose. I could pay off the late cable bill and kill the collection calls. Get my car up and running again. And if there was any money left, I was gonna get a shiny new, working smartphone.

"Smartphones are a waste of $$$," eight ball said.

Who asked you?

"Seriously. Y'all are like glued to those things. Do you know how many idiots end up here because they fell off a cliff taking selfies? We got a guy in here last week who fell into a dam of rabid beavers while he was playing Pokemon Go. Literally rabid beavers. He certainly caught 'em all. All the rabies virion, that is. You ask me, we shouldn't have let him in. We need to charge a dumbass penalty."

Jesus Christ, shut up.

"It's not His fault y'all are stupid. Well, okay, maybe it's a little bit His fault. God thought you'd be more fun to watch if we sprinkled a bit of dumb into the species, and that's totally true. But seriously, if you walk in front of an eighteen wheeler while tweeting, you kinda need to be punished for that."

I can't deal. I'm going to work. Can you please shut up until morning?

"Can you *not* do something stupid until morning?"

Okay then. You leave me no choice. I took one last bite of steak and put my money and the eight ball in my locker and bolted it shut—even though I knew the angel would find his way outta there somehow.

I waddled out of the employee lounge. Don't judge. Let's see how fast you walk with two twelve-ounce ribeyes in your belly. And despite the constant rabble of angel, for the first time in a long time, I felt deep down that maybe it was all gonna work out. Maybe it was the two delicious steaks. Or, maybe it was the wad of fat cash in my locker. Okay, yeah it was the money. People say money doesn't bring happiness, but that fat envelope sure did make me feel like my life might be on the upswing. That maybe DeeDee was right: This was my chance to make right *and* do good. This was my chance to matter. And get out of debt. It was one thing to know Demon Mart paid well, but it was an entirely different thing to actually see it all in cash.

Unfortunately, my high didn't last. I stepped out into the store and nearly froze into a Lloydcicle. *Brrrr.* It was so cold, it felt like the thermostat was set on Arctic Circle. My breath formed an icy white cloud as I exhaled. And there was a...*Oh. Shit. We're doomed.* A gigantic icy blue centipede was perusing the chip aisle. And I mean giant. He was twenty feet long at least, and hunching nearly in half so he could fit in the building, bumping up the acoustic ceiling tiles as he moved. He looked like he was made of solid blue raspberry gelatin. My knees turned to noodles. He was in the book. What was his name? Bongo? No. Bongala. Wait. "Bobura!" I yelled, emboldened by steaks and fat cash. "Stop right there!"

The blob undulated and blurped around to face me, moving like a behemoth Jello jiggler. "Get back in the cave, jerk!"

Well, that was a mistake. He didn't move.

"Uh, all right then." I tried to save face, faking brave. "You give me no choice but to kick your butt straight back to hell!"

"Hi. Ya!" It sounded way cooler when DeeDee said it, but I was committed now. I did my best Bruce Lee kick, to show it I was serious. He hissed at me, and his four huge insect mandible thingees with sharp spikes on the ends opened up to reveal a circular, razor-lined mouth. His belly rolled and rumbled, then he spit something that looked like gelled water at me.

"Duck! It's poison!" DeeDee flew threw the air. *Thank God. She's saving me!*

Well, kind of. She karate chopped me right in the leg, and I dropped like a sack of potatoes onto the pyramid of two-liter pop bottles behind me. The clear gooey poison water splatted the wall.

Gah. My leg. Ouch. Focus, Lloyd, Focus. Blue centipede monster. I nabbed the closest thing to me and prepared to strike. Unfortunately, that was a two-liter of Mountain Dew Code Red. *Welp.* It'd have to do. I shook it, fast and hard, and popped the top. The cap shot off, hitting Bobura smack between his eyes. Four. White. Eyes.

"Raaaahr." He grumbled and the building shook. The red stream of pressurized soda arched through the air and right into his open mouth.

Glug. Glug. Glug. He drank it all down. "Uuuuuuurrrrrppppppp."

Yep. He burped. Hard enough that his burp rattled the slushy machines. Welp. Guess I wasn't going to save the day with food this time. Plan B. His belly rumbled, his mandibles spread wide. Crap. He was gonna poison glob me again. I was scrambling around for another weapon when DeeDee jumped between us.

"Okay you two, cut it out." DeeDee had her arms out as if to hold us both back.

"What are you doing?"

"What are *you* doing?" She snapped.

"Putting him back," I said. "He's not allowed. Look at him."

His razor mouth frowned. (Razor-lined death sadness? Huh.

Interesting.) His four beady white eyes with little hairs around them drooped at the edges like they belonged to the biggest, saddest, ugliest Golden Retriever.

"He's not a threat, Lloyd," DeeDee said. "Look at him."

"I am. He's a giant gummy centipede!"

DeeDee huffed. "Look closer."

He had six bags of Smart Pop popcorn dangling from three pairs of centipede arms. And a red Netflix DVD-by-mail envelope in another...could I call it a hand? No. Grabber spiky thing. Dude looked like he'd just smoked weed and needed some munchies. And he looked sad. Maybe. Harmless? No way. He did spit poison at me a minute ago.

"You said they can't come out unless they look like people." I pointed at blob guy and his—could you call them shoulders?—seemed to slump even more, like I'd hurt his feelings. He blooped the top part of his blob so he could look over at DeeDee and give her the full-on sad eyes.

"It's okay, Bubby," DeeDee said. "He doesn't know. He's new."

Wow. This dude was really pulling her strings.

"Lloyd, Bubby has never once tried to hurt anyone. He comes up every Friday to watch a DVD and eat popcorn."

"Why doesn't he do that at...home?" Yeah, so it sounded weird to call hell "home" out loud.

"Netflix doesn't stream or deliver to hell," she said. "Besides, his roommate is a TV hog, so I've got a set up for him here, see?"

She pulled me to the end of the row and pointed to a giant flat screen TV bolted high on the wall in the back right corner of the store. A black leather Barcalounger the size of a Honda minivan sat in front of it.

"Has that been there the whole time?" I asked.

"Yeah, but the TV's not usually on."

Showed you how much I paid attention to my surroundings.

"The chair isn't usually here, though. He brings that with him. I let him watch here because he doesn't bother anyone, and I feel bad for him because he can't open the DVD envelopes. He doesn't have any fingers." She wiggled hers for effect.

Bubby had slugged up behind us so silently I didn't know he was there until his ice breath nearly frostbit the top of my head. He put a centipede claw arm around my shoulder and hugged me? *Oh Jesus.*

He urrrrrrp blooped and squeaked, and the noises rumbled my insides and rattled the glass beer bottles inside of the reach-in cooler.

"Bubby says he's sorry," DeeDee said. She grabbed the Netflix envelope out of his hand. "So, Bubby, what are we watching tonight?"

She opened it and slid out the disc. "Woah. Rock Versus Brock SummerSlam 2002? Classic! Excellent choice."

She high fived one of Bubby's centipede...arms? Hands? Spikes? Whatever. He jiggled in excitement. "He's a big Dwayne Johnson fan," DeeDee said to me. "Huge. But aren't we all?"

Oh. Hell. No.

Not about Dwayne Johnson, what's not to love? Hell no on the iceberg centipede part. I brushed his spiky arm bit off my shoulder. I was not comfortable watching wrestling with a twenty-foot tall, six-foot wide see-through gelatinous blue centipede from hell, okay? Did I mention that he, and all the air around him, was Antarctica-level freezing cold, too? "Can't he just pay-per-view that at home?"

"Uh, no. He likes The Rock, so that was back when WWE was WWF. That was pay-per-view, like, two decades ago. DVD is the easiest way to get it now."

Bubby slugged past me and settled into his Barcalounger. DeeDee followed him, put the disc into the DVD player then fiddled with the remote. "Lloyd, can you man the beer cave until I get Bubby set up?"

"Fine," I sighed. Yep. I'd lost this round. The giant freezing see-through jelly centipede was staying. I plopped down on the wood stool by the beer cave door. I could see a flicker of blue light reflected on the steel cooler wall. *Great.* Some*thing* was coming through. Where was that scanner thing?

I turned to the black cabinet behind me. (You know, the one DeeDee pulled a flaming sword out of to slay tentacle dude on the night I shoulda run on outta here and never looked back? Yeah, that one.) It was more like a black safe. The door was heavy, thick, some sort of indestructible metal with a large silver handle. I pressed it down, and the door opened. It was unlocked. And Hole. Eee. Crap. The stuff that was in there. So weird.

The once-flaming sword hung on its own mount. It was bigger than I remembered, at least a yard long, shimmering and gold. Real gold. But not on fire. *Hmmm.* Did you have to press a button to turn on the fire, kinda like a propane grill? There was a sharp gold dagger, with a curved blade like a bowie knife. There were rows and rows of sparkling gold knives, spears and arrows, many with gemstones embedded in the handles. Wow. The stuff in this case had to be worth millions.

I heard the sound of a stadium crowd roaring behind me. Rock vs Brock. So this was my life now. Friday date night with a giant Jello centipede from hell. *Think about the fat wad of cash in your locker, Lloyd. Think about the money! Okay. Okay. I will.*

The sword wasn't the only weird thing in the cabinet. A swirly purple, red and gold gourd, with a long thin neck and a big round bottom, sat in a glass case next to a glazed doughnut with pink frosting and rainbow sprinkles. The case was marked "Break glass in case of emergency." What was up with those damned doughnuts?

The cabinet held an odd assortment of CDs, too, like a grandma and a middle-aged metal head had combined their record collections. Tom Jones Live in Las Vegas 1969. Black Sabbath, The Dio Years. *Definitely Kevin's.* Zebra. Michael Bolton. I wondered if mullet ballad white guy knew his music could ensnare demons? Maybe I should write him a fan letter to let him know.

And, there was the angel eight ball. It rolled over. "Hey, stupid. When's it gonna sink in? You can't ditch me. Just for that, I'm not gonna tell you something snuck out of the gate. Oh wait...oops. I told you, didn't I?"

The triangle turned again. "Well, good luck. Try not to die. I need this job."

Oh God. Snuck out? My instant panic button dialed up to eleven.

There was a row of tasers and scanner thingies in the safe. Allrighty then. I grabbed a taser and waited by the beer cave door, once again in my best imitation Bruce Lee fighting stance. Well, okay if Bruce Lee were a six-foot tall white dude with shaggy hair and a little gut.

"Ha! A little gut?" It said. "Keep telling yourself that, buddy."

Jerk. Anyway, the blue light inside the cave still faintly flickered. But nobody. No thing? Had come out. *Huh. Was that gate supposed to stay open like that?*

I cracked the door and stuck my head in. The swirly vortex was tiny. Maybe a foot across. The whole wall had opened up when Morty popped through in his leisure suit. I didn't see any shadow forming to get through it either. I scanned the beer stacks. Nothing moved. Not so much as a shadow. No roaches. No hot demon strippers. No giant red devil hands. Maybe the angel was dicking me around.

That's when I heard...crinkling? A noise like someone squeezing potato chip bags. I could see the entire chip row from the beer cave door. Nothing looked weird. Just a row of Doritos, Conn's, Cheetos, Tostitos. You know, chips.

Crinkle. Crinkle. Crunch. Crunch. Crunch.

*What the...*The shiny plastic fronts of a few bags of chips dented in slightly, as if someone was casually running their hand across them. Their invisible hand. *Gulp.*

Crunch. Crunch. Crinkle.

I steeled myself and tiptoed over to the rack to investigate.

Crinkle. Crinkle. Crinkle.

I followed the rumpling chip bags. My pulse was pumping oh, about a zillion times a minute by this point. I still held onto a thin string of hope that angel eight ball was lying. Maybe it was nothing. Maybe a heat vent turned on and the air was hitting the bags. Yeah. That's it. DeeDee and the book didn't say anything about invisible creatures. They all had bodies, right?

That's when a bag of Fritos floated up into the air.

"Uh, DeeDee?" My voice cracked. *Way to be manly in the face of danger, Lloyd.*

"Yeah?" She called. The TV crowd erupted in applause. "Woah! Take that!"

"DeeDee?"

A second Fritos bag levitated in front of me. And a third. *Gulp. Stay calm, Lloyd.* Maybe whatever it was just wanted to make walking tacos. I reached out to the bag, a stupid move in retrospect, to see if it was an actual thing with an invisible body or just a haunted bag of floating ghost Fritos. You can probably guess what happened next. Yep. My hand ran smack into a squiggly nothing. Okay, a something. Something invisible. And squiggly, holding up the bag. "Oh crap."

Thwap. A party-sized bag of Fritos smacked me square in the face.

The next thing I knew, something had knocked my legs out from under me. I landed flat on my back on the floor, and all the air went out of my lungs. A dozen party-sized bag of Fritos rose into the air and then began to smack me across the face and body, and man it hurt! Dude, there were some sharp pointy edges on those bags!

Great. There was an invisible creature loose in the store, and it was a total jerk. Then the bags ripped open one by one, and to be frank, I opened my mouth hoping to catch at least one Frito as it fell. They're salty and delicious. Plus, you know, demon fighting fuel.

But no. The Fritos, like the bags, defied gravity, hovering for a moment in the air, before they began to swirl in a circle. The chip rack shook and all of the Frito bags popped into the air, splitting open, each Frito joining the ones already floating above me. I'll give this critter props. It knew what its favorite snack food was, and it was sticking with it. Now if that wasn't brand loyalty, I didn't know what was.

The Fritos kept on swirling, slowly gathering into distinct clumps. A line of Fritos formed what looked like a leg. An oval that looked like a wing. *Oh. No.* It was making a body. Out of Fritos. Welp. I'd never be able to eat one of those ever again.

"DeeDee," I yelled as I scrambled to my feet.

"What?" she snipped. "Wait? Triple H unsanctioned street fight? Bubby, this episode is gold!"

"Uh, DeeDee." Dude. Was she seriously still talking about wrestling? "How do we fight off a monster made of Fritos?"

"Wait. What?"

"Something came through the gate and it's making a body out of Fritos." Hold up. "Make that bodies, plural."

A half dozen flying things, with long legs, wings, and oh crap, long bitey-looking snouts were forming out of Fritos in the air above me. And they were nipping at each other, eating Fritos off of each others' wings and legs. Okay. They really *did* like salty snacks. *Wait.* Was I a salty snack?

"You're kidding," DeeDee said.

"I wish." My voice got louder and more forceful. I slowly backed away from the growing army of winged Frito mosquitoes from hell. "Hurry up, there's more than one!"

Unfortunately, my snipping at DeeDee got their attention. They stopped nibbling on each other and all turned their Frito muzzles in my direction, hovering there for a second as if sizing me up. The biggest one swooped at me. I lunged. The other Frito mosquitoes followed the leader, dive bombing me. I smacked one and the Fritos broke apart, only to reform into a foot-long mosquito hell beast just out of my reach. Another one jumped onto my shirt and jabbed its Frito beak into my neck. Gah! I punched it away, and it reformed again. In a split second, they were all on me and I was fwapping Frito beasts left and right.

"Help MEEEEE!"

DeeDee appeared at the end of the chip aisle. She looked at me, covered in angry dive-bombing corn chips, and said. "Well, shit." Then she walked away. *Walked away!*

This was the second time she'd thrown me to the wolves. Hot chicks could get away with murder!

"Don't leave meeeeeeee!" I meant it as an order, but it sounded like the whine of a drunk lonely man getting dumped by his long-time, live-in girlfriend. Ask me how I know.

So I swatted. *Fwap. Fwap. Fwap.* The chip monsters dive bombed me, then broke apart and reformed again and again. I was flailing like a hippie Phish fan hopped up on too many shrooms.

Swap. Fwap. Ow! One of the bastards scratched me. *Okay. Okay. Think. Where was my taser?* The answer was on the floor by the chip rack where you dropped it in absolute fear when the first Frito mosquito hell beast formed. I tucked and rolled. *Yes. Got it!*

I aimed at the biggest cloud of Fritos, pressed the button and the wires shot out. A couple of wires must have hit invisible bodies, because they stuck there, in the air, between corn chips. Soon the critters were swarming all over me. I hit the button again. A low, aggressive chanting in some ancient language rippled through the wires. The creatures with wires stuck in them let go of me and tried to escape, looping and twisting in the air so hard the taser nearly shook right outta my hand, but I held on tight.

Vrrrr vrrrrr vrrr vrrrrr. A really strong vibration rattled my teeth. *Plewp. Plewp. Pop!*

Apparently, that was the sound of the taser working. The Frito mosquitoes that I'd speared exploded. Thick, yellow guts that looked like pus and honey mustard pulsed in a blender rained down on me.

"Aaaaaaaahhhhhh! Bleeeee." *Gurgle.*

Yeah. I'm not proud of the sounds I made while all this was happening. It took me by surprise, okay? And yes, if you must know, I got some in my mouth, and no, I will never forget the taste. Let's just say it had heavier notes of pus than mustard, and definitely lacked a mellow, piquant after-dinner taste.

I immediately hunched over, spitting out hell guts, mouth watering like a barf sprinkler, when the creatures that weren't stuck on a taser wire descended on me again.

"Aaaaaah!" The bastards were scratching me!

That's when Bubby slugged up to the end of the chip aisle. The Frito mosquitoes backed off and turned to Bubby, hovering in the air as they sized him up. Bubby's belly rippled and undulated and he *uurrrppped* like he was either about to vomit or paint a toilet with epic diarrhea.

His spiky double mandibles opened wide, and the razor-lined circular mouth appeared. Only this time, his razor teeth were rotating like dueling miter saws. The Frito mosquitoes trembled, then ran. Right for the door. DeeDee jumped in front of the glass. She had a giant Pixie Stix in each hand. She started swirling them like they were nunchucks, busting apart the trembling Frito beasts, chips flying as they ducked and dodged and tried to reform.

Damn, that girl was fine. Capital F fine. And a badass. I watched her boobs jiggle as she fought off the beasts, striped sugar straws swirling. And I mean that in the most gentlemanly, I totally respect the hell out of this chick way possible. A straggling Frito beast hit me in the face, just to remind me that now was not the time to size up DeeDee's finer physical attributes no matter how much I secretly loved her.

By sheer dumb luck, I managed to grab it. By the invisible body. OMG. Woah boy. I wish I could take out my brain and rinse the memory of that sensation straight outta my synapses. It wasn't as bad as a mouth full of pus mustard, but it was pretty gross. The thing was solid. Invisible, yes. But solid, although it felt like one of those reach your hand into the mystery bucket gross-out games at a kids' Halloween party. The thing felt slippery, like oil, hard and crunchy like bug shells, and squishy like overcooked mushy rice all at once. *Dear Lord in Heaven, please erase the memories of that feeling from my brain.* Amen. And did I mention the thing was super strong and shaking? I held tight and my arms jerked left and right as it tried to get away.

Then my fingers started to go numb. And my nose. Because the temperature seemed to drop another fifty degrees, which was saying something considering Bubby already had the place dialed down to freeze pop.

"Anytime now, Bubby!" DeeDee yelled as she Pixie Stixed another Frito monster straight into next week.

Bubby's razor mouth whirred, and a low, rumbling sound reverberated out of him, so deep it shook me all the way down into my insides, like my very own personalized earthquake rattling apart my intestines. Then the air around me swished and whirled. Sucking. *In.* The wiggling hell mosquito slipped out of my hand, flapped its Frito wings desperately against the air, then twirled and whirled, somersaulting through the air right into Bubby's whirring saw mouth. Pus mustard exploded everywhere as Bubby sucked and slurped.

The other Frito mosquitoes whipped past me, one by one, smacking me in the face, trying to get a hold on my shirt, trying to avoid their date with Bubby the Gigantic Jello Jiggler centipede's whirring razor mouth of doom. As I swatted them off of me, one by one, they landed right in Bubby's mouth, squirting pus mustard like a cheap fast-food ketchup pack that'd been rolled over by a tank.

"Help me! Help!" A tiny voice flew right at my ear. *Shit.* It was Kevin, somersaulting through the air, right toward Bubby's razor teeth. "Help!"

I reached out and grabbed him. He wriggled in my hand. His legs tickling my palm like a wiggly giant roach. Ew gross. But I held tight. And he held tight to me, whimpering? "Don't let go, new kid. Please don't let go."

I held on as tight as I could, which was harder than it sounded because whatever magic suction Bubby created was an inescapable vacuum. At least for the Frito mosquitoes, powerless in flight against it, and for Kevin, who was being tugged so hard toward the saw mouth that I had to dig in my heels and pull as hard as I could against the force to keep him in my hands.

Strange. The force wasn't pulling on me, or DeeDee or any of the food or other stuff in the store. Just Kevin and the Frito mosquitoes. Everything else seemed unaffected.

I didn't have to hold onto whimpering Kevin for long. Bubby ate every single one of the Frito mosquitoes in three minutes flat, pureeing their invisible slime horror bodies into oblivion with his rotating blender blade mouth like they were honey-barbecued boneless chicken wings. When the last one had popped, and Bubby had used a long blue tongue to lick the pus guts off his cheek, he urrrrrrpppppped. Then he rubbed his belly. As if to say "Delicious."

Blech. I swallowed down the bile. *So. Gross.* But cycle of life, right? One man's disgusting, mustard pus nightmare was another man-centipede's finger-licking delicious appetizer.

I could feel Kevin trembling in my hand.

"Is it over yet?" His tiny voice squeaked through my fingers.

"Yeah. It's over."

I opened my hand. Kevin was curled up in my palm. A roach tear dripped down his cheek? *Wait.* Did roach faces have cheeks? He looked around, wiped away his tears, then unrolled his body and straightened himself out, running his legs over his carapace like a ruffled stock broker would smooth out his designer blazer. "Okay, dipshit. Put me back on the counter."

"You're welcome."

Kevin side-eyed me. Great. A roach that was too butch to say thanks. Whatever.

Bubby gurgled and vibrated. Er, talking?

"Bubby says he's sorry," DeeDee said, Pixie Stix hanging limp in her hands. "He'll be more careful next time."

"This is his fault?" I said it, then wondered if I should just stop asking questions and focus on staying alive (and getting rich) until Thanksgiving, as per the plan.

Bubby did the sad shoulder hunch again.

"Well, Bubby, by some weird quirk of biology, alters the gate," she said. "He can get through anytime, day or night, even if it's switched off and closed. The problem is the gate stays open behind him unless we manually close it. Yeah...about that. We forgot the closing part. And those things got out. And attacked you. So, oops. Sorry."

CHAPTER 12

Oops. Sorry? That was hardly an apology, I thought as Bubby's ice-cold, blue prehensile tongue licked the last of the mustard pus guts off my shirt and my face. He freeze-hugged me when he was finished, and gurgled what I could only guess was another apology. I looked down. I had to give him props. He was a clean plater. My clothes looked virtually untouched, like they'd never been splashed with hell beast innards. Because I'd been spit-shined by a gigantic hell centipede. Gulp. Yeah. That's fine. Totally fine. Nothing to see here.

"We'll finish SummerSlam next Friday, okay? It's probably best if you head home tonight," DeeDee said to Bubby, who shot DeeDee his biggest droopiest sad eyes. They hugged. Then he squeezed and blurped through the beer cave door and disappeared in a flash of blue light. DeeDee flipped what looked like a light switch, only red, by the beer cave door.

"This." She pointed at it. "Is the manual override. Flip it up and down twice to close the gate when Bubby comes in or out. Don't forget he has to be *all* the way in or out. If any bit of him is in the gate, it won't close. In fact, the gate will get bigger, and we definitely don't want that. Got it?"

I nodded, but I'm not sure how much really sunk in. I couldn't stop thinking about the pus guts. "What the hell were those things, anyway?"

"What things?"

Really? Did I really need to spell it out? "The...*things*. You know, Fritos?"

"Oh those. They were gnats." She shrugged.

"You're kidding."

"I wish."

"But gnats are tiny."

"If you hadn't noticed, gate bugs are waaaay, way bigger," she said. "And meaner. As a rule."

Oh God. There were giant bugs in hell. Which meant there were probably giant hell spiders. *Gulp.* I can't even go there. "But...why were they invisible?"

"Well, some people up here call them No See Ems. Maybe that's literally true down there? I'm not sure, honestly."

I closed my eyes and asked another question I probably didn't want answered. "What about Kevin?"

He wasn't a giant bug, but he was a talking bug, and he was nearly sucked into Bubby's mouth with the hell gnats. I had barely felt a tug, but Kevin was full-on wrapped up in Bubby's suction powers. Something was up.

"What about him?" She looked over at the counter.

Kevin was by the register, rocking back and forth in the roach equivalent of fetal position. (Would that be larval position? Ugh. So many questions!) He was clearly traumatized. Of course, I could hear the faint guitar licks of yet another Dio song pumping out of his speakers.

"Why did he almost get sucked into Bubby's mouth like those gnats, but we didn't?"

She snatched the meat of my arm and squeezed hard. "*Don't* talk about Kevin." She was forcefully whispering now. That wasn't good.

"But—"

"Shhh. Zip it." Then, in a voice so low you nearly had to be a T-Rex to hear it, she said. "He's unauthorized, okay? *Illegal.* So we can't talk about him, okay?"

"Wait. Illegal?"

She kicked me in the shin. "OW!"

"Shhhhh! Not so loud."

"But how is that even possible?"

"You know that saying 'as above, so below?'"

"Well, yeah." I guess?

"Think about that. We're border patrol. Border patrol here in the U.S. also comes with ICE. You know, enforcement? For the stragglers and the people who slip through? I've never personally met any, but I've seen enough to know that the other world." She pointed inside the beer cave. "Has their own version. And somebody." She pointed at Kevin. "Might be in trouble if he's found out."

"But. He's...*obvious.*" Kevin didn't exactly act like a dude in hiding. I mean, come on, his metal albums nearly made my ears bleed every night, he regularly used the intercom and he never bothered to hide or even shuffle off the counter when customers were around.

"We can't ever talk about it again, do you understand? We've said too much already," she looked around, as if waiting for SWAT to descend on us at any second. "I don't understand exactly how it works, but words have power. They manifest things, like celestial authorities,

114

gate guardians. Words draw attention if spoken aloud, okay? Things can be overheard. And we don't want *anybody...*"

She looked at Kevin, and then back at me. "To get deported or ushered through any gates they don't want to go through, okay? He's one of us. We look out for each other. That's all you need to know. Got it?"

She dug her glitter-polished nails deeper into my arm. "Got it?"

"Ow! Yeah, I got it!"

"All right, then." She let go. "Just relax. Roll with it. Don't ask questions."

"Let me guess," I said. "You don't know how it all works either."

"Nope. And I don't want to." She winked.

Okay. Full disclosure. I wasn't one of those dudes who could read a girl like a book, but I understood enough to catch that wink meant DeeDee did know something. Something I probably deserved to know, too. I was about to call her out on it when something rammed into my foot. *Gah.* It was the damned eight ball. Facing up. Of course. Always an opinion.

"Know that song from Frozen?" It said.

What?

The triangle turned and floated up through the red liquid again. "Let it go! Let it go-o-ooo!"

"Fine." I huffed.

"Listen to your friend." DeeDee pointed at eight ball.

"Oh snap," angel eight ball said. His triangle turned. "Better not tell you now."

"Relax. I don't need you," she told it.

She didn't buy the ruse. Who could blame her? Magic 8-Balls usually weren't so outspoken.

"You sure don't. You aren't a hopeless man baby who refuses to embrace adulthood," eight ball said. "This one here is a full-time job."

The triangle turned to show a hand, making the L for Loser sign, with an arrow pointing at me.

"What? Shut up!" I kicked it across the room, and I swear I could hear it cursing me out as it rolled, hard as a bowling ball, straight into the base of the hot dog station. "Jerk."

"Don't worry," DeeDee said. "Spirit guides don't last long around here."

Spirit guide? What was that supposed to mean?

I didn't get the chance to ask. The front door chimed, and Bob the Doughnut Guy stepped in, carrying a large pink box. "Sorry I'm late. We had a little, uh...incident, at the bakery, but the line's up and running again. You wanna check me in, new guy?"

"Sure." I went behind the counter. DeeDee went back to her stool at the beer cave door. And we were instantly back to normal, as if the Frito mosquitoes never happened. Jesus. Would I ever get used to this? This place was absolutely bonkers.

Bob the Doughnut Guy looked at his watch. "Where's Bubby? It's Friday night. I thought it was time to see what the Rock is cookin'."

He smiled and elbowed me, as if waiting for me to be in on his joke. I just stared at him, wondering what he was talking about.

"Not a wrestling fan, huh?"

I shrugged.

"Well, no accounting for taste," he said. "Let's get these doughnuts done. I'm behind schedule."

As usual, the case was nothing but crumbs, sold out. Except for the untouched row of glazed doughnuts with the pink frosting and rainbow sprinkles. Those ones never sold, even though they were equally, if not more delicious looking than the others. The pink ones literally called out to me, broadcasting their deliciousness, every time I walked past the case. I shouldn't have given it a second thought, but of course I did, and the more I thought about it, the more I realized that the doughnut case— like the rest of the Demon Mart—didn't add up. It wasn't as it seemed.

Who was buying and eating these doughnuts? Someone, obviously, and not just the guy in the track suit.

"Hey. You okay, space cadet?" Bob the Doughnut Guy snapped his fingers. *Huh.* He was wearing thick pink rubber gloves. Like industrial heavy duty gloves, when he opened the pink delivery box. Did he always wear those?

"Oh, yeah," I said. "Sorry. Just thinking."

"Don't hurt yourself."

"I like your gloves," I said.

He looked at them and shrugged. "New policy. New guy was careless and had an accident. We all have to wear these now. Just in case."

Bob the Doughnut Guy used his pink rubber-clad hands to load the doughnuts into the case, the same way he did every night. He took out the empty doughnut trays, shiny gold with lace-doily edges and littered with sprinkle shrapnel. He opened the pink box, lifted a fresh, full tray of doughnuts out of it and slid it into the case. Then, he lifted another tray of fresh, new doughnuts out of the box. And another. And another, until the case was filled with gleaming, steaming fresh-from-the-bakery fried and frosted deliciousness. More than could possibly fit into a normal, six-inch deep pink box.

A *bottomless* box. Every night.

And the steel beer cave wall was actually a doorway to hell.

And Kevin was a talking roach.

And a gigantic blue centipede came in every Friday to watch vintage wrestling.

And why was I still here?

Oh right. Money. Or, maybe I was in a coma. Maybe I had been hit by an SUV while riding my Huffy and I was actually in the hospital unconscious dreaming all of this. If only I were that lucky.

"Welp, all done." Bob the Doughnut Guy smacked me on the shoulder with his giant hand and said the same thing he said to me every night. "See you tomorrow, if you live that long."

He was out the door, squealing his pink truck out of the lot a few minutes later. Then, as if on cue, the desperate guy in the track suit jogged right on into the store, slid a devil's food chocolate doughnut with chocolate frosting into a bag, threw a couple crumpled up bills at me, and ran back out into the parking lot to chow down on his doughnut like he was a rabid, desperate squirrel.

Man. His timing! What, did he just jog behind the truck all night waiting for the deliveries? Track suit guy, as usual, was a serial litterer who left his doughnut bag in the lot and ran away, jubilant, crumbs still on his lips. Wherever he worked out, I was pretty sure doughnuts weren't on his officially-sanctioned diet, but it didn't seem to hurt him. He looked even buffer than the last time I saw him. He was starting to beef up like a Pumping Iron-era Schwarzenegger.

Hmmm. He sure loved those doughnuts. So did a lot of people. They sold out every day. I stepped closer to the case. The doughnuts called to me in seductive, quiet whispers, lighter than air. *Eat me. I'm delicious. You need me. Just a taste.*

Normally, I'd tune it out. I'd learned to do as much, to go do something else in another part of the store right after the doughnuts arrived. The pull was stronger when they were fresh and new. This time, I gave in. I peered into the case, my nose inches from the glass. Why was eating them specifically off limits to me, but anyone off the street could buy one for two bucks?

You know what? I had a lot of questions. It was time to get at least one straight answer. Knowledge was power, and knowledge began with a doughnut. I opened the display case.

Eat me, they whispered.

"I'm gonna," I whispered back. I steeled my nerves. *Which one do I pick?*

If I was gonna give in, I had to make it count. My hand hovered over the pink frosted. Then I thought of Pawnshop Doc and the pink one behind the emergency glass in the weapons safe. Maybe not the smart choice. I wanted a doughnut, not instant death. I went for the chocolate devil's food with the chocolate icing. I mean, the body builder ate one every night, and he was still alive. In fact, he looked better, stronger. At least I knew it wouldn't kill me, right?

I had my fingers on the doughnut and hadn't even lifted it off the bakery paper before Kevin jump-flew off the counter and landed on top of the display case. "Drop it!" He stood on his back four legs and waved his other two at me as if signaling an SOS from a sinking ship. "Drop it. Right now!"

"What if I don't?"

"Listen, dipshit. You have no idea. These doughnuts are a delicious assortment of absolute nightmares."

"Well, why are we selling them if they aren't safe?" Take that. Comeback of the year!

"Dude. I'm a roach not an existential philosopher. We sell soda pop, processed meat sticks, and deep-fried microwave noodles, too. People shouldn't eat that crap, but they do. The doughnuts are another level. Besides, we're specifically banned from eating them unless it's an emergency."

"This is an emergency," I said.

"Yeah? What's the problem?"

"I'm hungry," I said.

"Not good enough, fatty. You just ate two steaks. Rules are rules. Actions have consequences. And as your manager, I'm enforcing the rules. Drop the doughnut, or I'm writing you up." he squeaked.

"What? Write me up? This is America. It's my God-given, Constitutional right to eat a damned doughnut."

"Listen, dumbass. You haven't even eaten it yet, and look what it's done to you."

"What are you talking about?"

"Look in the case," Kevin said. He crossed all of his arms—legs?— smugly.

I shouldn't have asked. My hand, the one touching the chocolate doughnut, had ballooned in size. It looked like the hand of a giant. Fingers fat and long as bratwurst, puffed up and elongated, like a monster hand had been grafted onto my arm. And it was still growing. "What the hell?"

I tried to yank my hand out of the case, but it had swelled so much it was stuck. "Kevin. Help!"

"Nothing I can do," he said. "It's also your Constitutional right to pay the price when you write a check your ass can't cash."

"Dude. Seriously! Help me." My hand was super warm, and the skin was so tight...so so tight, like a fat lady's yoga pants, stretched to the max, holding on for dear life.

"Hey. I told you not to touch the doughnuts. You touched the doughnuts. What did you expect?"

"Well, not this! Help me!"

"I can't." He shrugged.

"What do you mean you can't?"

He rolled his beady black eyes. "You haven't read your employee manual yet, have you?"

"What—HELP ME!"

"Look. I *can't* help you. The doughnut spells are irreversible."

"Spells? What? Like magic? Like, witch spells?"

He shook his head. "You're just gonna have to wait until it wears off. There's no reversal. It's time-based. On the plus side, if you jerk off today, it'll feel like you're getting some strange. That'll be fun for you."

"That's not funny!"

"It's kinda funny. Speaking of jerking off." He thumbed a leg behind him as DeeDee walked up to the counter. "You're number one spank bank star is on the move."

"Is everything all ri—oh my GOD!" She put her hands over her mouth, but I could still see the shock in the rise of her perfectly tweezed eyebrows. And it wasn't making me feel better about my situation. "Lloyd! Your HAND!"

Okay, yeah. I know. It was shocking. I get it. It was a super giant-sized hand now, and my still normal-sized wrist was having trouble lifting the weight of it. And oh, did I mention it was still stuck in the case and now, oh boy, it was so big it was starting to seriously pinch. I was running out of room in there.

DeeDee freaking out wasn't helping me get through it. "Help MEEEEEEEE!"

She snapped to. "Oh, yeah. Right."

She hopped over the counter like a parkour master. A second later, she'd snapped on some black rubber cleaning gloves like she was a surgeon on a prime time television medical drama. She grabbed my wrist and started twisting, trying to angle my hand out of the case. "Try not to touch any of the other ones. We don't want to make it worse," she said.

"Worse? How could it get any worse?" Nope. Don't answer that.

"Just try, okay?" She twisted and turned but my giant hand was not coming out. "We need lube."

She hopped the counter and ran to aisle four.

"That's what she said," Kevin said. Then he roach chuckled. *Gah.*

Dickhead.

"Thanks for your help, Kevin."

"Dude. No means no. You're the one who went all rapey on the doughnuts. This is all your fault, not mine."

"The second I get my giant hand out of the case, I'm gonna pound you into oblivion," I growled like an injured animal.

"Whatever, monster mitt."

DeeDee emerged from aisle four with a giant tub of Vaseline. A minute later, she was behind the counter slathering it onto my giant hand. She jammed her fingers inside the case and rubbed the lube onto my ever swelling—so I wish this story was going in a different direction, but no—freakazoid giant troll hand.

My head started to spin a little. Okay. A lot. "I think I'm gonna pass out."

"Your heart's probably not pumping enough blood to fuel that massive meat mitt," Kevin said. "Unless you're hiding a Stallone arm under that polo shirt, your jerk off plan is probably shot, too. No way you'll be able to lift that thing!"

"I'm glad you're finding this so amusing," I said. Room. Spinning.

"Hey. I'm a talking roach with a pack of dickheads for roommates. I have to find joy wherever I can."

And that was the last thing I remember.

CHAPTER 13

I woke up with my cheek pressed against the softest velvet I had ever felt in my entire life. Soooo smooth, luxurious, and absolutely soaking wet. With drool. *Crap.* My drool, because I had fallen asleep face down, snoring, leaking fluids like an over-topped dam, mouth-breathing like an orc. All night.

Wait. Whose couch was this? Where the hell was I? I opened one eye to peek, assessing for danger. Kinda like I was the star of those spy movies where the bad guys were right next to me and inexplicably waiting for me to wake up before they hurt me? But the good guy pretended to be asleep so he could listen to the bad guys outline their plan? Yeah. Just like that.

The room was dim, but not totally dark. My one eye told me I was face down and had completely drooled-up a red velvet fainting couch that looked like it'd been lifted straight out of Dracula's boudoir in Victorian England. There was another one exactly like it right across from me. There was a polished black coffee table shaped like an old-timey coffin in between. All on top of a very black, very shaggy rug.

Great. I'd been abducted by vampires. I was dinner. They just hadn't eaten me yet.

I got brave and opened both eyes to scope out the scene and hopefully plan my escape. I was in a long, open room in a trendy, expensive loft by the looks of it. Exposed ducts and heavy wood support beams ran along the ceiling. The walls were brick, and the few bits of actual drywall were painted black. There was a wall of windows, but the curtains were black and pulled shut. Bright white sunlight blazed around the curtain edges. *Thank God. It's daytime!* I could open the curtains and burn my captors to dust!

I sat up. All the furniture was either black or blood red. Geesh. Textbook vampire! I was about to check my neck for bite marks—you would too if you'd seen what I'd seen—when I practically yanked my bicep clean off the bone trying to lift my hand. It was so heavy. *Crap.*

My giant hand. That wasn't a dream. That happened.

My hand was wrapped in a red towel, on the red velvet sofa, surrounded by ice packs that had clearly fallen off during my (hopefully not undead, because how would I tell Mom I'd been turned into a vampire?) slumber.

Srnnk. Churrrr. Snort. Snort. A loud grumble came from somewhere in the apartment. *Uh oh.* I wasn't abducted by vampires. I was abducted by a moaning Frankenstein's monster. Well, a snoring one. I had to get out of here.

"Good afternoon, sleepyhead." DeeDee walked out of a doorway cut into the brick wall.

"Shhhh! Quiet, DeeDee. Vampires!" I yell whispered.

"Are you still dizzy? You're talking crazy." She wasn't fazed.

"Didn't you hear that groaning?" I whispered. "Monster! Let's get out of here!"

"I'm not leaving. This is my place. No monsters here." She glanced back at the doorway she'd walked out of. She looked a little uncomfortable. "No real monsters, anyway."

She rustled around in the kitchen for a few minutes then carried two mugs over to me. She plopped down on the blood-red (see the theme?) velvet armchair next to me. She wore only a large T-shirt for some indie rock band I'd never heard of. And black panties. And I know that because I could see them for a split second when she put her leg underneath her to sit down.

Gulp. Tea Cups. Rainbows. Unicorns. Fat dudes. Think of anything but those panties. I didn't have enough blood flow to support a giant hand and a giant hard-on.

"I don't know what you like, so I figured coffee was a safe bet." She sat a mug shaped like the Bride of Frankenstein on the coffin coffee table between us. She sipped something bright red out of her own matching mug.

Something red. "Great. You're a vampire." I threw my hands up in defeat. Okay, I threw one hand up. I still couldn't lift the other one. "I should have known."

"Why would you say that?"

"Look around. This place looks like the set of, oh, every vampire movie ever made? You work nights. All the monsters at the store don't faze you. And now you're drinking blood."

She looked at her cup. "It's Raspberry Zinger. Caffeine makes me crazy."

"Well, this place screams vampire. Vampires always have fancy houses." I'd seen Twilight, but I wasn't gonna admit that out loud. "And, how do I know you're not lying about the tea to make me feel better?"

"Taste it." She held it out, but I didn't take it. "And all this?"

She waved her hand around the room. "It's called goth girl with a job. I bought all of this stuff off the Internet, and it came in flat-packed in boxes. I used coupons, too, so it can't be too edgy. I would hope real vampires could afford real antiques."

"You aren't just saying that to make me feel better?"

"Vampires wish they had this much style," she said. "How's your hand?"

"I don't know. I'm scared to look." I may have never uttered a truer statement.

"Then close your eyes, and I'll look."

She put her mug down, crawled across the shag rug, and knelt down in front of me. *Woah boy.* I'd seen a few X-rated scenes that started like this. Her pale skin was smooth and flawless. Her face perfect, even without a hint of makeup.

"Ready?" she asked.

"No. But do it anyway." I closed my eyes and felt DeeDee gingerly moving the towel around. Then silence. Dead silence. "That bad, huh?"

"Actually it's about half the size it was when you passed out. At this rate, it should be close to normal before work."

"Really?" I opened my eyes and made the mistake of looking. Holy hell. It still looked like someone had sewn a monster hand onto my wrist. And it wasn't just puffy skin. Even the bones looked bigger.

"No permanent harm done. At least now we know what happens when you eat a chocolate doughnut. That's a win."

"But I didn't eat it."

"Yeah. About that," she said. "Customers come in and buy doughnuts all day long, but I've never heard of anyone getting a reaction from only touching them. I'm guessing you're allergic. Or just more sensitive. I don't know. The doughnuts are another magical mystery. The manual says they impact everyone differently. It's all very personal."

"A mystery? How can you be so cazh about the doughnuts, and all the weird shit you've seen?"

She shrugged.

"Oh God. Let me guess. You're from hell. You're one of them and you didn't tell me because you didn't want to freak me out."

"You're hilarious. You know that?" She reached up and pushed a piece of my hair back off of my forehead. "I'm a plain old human being just like you."

DeeDee was hardly plain. Most people never got the chance to walk around in a body like that.

"Maybe I've had more time for all of it to sink in," she said. "I've also been a goth chick who loves horror movies since I was thirteen, so monsters aren't exactly out of left field. Here. Have some coffee. You'll feel better."

She handed me the mug. I took it and did a quick check for traces of blood. (Couldn't be too careful.) Nope. Just creamy coffee.

"Where are we anyway?"

"This is my place. I couldn't risk sending you out into the world with a giant monster hand. If a normie saw that, it'd raise too many questions. We don't need the attention," she said. "Besides, you blacked out. I don't know where you live. You couldn't ride your bike there unconscious. And I sure as hell wasn't sending you home with Kevin. His roommates are the absolute worst. So, here you are, safe and sound."

"This is *your* place?" I scanned the room. It was a vampire love nest, yes, but it was also deluxe. Sure, there was a framed Evil Dead 2 poster on the wall, the one with the hand reaching out of the ground choking the babe? Yeah, that one. Next to a framed Frankenstein poster, the one with the moody green Boris Karloff. But other than the color scheme and the monster movie posters, the place was posh, modern, like something only the well-paid upwardly mobile could afford to live in. It had that fashionable open floor plan Mom always pined for after she watched too much HGTV. We were in the living room side, along with the stereo system and flat-screen TV, and the kitchen was on the other side.

"So, this is where you live? All the time."

"Yep. Home sweet home, mine all mine."

"Yeah right," I said. "You mean landlord sweet landlord."

"No. It's mine. I own it. It's a condo. Look out the window. We're on High Street. Short North."

"Gee. Aren't you tragically hip?"

Yeah, okay. I tried to play it cool because I felt a little hot around the collar. *Dude.* I still lived in my childhood bedroom. With my parents. In the suburbs. Could I get any less cool? Oh, you know I can! I had no money. I owned nothing but a busted smartphone and a car that didn't run. And here was DeeDee, sitting in her own condo on the hippest, most expensive street in Columbus. Suddenly, it dawned on me that DeeDee was a lot like Simone. All goals and achievement. Why were chicks so put together? Us nice dudes never had so much as a hope to ever keep up.

"It works out," DeeDee said, oblivious to my inner turmoil. "It's a hike to work, but I can walk to class."

"Class?" I had a feeling I was about to feel even more like a loser.

"Yeah. I go to Ohio State. I've got about a year left."

Yep. Called it. Might as well raise my hand and say "community college drop out here." I didn't have the grades to go to Ohio State, even if I wanted to. Not even one of the branch locations. I was a budding Homer Wiley, failed subreddit cult leader, if there ever was one.

"Philosophy major. Ironic huh?" She chuckled. "That's probably why I like the job so much. I'm a goth philosophy major for God's sake. Ruminating about life and death is my bag. I spent years wondering what was out there, what was on the other side. And what it is to be good or evil. And vampires, because, you know, goth."

"Vampires aren't real. Get serious." I chuckled.

She wrinkled her eyebrows, looking at me like I was stupid. Again. "Anyway. All the mysteries of life. All the things humans can't understand but try to, the essential truth that we're all searching for in the dark, so close and so out of reach. I mean, how lucky are we? We see the mystery every single day. We see it all in person. Monsters. Demons. Heaven. Hell. It's all real. Right here, running right alongside the mundane world every single day. That job changed my life. I love it."

"Aren't you terrified?" I took a sip out of my mug, trying to control my shaking hand. *Mmm.* The coffee was delicious. Creamy and strong and mocha. I should know. I was a barista for three hours once, remember? "It hasn't exactly helped me sleep at night."

"Or helped you make better fashion choices." She pointed at my pastel blue polo shirt.

Okay, so yeah, I was still on the church camp kick, because I still wasn't convinced my soul wasn't in danger, okay? Knowing made DeeDee excited. Knowing made me want to hedge my bets.

I wasn't taking chances. I wasn't gonna end up in a fiery pit of hell spiders. If the gnats were bad, and the centipedes were twenty feet of frozen jelly, think of the spiders! But of course, the only thing I could articulate was, "You don't like my T-shirts."

"Your T-shirts look like they came out of a cheap souvenir shop in Branson, Missouri," she said. "Wear something that doesn't hurt my eyes when I look at you, something with personality. But not 'church camp' or 'dumb frat guy.' Seriously. You don't have anything else? Isn't there, like, a gamer chic look? You're cute, Lloyd. You need to show it off."

And...I got a full-on chub. Yep. There it was. One smile and a compliment and I was tingling all over. She owned me. I may as well lie face down in a ditch filled with mud for all eternity, because I would do it just in case she might need to step on me that one time to keep her shoes clean.

"We can work on the clothes," she said.

Oh God. We. I'm cute and 'we' can work on my outfits. Isn't that, like, step one on the twelve-step program to steady girlfriend? They dress you and improve you. That's what chicks do. And we let them because, dude, vaginas! Wait. Wait. Focus, Lloyd. Focus. Not on panties, on the big picture! "How can you afford all this? How long have you worked at Dairy...uh...Demon (gulp) Mart."

I tripped on the words. Some things felt worse and more sinister when said out loud.

"Almost three years now. And you know how well we get paid. That job is a golden ticket."

"I don't know. Money's evil. That's why rich dudes are assholes."

"No, silly. Assholes will be assholes, rich or broke. Money is neutral. It's a tool. Use it well, and you can get the life you want. This is what I want: A college degree and a condo that I own, free and clear. Well, and to be a ninja, but money can't buy that. It's still a work in progress. What do you want, Lloyd?"

I didn't answer because it was too embarrassing. I wanted to be able to see the sky from the bottom of the deep hole of debt I'd dug. I wanted to break even. Start fresh. Actually building a future, owning something, seemed as possible to me right now as flying to the moon by flapping my arms really hard. DeeDee must have judged from my clueless silence that I didn't want her to press the issue. She was kind enough to change the subject.

"Did you know Junebug worked the graveyard shift for seven years? Seven! She's a legend," DeeDee said. "No one's ever lasted that long. Word is she went out in a blaze of glory, too. Fought off a horde of flesh-eating ghouls with her silver sequined scrunchie and a fistful of Slim Jim Monster Meat Sticks."

Help me, Jesus. Did she say flesh-eating ghouls? As in... "zombies...?" My mouth had suddenly gone bone dry. "Are...real?"

The words barely squeaked out. I broke out in a sweat.

DeeDee was giving me the same look of "Are you stupid?" she'd given me when I asked about the vampires. Something hit my ankle. I looked down. Angel eight ball rolled partially out from under the sofa, triangle face up. Of course. Always an opinion. "Zombie rule number one: Cardio."

Shut up. I kicked it back under the sofa.

"Junebug moved to day shift after that. Guess she felt she couldn't top it. And, you know, for Ricky."

"Ricky?" The porcine, terrified day manager who was eternally painted head to toe in size too small plaid polyester? I looked down at my polo shirt and too-small khakis. Okay. I was going back to cargo shorts and T-shirts. Man muffins were not a good look. "Why? Are they like, a thing?"

I'd have to kill myself if a guy like that was getting sweet love on the regular, but I wasn't.

"No, it's not like that."

Phew. One less reason to kill myself.

"Junebug is super protective of Ricky, like an aunt. She's friends with his mom. They're neighbors. They all live in the Paradise Isles trailer park off of Emerald Parkway. Anyway, Ricky was hired for graveyard, but his first night was his last. I mean, ghouls on your first night? Can you imagine?"

Uh, I got a snake dude in a trench coat sucked into a Michael Bolton CD on my first shift, so yeah. I can image.

"Junebug talked Faust into moving Ricky to days. He needed the job, but he couldn't hack the graveyard. Long story short, his mom has some serious health problems or something and he takes care of her. Yes, Ricky still lives with his mom," DeeDee said. "But you probably guessed that by looking at him."

Yep. Mouth even drier, body even sweatier. I still lived with my Mom. Could she—could other people—tell by looking at me? Was my life path leading me to either be a Homer Wiley or a Ricky the Day Manager?

I was afraid of the answer, so, naturally, I changed the subject. "Faust is the devil. Aren't you the least bit worried about hell and eternity? He said there was a gate for doomed souls. Do you want to end up in there, like Homer?"

"Who?"

"The reddit dude who possessed Caroline Ford Vanderbilt!" How could she forget? I hadn't stopped thinking about it.

"Oh God, her. She's suing the store, you know. Good luck with that," DeeDee chuckled and took a sip of tea.

"Gah. But, hell!"

"Okay. You need to relax. I've already said you aren't gonna burn in hell or suffer eternal damnation because of your job. Well, unless you run a leveraged buyout hedge fund. I'm pretty sure there's a commandment against that," she said. "Maybe number twenty-five? I'd have to double check."

"But there are only ten commandments."

She rolled her eyes. "You haven't read your employee manual yet, have you?"

Gah. Enough with the lectures! "How can you be so sure all this is on the up and up?"

"I'm a philosophy major. Duh," she said.

I blank stared.

"Are you familiar with the concept of free will?"

I may or may not have blank blinked a few more times.

"Free will is the idea that you, through your choices, thoughts, and actions, control the outcome of your life and the fate of your eternal soul. Plato. Aristotle. Aquinas. Descartes. Kant. Sartre. Philosophers have grappled with what free will means for literally millennia."

Blink. Blink. Did you catch that? Me either. "Sum it up." I also wanted to say 'and keep it simple, like third-grade reading level,' but those weren't really the words that make smart chicks respect you.

"I've read all the theories. All the long, blathering arguments. It's easy to make it complicated, but it's really very simple. Every day, we make choices. Your choices either hurt people or help people. If you hurt people, and you don't care. If you only care about yourself, at the expense of others, you're gonna burn."

"That's it?"

"That's it."

"It can't be that simple."

"Yes, it can. It's all right there in the bestselling book of all time."

"The Cat in the Hat?"

"The bible, stupid." She eye-rolled me. "Book of Revelation: 'God searches hearts and minds, and will repay each of you according to your deeds.' Romans two: 'He will repay according to each one's deeds. Glory and honor and peace for everyone who does good'."

"I never pegged you as a bible quoter."

"I read. A lot, but sometimes the first source is the best source," she said. "TV preachers these days say faith is all that matters, but I call bullshit. It's about actions. How you treat people, especially those who are poor, who are different, down on their luck. Me and you? Faith wouldn't be enough anyway, because we know. We *know* it's real. Heaven. Hell. Demons. Angels. All of it. So we have to rely on doing good things. And what bigger, better good thing is there than keeping monsters in hell where they belong?"

Wow. So, this was a lot to process.

"Anyway, working for Faust doesn't damn us, our choices do."

"And you trust Faust? You don't think there's a catch? That the money, all of it, is too good to be true?"

"The money is hazard pay. And protection against bribery. You can't be trusted to do a good job if you aren't being appreciated. Corruption and temptation would be too dangerous," she said. "And, yeah, I do trust him. Faust respects free will. He's an excellent judge of character. He knows us better than we know ourselves. He knows what lies in our hearts."

Gulp. "About that..."

"Relax. It's on the up and up. He wouldn't abuse that knowledge," she said. "My point is, you don't need those church camp clothes. Faust hired you. That alone proves you're worthy. You have a pure heart. So do I. So does Kevin, as hard as that is to believe. So do Junebug and Ricky. Pure of heart, all of us, deep down. That's a job requirement, so you're already on the right path."

"Why would a pure heart (whatever that means) matter?"

"Because sketchy people can't be trusted to hold the fate of the world in their hands," she said. "Look how that's working out in politics."

"Good point."

"The world is a shit show, Lloyd. We're neck deep," she said. "Every one of us is born with a shovel. At the end of your life, you'll be judged by one thing: Did you use your shovel to clean up your little corner of the world? Did you, by existing, make the world less shitty? Me? I'm using my shovel. I've chosen to start digging. I'm going to leave my corner nicer than it was when I found it. Part of that is my job. So, Lloyd. Tell me. Are you going to dig, too?"

CHAPTER 14

Right about now, you probably have two questions. Yes, my hand did shrink back to normal size, thank you very much. And no, I did not get the chance to jerk off using my monster hand, so I will never know if it would have truly felt like the caress of a stranger. And since we're being totally honest here, I'm a little bummed about that in retrospect. Get it while you can, right? Seriously, don't judge. I'm lonely.

Wait. Those weren't your questions? Okay then. Nothing to see here.

In other news, if you must know, I was not planning to go anywhere near the doughnut case ever again, no matter how much the stupid things called out to me. If touching one was enough to give me a troll hand, I didn't want to find out what would happen to me if I actually *ate* one.

So here I was, back at work, steering clear of the doughnuts. And I'd survived to see another payday. I'd thought a lot about what DeeDee said about money being a tool and using your shovel, yada yada. I wasn't sure selling slushies and forties, or making sure succubus strippers made it to center stage at Sinbad's on time, qualified as shoveling shit out of my corner of the world as far as getting to heaven, but DeeDee did get one thing right. Cold hard cash, used strategically, could change your life.

For the first time probably ever, I had crawled far enough out of my debt hole to see grass at eye level. Exterminator bill? Paid. Car repairs? Done. (I still couldn't afford insurance, though. Dudes under thirty practically had to sell a kidney to pay for a policy.) Cable bill sent to collections? Paid in full, debt officially erased. Student loans? Okay, not paid off, but today was Friday. Payday. With the cash in my locker right now I'd be able to make all the payments I'd missed, plus interest and fees, and get current on the loan. If I was lucky, I'd even have a bit of extra cash to put in my pencil case in my sock drawer. That hadn't happened since I was eleven.

If I played my cards right—as in, avoided being slain or mutilated by hell beasts until *next* Friday—I might actually be able to pay my parents back for that semester of community college I totally borked up.

I never, ever thought I'd say this, but being responsible felt *good*. Like, *really* good. (Pinkie swear RIGHT NOW you'll never tell my Mom I said that because she'd hold it over my head forever.)

If you really must know, things were different, warmer, between me and DeeDee since that day at her apartment, too. She smiled at me more and eye-rolled at me less. We'd become pals. And maybe, just maybe, if I played my cards right and the stars aligned, we could be more than friends. I think she liked me. If I was smooth, I bet I could convert that into *liked* me liked me. Need I remind you, she said I was cute?

"Keep dreaming," Kevin said, snapping me out of my sentimental haze. "She's way out of your league."

Dude. How did he zone in on my brain waves like that?

"Your name tag, dipshit. That's how we communicate. I don't have human vocal cords, so I'm not actually talking out loud. This is all smoke and mirrors. Psychic gypsy New Age Wicca crap," he said. "It's in the manual which, let me guess, you haven't read yet."

I stared. He shook his head, annoyed, then scuttled across the speakers, pulling a thin copper wire behind him.

"What are you doing?"

"Hand me a couple of rocks." He pointed to the pile of weird crystals under the counter.

"Can you be a little more specific? There are hundreds of them."

"Hold on. I made a list." Kevin looked at a tiny piece of paper he was holding in one of his teeny roach hands. "Don't just stand there. Get moving, noob."

"Fine." I squatted down in front of the rock collection. There were tiny labels on each cubby, but the letters had faded. Why did we need so many magic rocks, anyway? Everyone knew healing crystals were all hippy-dippy crap.

"I hate hippies, too, kid," Kevin said.

Gah. I was not cool with this psychic mind-reading connection.

"Not my fault," Kevin said. "Just keep it clean, okay? I don't need to know what you're thinking when you're standing by the porno mags."

"Wait. I—"

"Zip it. Moving on," Kevin said. "I need a selenite and a pyrite."

"That isn't helping me." A rock was a rock, as far as I was concerned. Although, this collection was a lot more sparkly than gravel.

"Um...one looks like a white crystal tube with brown spots on the ends. And the other is fool's gold, so it looks like a bunch of little gold spray-painted chunks all stuck together."

It took me a few minutes, but I found them. At least, I found rocks that kind of fit those descriptions. I handed them to Kevin. Okay, I couldn't technically hand them to him. They were bigger than he was, so I sat them on the counter next to him. He wrapped the copper wire around one rock, then looped it around the next, connecting them together. He plugged one end of the copper wire into the speakers and the other into the intercom system.

"What are you doing?"

"Dialing it up to eleven. Literally," he said. "These rocks should amplify the sound, so we can feel the spirit of Dio rocking directly in our souls."

"Great." You know I didn't mean that, right? But he was my boss, and he had stereo dibs. No use arguing.

"You're welcome," Kevin said anyway. "Hold on to your butt, kid. I'm about to press play."

I waited for "Rainbow in the Dark" or maybe "Stand Up and Shout," or "Straight Through The Heart," or any of the too many of Kevin's favorite Dio songs I now had stuck on a loop in my brain, to rip across the speakers. But it didn't. Kevin had his hand on his Zune, but he didn't press play. Instead, he stared at me and made a subtle motion with one of his legs. A move that looked eerily like a "look behind you, but don't make it obvious."

Gulp. Dear Lord, if you're listening? No hell spiders. Please don't let it be hell spiders. That's when something cold and hard pressed against my temple.

"Don't move," said a man in a shaky growl. "Put your hands up where I can see them. Then turn around real slow and open the register."

Oh, boy. It's a gun. We're being robbed.

"Duh, Sherlock," Kevin said. "FYI, this guy looks totally nuts. You've probably got about a seventy percent chance of taking a bullet on this one."

Suddenly, my knees turned to noodles, and I was wobbling in sheer terror. I tried to contain it because no sudden movements was kinda rule number one in the don't get shot playbook. Okay, yeah. On a one-to-ten scale of terror, demon Frito gnats should probably rate higher than a desperate human with a gun, but see how rationally you react with a bullet pointed right at your brain.

I turned around as slowly as I could, hands up like I was the perp on a cop reality show. I took one look at the guy with the gun and yep, I was going down. The robber didn't scream stability or strategic planning, or "I care enough about my future not to kill a dude and add a manslaughter charge to my rap sheet."

He wore a pair of those nineties wide-leg raver pants. What were they called? Oh yeah. Phat pants. And he looked like he'd been wearing them since 1998 without washing them once. He was bone thin, gaunt. His body and his gun were shaking. And not the 'I'm scared to be committing a crime' shakes, more like coming down off a high and need a fix, stat, and I don't care who I need to kill to get high, shakes. Addict shakes.

Great. I was gonna get shot, just when my life was on an upswing. Can't win for losing, right? Grandpa was onto something.

"Give me the money. All of it." He bared a row of rotten yellow teeth. He looked like one of those mugshots on the news, the meth heads caught in police stings who looked about fifty when they were actually in their twenties, worse for wear. Road hard.

Kevin was on the register now, waving some of his legs to get my attention. "Follow the robbery protocol, step by step," he said. "And be careful. This joker made it past the Go Away charm, so he's super desperate. Don't die here or you'll end up like me."

"What the fuck is that supposed to mean?" I was so stressed, I said it out loud. I totally forgot Kevin could zone in on my brain waves. The robber thought I was smack talking him, so naturally, he was angry.

"It means give me the money, asshole," jittery meth-mouthed robber said. "What are you, stupid?"

Stupid. Why did everyone keep calling me that? It was starting to hurt my feelings. I hit the no sale button on the register, and the cash drawer slid open. I glanced over at Kevin because it seemed like he was going to coach me through this robbery protocol thing step by step. But no. The register was roach-free. He'd tucked and rolled.

At that moment, DeeDee walked up next to me. *Thank you, Baby Jesus!* She hadn't hung me out to dry. For once.

"Where did you come from?" The robber yelled at her and then aimed his shaking gun at DeeDee. I tried to slide in front of her because, you know, gentlemen take bullets for ladies they secretly love and one day hope to put their penis inside of, but DeeDee pushed me aside. "Hands up, bitch!"

"No need to get nasty." She put her hands up. "Do you want the money, or do you want my hands up?"

"What?... shut up!" The robber was sweating bullets. (I probably should choose a better metaphor here, but I don't perform well under pressure.) His eyes darted nervously between us and the register.

At that point, I'd also wished I'd paid more attention in geometry class because I was having a lot of trouble calculating exactly what angle the bullet would travel if I grabbed the gun and tweaker pulled the trigger. Should I push the barrel up or down? Before I decided to make a move, I kinda needed to know which one of us might accidentally get shot. And then there was the whole was I even strong enough to overpower this dude? Maybe I should have listened to angel eight ball and taken some fitness classes.

And wouldn't you know it, the stupid ball chose that very moment to roll out onto the counter, triangle up.

"That's right, fatty. If you'd listened to me, you'd have this jerk pinned. You'd be DeeDee's knight in shining armor already."

Always an opinion.

"Where did that come from?" The robber pointed his gun at the angel eight ball.

"Please. Do me a favor and shoot it."

But no. He put the gun in my face instead, and I mean really in my face, into my nose so hard it pushed my nostrils flat. This is the part where I would have pooped my pants if all of my orifices hadn't been squinched up so tight with fear.

"Hey. It's okay. You don't need the gun." DeeDee smiled at the robber. "Take the money. We don't care. You can have it."

The robber looked at her. Then at me. Then at the fat stack of cash in the open register drawer. "No funny business," he said. "Hand it over."

"Okay. I've got to put my hands down so I can get the money."

He nodded, anxious, but still unsure if he should trust our plan.

"Life in prison for killing us isn't worth the cash," she added, cazh as usual. She stacked up the bills. Twenties, then tens, then fives, then ones until the drawer was empty. She took one shiny gold coin out of a side compartment and sat it on top of the bills. It looked like actual, pure gold. And ancient, with some weird design on it. *What was that?*

She held the money out to him. He took the wad with his other, equally trembling hand. He stuffed it into the pocket of his giant-legged raver jeans. Then he grabbed the eight ball. "This is mine now, too."

"Good luck with that," I said. Man. When was I gonna learn to keep my lips zipped?

"What? Shut up!" He backed away. The gun was no longer touching me, but he was still pointing it at me. Then DeeDee. Then at me. His eyes were so wide, the whites above his irises were clearly visible. Great. He literally had crazy eyes.

"Don't call the cops," he yelled as he rounded the end of the counter. The jerk still had his gun on us when he stopped to load his pockets full of cheap smokes from the display racks.

DeeDee leaned close to me and whispered. "You're wearing your name tag, right?"

I glanced down. "Yeah. What? Why?"

"Make sure it's straight. Then say 'Have a nice day' to the guy before he walks outside. Okay?"

"What? No!" I whisper screamed. "I hope he has a shitty day. He deserves the worst possible day."

"Just do it. You have to do all the steps, or it won't work."

"What won't work?"

"The robbery protocol!"

She straightened my name tag, then hers, and said: "Have a nice—"

That's when the intercom vibrated to life, with ear-splitting feedback, and "Hungry for Heaven" screeched out of the speakers. *Gah. Why did I know that? Kevin and his Dio! Really? Now?* And when I say screeched, I mean it felt like every note was a talon ripping my eardrum apart piece by piece and pulling it out through my nostril. I put my hands over my ears, but the music was so loud it rattled my insides.

"Sorry!" Kevin said. "I accidentally walked across the play button."

The nervous robber apparently didn't like Dio either. He scowled and held his ears. "Turn it off!"

He pointed the gun at the speakers and pulled the trigger. I don't know where Kevin bought those speakers, but he got a good deal because they appeared to be bulletproof. The bullet sparked when it hit one, then bounced off. It was ricocheting all over the place. It bounced off the counter and hit me straight on the name tag. "Gah! I'm DEAD!" I screamed.

I did a quick assessment, running my hands over my chest, but nope. Phew. No bullet hole! No bullet? Huh. I heard a chink. The bullet had stopped cold, lodged in the front window.

"On the floor or I'll kill you!" Except, the robber didn't give us time to do anything before he pulled the trigger again.

Bastard! But that bullet bounced, too. What, was his ammo made of rubber? At that point, the holy-shit-I-just-got-shot-and-there's-another-bullet-coming nerve impulse kicked in, and I screamed like a terrified toddler. DeeDee ninja-kicked me to the floor and landed on top of me. *Oh. Hell. No.* She was not going to save *me*.

We tussled for a hot minute as I attempted to roll over on top of *her*, to shield her from the bullet like the gentleman my Mom raised me to be. But no. She pushed me off, reached up, and clicked Kevin's Zune off. The music stopped immediately. My ears were still ringing. DeeDee shook her head and sat on one knee for a hot minute, getting her bearings, before she bounded—in one move, no joke—over the counter, somersaulting over the cigarette displays. I followed her yelling "nooooooooooooo!" terrified that one of us would be shot. Again.

She knocked the shaking addict to the floor. The gun slid across the linoleum. He went after it, but he wasn't exactly in peak physical condition. DeeDee got to the gun first, grabbed it and turned it on him. The robber looked like he might actually poop his pants. He started emptying his pockets and pleading for his life. "Keep the money," DeeDee said, holding the gun like she was a trained assassin. "Just get out. Now."

He scrambled to the door, but before he was all the way out, DeeDee called after him in the most high fructose corn syrup sticky-sweet voice I'd ever heard. "Have a nice day!"

The door shut behind him.

"I'm calling the cops!" I squealed.

"No. Don't." She flipped the lock on the front door and held on to the push bar white-knuckled. "Robbery protocol. One. Secure your name tag. Two. Give the perp the cash. Three. Say have a nice day. Four. Stay still. Justice will be served immediately. Whatever you do, don't move."

All three of us looked out the window. The robber was limp-running across the parking lot. He stopped at the base of the neon 24/7 Demon Mart sign. I could see his face in the red glow, looking around. There was a sound, a deep vibration.

Whoop. Whoop. Whoop.

It sounded like flapping, like the wings of a bird, but amplified and in slow motion.

"Remember, don't move," DeeDee said, eerily calm. "It'll get him faster."

"Who'll get what faster?" Nope. Don't answer that. La la la la, forget I said anything.

The building vibrated, rattling things off the shelves. The robber started running again. Scrambling, actually. He tripped over his Phat pants, falling face-first onto the asphalt. He started to crawl. He looked back at the pitch-black night and screamed, "No! No! No no no no no!"

"I hate this part." DeeDee's voice was shaking. "Whatever you do stay still, Lloyd, or it'll come after us."

"What will come after us?" Jesus. I needed to shut up because I really didn't want answers to these questions. I stared out the window, frozen in place with terror, eyes absolutely dry because I was too scared to blink.

At that moment, a black shadow descended on the robber, swallowing him in total darkness. No, not a shadow. The edges came into focus in the neon light. The robber was wrapped in a gigantic, pitch-black wing with feathers like a bird. A big bird, and not the nice yellow one. I couldn't even see the guy. The wing was wrapped up tight around him. My heart was kicking my sternum so hard it was knocking me sideways.

Wow. Junkie or not, I wasn't sure anyone deserved whatever this was. Just then, a gold shimmering eye emerged from the black feathers. It looked into the store.

"Don't move," DeeDee whispered.

Kevin was clinging to my shirt, trembling. The gold eye looked at us, then away. The creature's massive wings flapped, and it took flight. The addicted robber screamed. His legs kicked against air, as the creature carried him away into the night, gripping him in leathery clawed feet.

"That," DeeDee said, "is why no one ever robs us twice."

CHAPTER 15

"We need to talk about the music, Kevin. You turned it up on purpose, didn't you?" DeeDee asked.

We were all behind the counter, reloading cheap cigarette packs into the display carousels and generally tidying up after our attempted robbery/colossal demon bird-napping. "You nearly got us killed," she said. "You know the protocol. What were you thinking?"

"If you must know, I was trying to summon the spirit of Ronnie James Dio. I started while dingus was robbing us because I thought it would be awesome to watch Dio swoop down and scare that tweaker away before he hung out with us."

DeeDee gave him some serious side-eye.

"Don't give me that look. It was a sure thing. I consulted the book. I did my homework." Kevin's leg pointed at the big creepy old monster manual behind the counter. It was open to the page with Bubby and a bunch of other unfathomable horrors in a circle around the hungry angler-fish guy. Right next to the page with illustrations of rocks and lists of their magic powers. "So I picked the wrong rocks. You know how this goes. It's art, not science."

"Maybe next time don't test your spells during an armed robbery?" She said. "Still, your rocks did something. That bouncing bullet thing saved Lloyd's life. Of course, we probably wouldn't have been shot at if you hadn't blown that poor guy's eardrums out. You and your stupid Dio."

"Watch your mouth," Kevin snapped. "That man was a world treasure. No man is more metal than Ronnie James Dio."

"Wait. What?" I was a few steps behind on the conversation, still reeling from watching a man-eating devil bird fly off with a drug addict. "The bullet. That was the rocks?"

"Pretty sure." She pointed to the whitish one. "Kevin, why were you using clear quartz to summon a spirit? It's a power amplifier, not a conduit. Don't you need selenite to reach the other side?"

Kevin glared at me. "I asked for selenite and you gave me quartz?

No wonder it didn't work, dumbass."

"Dude. If it was the wrong rock, you should have said something!"

"I'm not a rock expert. I thought it was the right one," Kevin snipped.

"Well, so did I!"

DeeDee examined the copper wire linking the stones, unfazed by our argument. "The pyrite. That's defensive, a shield. That's probably why the bullets bounced," she said. "I'm not sure how you planned to help Dio cross over with pyrite, but the quartz must have amplified its defensive properties. That's why the bullet didn't kill Lloyd. It bounced instead. Nice setup, Kevin. Maybe we could use it if things ever get really bad around here."

"Oh, my God. I seriously almost died?" I suspected it, but now that I knew for sure, it was way more intense.

"A drug addict shot a gun at you," Kevin said. "Duh."

"But...they're just stupid rocks! Rocks are rocks. They don't have superpowers."

They both looked at me like I was stupid. Again.

"Do you even know how to read?" Kevin asked.

Yep, I'd been shamed. By a talking roach.

"Ack! I can't deal." They weren't even the least little bit freaked out by my near-death experience, but I sure as hell was. What good was paid off debt if you weren't alive to enjoy it?

"Listen, Lloyd. We can talk about the details later. Right now, relax." DeeDee hugged me then smoothed out the wrinkles in my "Who farted?" T-shirt. Please don't lecture me on my fashion choices. I'm not in the mood.

"It's fine. You're fine. Don't worry. That dude will never bother us again," she said. "But Jesus, you might kill me with this shirt. Next day off? We're going shopping."

I blushed. Shopping. It's a date! Wait a minute. She couldn't smooth all this over that easily. "Don't worry? That's easy for you to say," I said. "You didn't get shot."

"Uh, yes she did." Kevin held up a smooshed spent bullet. "While you were screaming like a sorority sister."

"Says the roach who was holding onto me for dear life. And what the hell was that thing in the parking lot, anyway? Why are none of you talking about *that*?"

"It's not our first robbery," DeeDee said. "We don't need to know its name. Just always–*always*—give the thief a gold coin. It helps *it* find him faster. You do not want it flying in circles around the store any longer than it has to, because that is some seriously freaky shit."

She slipped the last pack of Pyramids into the display rack. "See? All better. Back to normal." She put her hands on her hips and surveyed our clean-up job. "You all right, Lloyd?"

I stared at her. Uh. No. Duh!

"Okay then. I'll take the gate, you relax for a while. Pull yourself together," she said. "Bubby will be here soon. Why don't you watch some wrestling with him? Take it easy. Eat some popcorn. Have a laugh. You'll feel better."

She smiled, sat her curvy bottom on the counter, then flipped her legs over. A second later, she was at the beer cave door scanning the passport of a man in a tan trench coat. He looked like a middle-aged detective. Except for his orange feathered ostrich legs. Woah boy. Didn't need to see that.

"You're good to go, honey, but only if you put on some pants," DeeDee said to him. His shoulders slumped, disappointed. DeeDee handed him a pair of khakis out of the weapons cabinet, and he slipped them on, fumbling to get the cuffs over his bird feet.

Nope. No way. Hanging out with a giant jelly hell centipede was not going to make me feel better. None of this was making me feel better. Stupid debt. I was literally trapped in debt hell! I stomped off.

"Where are you going?" Kevin asked.

"I'm getting a slushy." A big one. And probably another one after that. I was gonna slam icy sweet goodness like cheap tequila shots until I was on a happy sugar high. Don't judge me. Sometimes you have to eat your feelings.

"Wait a minute," Kevin said.

"What!" I turned around.

Kevin pointed down. A big, muscle-clad red arm was emerging through Kevin's swirling green vortex. "Get one for my dickhead roommate, or we'll be tripping over his stupid claw hand for the rest of the night."

"Fine," I huffed. Talking roaches. Disembodied demon arms. Armed robbers carried off by giant birds? Literally being shot in the chest. Nope. Nope. More nope. How many more weeks until Thanksgiving? Because I am out!

So, I was at the slushy machine pouring out a Brimstone Blueberry for Kevin's dick roommate, calculating exactly how many more shifts I had to work to be debt free, when I heard an alarm go off behind me. It was an ear-splitting low-pitched, blurp blurp blurp. Like the red alert on a movie submarine.

Holy hell. What now? I had learned one thing since I started working here. When it rained at the 24/7 Demon Mart, it poured. The quiet nights were super quiet, and the bad nights were super bad. So, here we go. The robbery had opened the floodgates. Tonight was shaping up to be about as fun as being neck-deep in a dumpster filled with burning devil turds. I gave myself a quick pep talk. *Only a couple more weeks and you'll be debt free. Maybe you can find another side hustle to speed that up. And, DeeDee's taking you shopping. That's step two on the twelve-step path to boyfriend. Eyes on the prize!*

Okay then. Nerves steeled. I turned around to see what the alarm was all about. The hot succubus strippers sashayed toward me, licking their glossed lips—woah boy, so hot—hips swinging. "Hi, cutie pie." The brunette bombshell stroked my neck with the dark red nail on her perfectly manicured finger as she walked by. "You ever need a ride, sugar, you know where to find me."

She winked, the other two tittered. Jesus, was it hot in here? I watched their curvalicious lady bits bounce as they strutted across the parking lot and into the side door of Sinbad's. No man was leaving that dump with a full wallet tonight.

It was Morty, the smarmy incubus, who must have set off the alarm. He was arguing with DeeDee at the beer cave door. He was dressed in full police uniform, but even in authentic gear, he still had the aura of a low-budget bachelorette party stripper.

"I'm sorry, but the scanner reads red. You can't come out. You know the rules."

"But I have to, Sweets. I've got a three-way lined up with two horny housewives. They're in the adventurous stage of their mid-life crises. Totally desperate. Nearly rock bottom. Prime pickins. I've been working them for weeks. Opportunities like this don't come along every day. You know I need it, honey. Need it!"

"You know the rules, Morty. Go home and get it sorted out, then come back. It's early. You've got time."

"But those two ladies are rearing to go. I can smell their ovaries from here! I'm only going next door. Look, if it'll make you feel better, I won't leave the bar. I'll do them in the storage room. It's right next to this wall here. That's as good as staying in the store. It's only two feet of concrete wall out of bounds." He pointed to the wall where Bubby's TV hung, awaiting the wrestling stylings of Dwayne Johnson. "If I'm late, they might go home. Or worse, find some other man. A *human* man. Do you want them to waste their wild streak on a night of disappointing sex? Dash their hopes and dreams? Or do you want them to feel true ecstasy, one time in their short, miserable lives?"

"I'm sorry, Morty. I can't let you out. Those are the rules," she said. "Take care of your documents. Talk to your...boss? Well, whatever you've got down there and then come see me."

"Come on. You know me. I couldn't hurt a fly! You can let me through this one time. What's one little red light between old friends?"

He turned on a crooked grin and a lot of charm. Dude. I could see why lonely married broads and divorcees were easy pickings. He was a big-time schmoozer, smooth as glass. Morty could use cheesy lines from one of those 1970s How to Pick Up Women guidebooks and actually pull them off. I could tell by the way he was looking at DeeDee that he'd elevated sliding his hooks into human women to an art form. He lathered them up, looked at them like they were the sexiest creatures on earth, the *only* woman for him, the moon and the stars, until their panties dropped right off. In the sketchiest way possible, of course.

My guts sank. *This guy gets laid, and I don't.* Nice guys do finish last, don't they? Something hit my foot. I looked down. Stupid angel eight ball. I thought it'd been carried off along with the robber. He must have dropped the ball when DeeDee wrestled the gun out of his hand. Just my luck.

"Dude. Were you seriously gonna let that jerk walk out of here with me? What's wrong with you? I thought you had my back!"

"Nope." I kicked the ball away and walked back to the counter. Judgmental prick.

I leaned over the counter, handing the Brimstone Blueberry to the impatient devil hand poking out of the mystery wormhole that I was pretty sure led to Kevin's...house? *Cupboard? Ring of hell?* Not gonna ask, didn't want to know. When I stood up, a guy stepped *in* the front door. *In.* And not just a guy. Worse. A hipster.

Sigh. Here we go. I sized him up, trying to determine what kind of desperate he must be to have gotten past the Go Away charm. The robber's desperation was obvious. This guy? Not so much.

He was slim, but with muscles. He kinda looked like a photocopy of Adam Levine made on a machine running low on toner. If you squinted, they looked exactly alike. Dark hair, tight skinny stretch jeans. Tattoos poked out of the collar of his combination cardigan/smoking jacket. (Where do you even buy something like that?) And his hair. Ugh. It was shaved short all around, about the same length as his stubbly well-groomed hipster beard, and there was a pile of hair on top with lots of gel holding it in a perfect coif. He clearly had a stylist. And he screamed chick magnet.

I looked down. I had a budding beer gut and a Taco Bell sauce stain on my cargo shorts. What did I scream? Never mind. Don't answer.

Well then, I better get this tragically hip lame-o out of the store before the giant bouncing blue hell centipede blops out of the beer cave, and this hipster Facebook live streams us all out of a job. I walked over to him. "Hey man, can I help you?"

"Yeah. You can get out of my way." He pushed me to the side.

Well, he sure was charming. For a hot minute, I thought what's the rush? It'd be fun to watch a swarm of Frito-based hell gnats rip him apart. "Can I help you find something?"

"I'm here to see DeeDee."

"And who may I say is calling?"

"I'm her boyfriend, loser," he snipped. "Now get out of my way."

Boyfriend? *Aaaaaaaaaaaaaaaaaaaaaaaaaaaaaaahhhhhhhhhh!*

That was the sound of my heart exploding into shards, erupting out of my rib cage like a Xenomorph chest burster, then sliding down my leg right onto the floor. Sure, go ahead. Tap dance on the bits. It couldn't hurt any worse.

"When you're a hot chick, it's always a seller's market." Kevin stood on the cash register, taking nips off a mini bottle of Wild Turkey. "You had to know, right? Babes like DeeDee are drowning in dicks. You didn't actually think you stood a chance, did you?"

Gulp. Yeah. I did. A tiny shred of one, at least. Clearly, my assessment of my prospects was too rosy.

"That's an understatement." Kevin shook his head and took another drink.

"Stay outta my head, roach! And should you be drinking that? You're underage." How long did roaches live? Maybe a year?

"I'm fifty-seven, so shut up. And don't judge me," Kevin said. "It's been a rough night."

Fifty-seven? Did he mean days?

"Yo, DeeDee," the hipster called out.

Gah. His hipster hair and clothes and perfect body were bad enough, but did he have to start a sentence with "Yo?" Hello, douche bag! The hipster strutted toward DeeDee, his perfect, angular cheekbones slicing through the air like it was butter. He was tall and broad-shouldered and fashionable, everything I wasn't, and I totally hated him for it.

DeeDee stopped arguing with Morty. "Tristan?"

Jesus. Tristan? Seriously? Shoot me. Even his name screamed panty dropper. Lloyd? That screamed la la loser. Remind me to legally change my name to something hot, like Mr. Sexy Sleekpanther. (I'm officially taking suggestions.)

"What are you doing here?" She asked. "How did you even get *in* here?"

"What do you mean? I walked in. It's a store. Anyone can walk in," he said.

Her eyes were wide. I knew she was referring to the Go Away charm, but Romeo, *oh excuse me Tristan*, didn't. I was marginally consoled. By the very fact that he made it inside, we all knew he must be some flavor of desperate, no matter how good he looked on the outside. *Take that, Tristan. Mr. Sexy Sleekpanther's got your number.*

"But it's after midnight." DeeDee was still thinking about the charm.

"I had a show tonight. Remember? At the Ace," he said, clueless.

"Are you all right?" She asked. That's right. Fish it out of him, girl.

"Who is this guy? Are you dating a cop now?" Tristan looked Morty up and down.

"Who am I?" Morty grinned, obviously amused. "I'm a real man, Loverboy. Who are you?"

High five, Morty. Troll him!

"Wait." Tristan turned back to DeeDee. "Is this the guy who was at your place the other night? I heard a voice. Was it him? You said he was just a 'friend'."

Yes, he actually made air quotation marks when he said friend. Ohmigod, I hated him. Then, it hit me like a ton of friendzone bricks. The other night? Wait. Tristan heard *my* voice. That monster snore? It was Tristan. Oh, my God. He was there, snoozing it up in her bedroom while I drooled up her sofa! Yep, that's right universe. Keeping stomping on the exploded remnants of my heart.

"She wishes it was me," Morty said.

"A cop? Are you serious?" Tristan sized Morty up, shoes to hair then back down. "And even if he weren't, he's so..."

Astringent, full-bodied with a hint of sketchiness and a deep, strong smarmy note? Yep. He sure was.

"Gotta go, sweetheart. The window of opportunity on my three-way is closing fast. We can sort this out later." Morty snorted and adjusted his, um, package, if you get my drift. (Dude, he really was carrying a nightstick down there.)

"Stay away from my girl," Tristan said, trying to feign tough with a threatening index finger pointed at Morty's chest.

"Slow down there, Loverboy. She's her own girl. But don't you worry, champ. When she's done with you, I'll be around to pick up the pieces." Morty rolled on over to me. "I'm good to go. The red light was a mistake. I owe you one."

"Lloyd. Do NOT let him leave here, do you understand?" DeeDee said. "Keep him busy while I sort this out."

Great. I stepped in front of the glass doors, a deflated, friend-zoned husk of a man.

DeeDee turned to Tristan. "What are you doing here?"

"You missed my last two shows. You haven't returned my texts. You stopped liking my Insta posts. What's your deal?"

"Is that why you're here? You know I'm busy. I work, and I go to school. I've got a lot going on. Things to do," she said. "Honestly, I don't understand why you're so upset. We aren't, like, serious."

Aaaaaaaaah. No, that wasn't a scream. That was the sound of relief, a lifting, ever so small, of my spirits. DeeDee was giving Tristan the blow-off. Praise Jesus!

And, bonus. Morty didn't make a run for the door like I'd anticipated. Instead, he put his arm around me and turned around to watch the Tristan/DeeDee drama unfold. He was tuned in on them like it was the last game of the NBA finals, the clock was about to run out, and the score was tied. "You might get a shot at her after all, kid," he said. "Bet you twenty this guy's going down in flames."

One can hope, right?

"Not serious? You're kidding." Tristan the ever so hip and handsome ran a shaking hand carefully over his needlessly complicated hair. "You've been all over me for weeks, flirting like your life depended on it. Hanging out every day. And don't forget all those things you did to me when we were alone. I know you want me. You can't get enough of me. Now you're saying it isn't serious? I don't think it gets more serious."

Gulp. La la la la. I'm not hearing this. Except I totally am, and it's breaking my mushed heart even more, and it's kind of pissing me off a little! What did she do to him when they were alone? No. Shut up. Don't answer.

"Trist, listen. We had fun, but it was only a fling. A whirlwind. And that's all it was ever going to be. We talked about it. You straight up said you didn't want a girlfriend, and I told you I was cool with that," she said.

"Hey, who said anything about girlfriend? You're the one who brought that up." Tristan tried really hard to play it cool, aloof. Look, I'm pretty dumb when it comes to relationships, but I know what going down in flames looked like, and this guy was on fire.

"Trist. It's been epic. We've had fun, but neither of us is ready for a real relationship, so let's just enjoy what we had."

"Oh yeah. This is getting good," Morty said. "I need a snack to go with this show. Hey Kev, you got anything good back there? Can I have a swig of that?"

Morty slid over to the register, took the Wild Turkey from Kevin and drained what little was left out of the bottle. "Seriously?" Kevin said. "Do you know how long it took me to open that thing? Roaches aren't known for their grip strength. You're buying me another one."

"Whatever you say, little dude." Morty went behind the counter and started rummaging around underneath. God only knew what for. There wasn't anything but rocks and weird trumpets back there.

"You know what? It's cool, babe. You're right. It didn't mean anything at all," Tristan said. "I mean, I came here to end it. Because you ruined it when you went all 'I love you'. Why d'you get all needy? It's not a good look for you."

"Um, no. That wasn't me, that was you. You said you loved me, and that's why I ended it," DeeDee said.

"Oh snap," Morty popped up from behind the counter. He had that weird, old dusty purple gourd in his hand. "DeeDee is stone cold. That's my girl."

"Hey. I'm sorry if you're hurt. This was all about fun," she said. "I stopped seeing you because I don't want to hurt you. It's not fair if we're not on the same page. I'm not the type of girl who leads people on."

"Hurt? Me? Nope," Tristan said. "No way. I'm fine."

"He is so totally not fine." Kevin sat on my shoulder, his four legs holding onto a single piece of popcorn. He was swaying, and he reeked of whiskey. I winced. I didn't even feel him crawl up there.

"You're totally drunk, aren't you?"

"Little bit," Kevin said.

Tristan was pacing now, his boots carving tragically hip circles in the linoleum. He looked like the type who would have posted ten selfies by now if his face weren't flushed and his eyes weren't wet. He was blinking hard, trying to disguise tears. Nope. Not working. Not so much. *We all know you're crying dude. You're not fooling anyone.*

"I will not be ghosted. Girls don't ghost me, I ghost them. That's how it works," Tristan said. "Get it?"

"Yeah. That's right. Chicks love it when you turn the tables on 'em. Works every time. Not," Kevin said. "Good luck with that, dude."

"I've got girls lined up, falling over me. DMing me. Swiping right. Waiting backstage after every show, totally getting off on my music," he said. "You're not special. You never were. I don't need you."

Oh, great. He was in a band. Of course, he was.

"Trist, don't be like that." The intimacy in DeeDee's voice, the nickname. Gah! I couldn't stand it. Yep. Nice guys finished last. If DeeDee tossed away hunky indie rock frontmen like fast food wrappers, what chance did I have?

"Phew. I'm starving. What did I miss?" Morty walked up to us. He was about to take a bite of the dusty old gourd that'd been behind the counter for God knew how long when Kevin jumped onto his face and started smacking him with his two front legs.

"Drop the pumpkin!"

"No way, man. It was the only thing back there that was edible! I've gotta fuel up the love machine, you feel me?"

"Fine. Go ahead, then. Eat it," Kevin said. "But remember, you eat it, then it eats you. I've never personally seen it work, but I've heard it melts your guts out."

"What the!" Morty dropped the gourd. It thwacked against the linoleum then rolled, unscathed, into the candy aisle. "Why do you have that?"

"Duh," Kevin said. "Not everything that comes through that gate is a harmless hell perv."

"Good point. Guess I could do with some Twizzlers instead," Morty said. "What did I miss? Is Loverboy still going down in flames?"

"Oh Yes. Yes, he is." Kevin jumped back onto my shoulder. Gah. I'd never get used to the feel of a roach crawling on me, even if he was sentient.

Tristan had changed tactics and was now pointing out all of DeeDee's faults in a bid to convince her that he would be the only man who would ever love her. Jerk.

"Boy, Loverboy does *not* know how to sweet talk a lady. I mean, read the room, dude. She is not the type of broad you can win back with insults." Morty was like a live sports commentator at this point, calling out the play-by-play. "You gotta lay icing on a piece of cake that fine. Amateur. I can't believe she let him into her delicious panties in the first place. Jesus, they're probably hanging onto that ripe ass for dear life right now."

"Amen to that," Kevin said.

"Can you not talk about DeeDee like that?" I squeaked.

"Aw, looky here. We got a gentleman." Morty punched my arm. "I like that. It's classy 'n' shit. Oh man!"

Something caught Morty's eye. He whirled around and pressed his face against the door glass. "The redhead portion of my three-way is walking into the bar right now. Mmmmm. Mmmmm. Hot damn. She's wearing her fuck-me pumps, too. Yeah. You're keeping those on tonight, honey. That's right. Daddy likes them spike heels. Mmmm. Mmmm. Dammit."

Morty rifled through his pockets and checked his cop belt. "I forgot my hand cuffs. Shame. She woulda looked good in 'em."

"Zip it, pervert." Kevin took another bite of another popcorn kernel. Dude. Where did he get that? "I don't want to miss anything. Oh, wait. I think Loverboy's on his way out. Show's over. Boo!"

Tristan was stomping toward us, eyes pink from crying. Or

blinking-not-crying. Either way, pink.

"You!" Tristan grabbed Morty and spun him around. Now, to be honest, I was expecting Morty to get punched directly in the nose. It looked like Morty was expecting one, too. But that isn't what happened. Tristan, instead, clutched the crisp polyester collar of Morty's police shirt and...sobbed. Oh yeah. He let loose. Projectile tears. Snot rockets. The works. "What do you have that I don't have? Hurp. Hurp. Hahurp."

And no, I didn't add that last part for dramatic effect. Loverboy was seriously ugly crying. Hard. I found it mildly satisfying, but at the same time terrifying because, hot damn, DeeDee was a heartbreaker. She didn't seem ruffled at all, maybe a little annoyed, as she checked another demon-critter-thing in a people suit out of the gate.

"Get your hands off me, man." Morty grabbed at the door, trying to get away.

"I can't live without her," Tristan blubbered. Snot dripped into his artisan-curated medium-stubble beard. "Please. Stop seeing her so she'll give me another chance. I promise I'll make her happy. Hurp. Hurp. Huhurp. I can't live without her."

Jesus, his crying noises were getting worse. At this point, I'd like to say I was gloating, and I'd like to take the high road and say I didn't cry this hard when Simone kicked me to the curb after three years together, but nope. I can't. I hate you Tristan and everything you stand for, but I feel you dude. Been there.

Morty, however, had no such sympathy. His eyes were wide with terror, his mouth twisted up in disgust. He clawed at the glass trying to get away. Tristan's emoting was making Morty's hard-on of overconfidence go limp. Seriously, he overall seemed a little smaller and more shriveled, as if he himself was phallic. "Get off me, man. You're harshing my vibe! This is not sexy, man. Not sexy! Pull yourself together. Have one of my ladies! I got some spares."

Tristan sobbed some more. He wiped his nose on Morty's chest.

"No! Not the uniform!" Morty shouted. "I've got ladies waiting, hot to trot! Get him off me, guys! Help!"

"Sorry, man," Kevin said. "This is priceless."

"Really, roach? So much for helping a brother out. Nope. I can't. Can't do it. Game over, man!"

Morty grew a little taller and harder as he gripped Tristan by his needlessly complicated smoking jacket cardigan thing and threw him up and away. As in, really hard up and away. Literally. As in, airborne. Right into the cheap cigarette racks we'd just refilled. Tristan slid across the counter, smokes flew in all directions, and then Tristan thump-landed on the floor behind the register. Wow. I did not see that coming.

"Really, Morty?" Kevin snipped. "We just cleaned all that up."

Morty smoothed out his uniform. "It wouldn't be messed up if y'all had helped me. I can't even with the crying. Desperation is not sexy, and sexy is my jam."

His breath turned into a white cloud in the air as he spoke. *Brrrr.* Goosebumps skipped up my arms. Damn, it was cold in here.

"Oh no." I turned around. A gigantic icy blue face with four white eyes was ducking out of the beer cave. "Bubby's here."

Tristan stood up behind the counter, wiping tears and dust from his pink face.

"Get him out of here. We can't let Tristan see a giant centipede coming out of the cooler!"

"Relax," Kevin said. "That emo douche won't see anything. You can't see anything without a name tag."

"But he saw Morty." Duh.

"Totally different species," Kevin said. "Morty and the chicks are designed to be seen. Bubby's ancient, an old one. Made of primordial goo or something. Why do you think he's so flubby? As long as he stays inside the store, he's invisible. Unless you've got a name tag. That's part of the magic."

"But what if Bubby bumps a shelf or something," I said. "Will Tristan see it move?"

"Shit," Kevin said. "Hadn't thought of that. No one's ever stuck around this long after midnight. Okay. New plan: Get Loverboy outta here."

DeeDee was holding the door open for Bubby, who was hunched way down squeezing through. She had a DVD in her hand. "It's finally here! World Wrestling Federation, New Orleans, March 1999. Sold-out crowd. Undertaker versus Big Bossman. And headlining? Your favorites and mine, Stone Cold Steve Austin and Mankind versus the Rock and Kane in a Texas Tornado match! Best Friday night, ever!"

She high-fived one of Bubby's spike arms, walked over to the TV and popped the DVD into the player.

"Come on, kid," Kevin said. "Let's get Loverboy out of here."

I turned around, ready to usher the sniveling indie rock god out of the store. He was still standing behind the counter, but he had a page from the big, old creepy book in his hand.

"That's not good," Kevin said.

"DeeDee. I love you! This poem says everything I feel about you. Listen. Please!" Tristan began to read off the page. "I offer myself to you with an open heart. For you, I sacrifice my body and my soul. I will burn forever for you, with an open heart. My love will sever the barrier between worlds."

"Shut him up! Shut him up! Shut him up!" Kevin screamed and poked me in the neck.

"I don't want to know what he's doing, do I?" Nope. I don't. Because he's reading the fancy words in the scrolly gold and red ink off that page with the giant hell spider on it. Gulp. Why did it have to be the spider page?

Bubby began to howl, like a wolf at the moon.

"That ain't a love poem." Kevin yelped. "He's summoning Lagopex the Devourer. He's offering himself up as a willing sacrifice. He's professing his love for the old gods. God, I hate hipsters!"

Well, that wasn't good.

"Don't let him finish it, or we're screwed! Go! Go! Go!" Kevin grabbed tight to my shirt. My adrenaline surged, and I ran, full speed, or as full speed as a chubby guy who spent most of his sedentary life playing Xbox could go, right at Tristan.

"I will disrupt the stars and part the heavens so that I may look upon your face forever—"

I jumped over the counter. Okay yeah. I tried to jump over the counter, but instead rammed myself right in the gut and then fumbled forward, half-landing on Tristan. And holy hell did that hurt. But mission accomplished. I snatched that paper right out of his hand. Aha! Victory! "I got it!"

"Too late." Kevin sighed and rubbed his brow. "He finished it. We're screwed. What a waste of a whiskey buzz. Well, kid, if we make it through this, we'll be getting some fat hazard pay. I've got my eye on a giant flat-screen TV. Eyes on the prize, right?"

"Kevin! Forget the TV!" I screamed. "Look!"

Bubby howled and writhed. He was stuck in the beer cave door. Not stuck, more like webbed. Strings of something white and thick and goopy crisscrossed his belly, holding him in place. He pulled and struggled against the goop, but the stuff wasn't budging. DeeDee was tugging on it, too, trying to free him with one hand, while desperately flipping the emergency switch up and down with the other. "Guys. The manual override isn't working. He's stuck in the door!"

Tristan, completely unaware of the true horror unfolding before him, turned to me and said, "Do you think she liked my poem?"

"Way to go, Loverboy," Kevin said. "I always knew hipsters would destroy the world."

"What's happening?" I said to Kevin.

"Well, Loverboy here just kick-started the end of the world. The monsters on that page are on their way up here right now," Kevin said.

"Jesus. That's why dudes aren't supposed to talk about feelings. They always mess it up. Always!"

"What do we do?"

"All right, kid. Listen up," Kevin said.

"Do you think she'll take me back now?" Tristan blubbered.

"Shut up!" I snapped at him, then, I held my breath and focused intently, like I've never focused before, so I could absorb every word of wisdom Kevin was about to give me. Because, a category five turd hurricane was hurtling toward the proverbial fan, for sure, and I was not going to get eaten by giant insects from hell.

"Whatever happens. Nothing gets out the front door. Got it? *Nothing*. No matter what," Kevin said. "Oh, and don't let the fish guy eat Loverboy, or the store blows up, the gate flies open, the deal is sealed and the world ends."

Kevin crossed his two front legs over his head and swan dived off my shoulder. He landed ever so gently on the counter. He stood up stick straight, steeling himself, then looked back at me and said, "It's time to rock."

CHAPTER 16

"Ah! A roach!" Tristan screamed and swatted at Kevin, who flipped him the bird as he scuttled to safety under the doughnut case.

That's it. Over him. "Okay, time to go." I grabbed Tristan's arm and started yanking him out from behind the counter.

He dug in his heels. "I am not leaving until DeeDee takes me back."

"We don't have time for that, bub." I sounded like a ten-foot-tall three-hundred-pound bouncer, even though I was terrified goo on the inside. My overall anger at Mister Tragically Hip had trumped my anxiety about what was coming. "Sorry. You're leaving."

"Don't touch me, fatty." He yanked his arm out of my hand and recoiled from me like I was some kind of contagious freak.

Oh. Hell. No. He wasn't gonna treat me like that, especially after he insulted DeeDee. She might not want me, but that doesn't mean I would stand by and let some other guy treat her like crap.

"Store's closed. Get out," I said.

"You're open twenty-four hours. You never close," he snipped.

"Who works here? Oh yeah, I do. I say we're closed. Now get out!"

I grabbed him by the collar and pulled on him as hard as I could. He held on to the counter and wouldn't budge. Honestly, I didn't care if the hungry fish ate this guy. Good riddance. Slut-shaming DeeDee? Nope. And, hello, end of the world pending? Two strikes, you're out. "We're closed. Emergency maintenance. Some dumb ass let loose a bunch of bugs and the exterminator's coming."

Too bad Tristan did not know how epically true that statement was.

He pulled away from me, and when I tried to grab hold of him again, he swatted my hands away. That's when the floor started shaking under our feet. *Oh. Shit.* Tristan grabbed onto me and squealed. The floor rumbled, and the racks shook. Slow at first, a gentle rocking, then faster and faster until one of the end caps rattled loose and fell over, sending boner pills and smartphone chargers sliding across the linoleum. Okay, then. We were having an earthquake in Ohio. Sure, that was totally normal. Not.

Morty strolled out of the candy aisle with a torn-open bag of Twizzlers. One hung partway out of his mouth, flapping up and down as he chewed it. "Show's about to start," Morty said. "This is gonna be good."

Bubby was still trapped—webbed?—in the beer cave door, but here's the kicker: The door was no longer a steel and glass rectangle with "Beer Cave" written in melty monster ice font. It was a halo of bright blue light as if that part of the wall had disintegrated and had been taken over by the swirling blue vortex. The gate, it seemed, was stuck open, and it had gotten bigger.

Suddenly, Tristan went slack in my hands and slid to the floor. He was crying again, only with a decidedly more panicked look on his face. He was rocking back and forth trying to protect his hair from the fine dust of plaster that was shaking loose from the ceiling as the store quaked. "Oh, God. It's an earthquake. It's an earthquake. Help me! Help me!" He whimpered.

Gah. Jerk! "You!" I gave him the sharp point of my index finger, just so he knew I was serious. "Stay here. Stay down." *And don't get eaten by a giant fish monster from hell, even though you deserve it.* "Got it?"

"Hurrrr hurrr hahurrrp," he cried. "Please, God, please. I don't want to die. Waaaaaaa!"

This guy was seriously killing my soul, but I had bigger fish to fry. Maybe literally. Thankfully, I still had the page Tristan had torn out of the book in my hand. I smoothed it out. Maybe there was a poem to close the gate? Let's see. Red letters. Yada yada. And nope. Nothing. Only the summoning spell. *Crap! Crap! Crap!* That's it? Where's the book? There must be something else, a reset button, something to cancel it all out.

It took me a while to find the book. Tristan had knocked over the stand, and just about everything else, when Morty threw him over the counter. But there it was, upside down, pages loose and scattered in with the mess of cigarette packs and display racks piled up on the floor.

The room was still shaking, Tristan was curled up in a ball crying, and I was gathering up pages when DeeDee screamed. "Lloyd, Help!"

Uh oh. I popped up, but I didn't see her. Where was she? She wasn't at the switch. I did my closest approximation of a ninja-jump over the counter. And yeah, that move takes abs I do not have, and I didn't make it all the way over, so it was more like a roll. And it hurt quite a bit thank you very much. As I ran toward Bubby, I checked the aisles for any signs of DeeDee amidst the rattling racks and falling shelves. I didn't see her. *Shit. Shit. Shit.* Fear fueled me. My heart was pounding like that night I drank six Red Bulls on an all-night game binge and nearly went to the ER. "DeeDee?" I called out. "Where are you?"

Bubby howled and pulled, unable to free himself from that weird goo. The air all around him was arctic-level freezing. Even the beer was freezing, expanding in the glass bottles, exploding in their racks, littering the floor with broken glass. The wall of reach-in cooler doors cracked and lurched as the vortex inched its way farther out, a growing, swirling blue hell circle spreading out from Bubby.

When I got to him, Bubby bent down and put his forehead against mine and made a whimpering noise that sounded either like crying or a desperate, honest plea for help. Sadness tingled inside me. Poor guy. He might be a gigantic freezing jelly centipede with a mouth of whirring razors, but he did seem like a nice dude otherwise. And he was suffering. I pulled at the goo holding him in place, but I couldn't get it to budge. It was super sticky, and tight around his belly, cutting into his abdomen. What was this crap? Bubby nudged me away, and when I looked up at him, he tilted his head.

"Lloyd. Over here." A whisper. It was DeeDee. She was kneeling on the floor, holding on tight to the weapons safe. Holding on tight because once Bubby wasn't in front of me, it was windy in here. The air pulled on us, not like a vacuum, more like a drain swirling us down into the center of the vortex. It took some very steady, deliberate steps to make it to DeeDee. She was holding tight against the suction, while also loading up with weapons. She stuck the taser in her boot, along with a golden knife.

"Here. Take this." She handed me the sometimes, but not currently, flaming sword. "Bubby's stuck in the gate. It'll keep getting bigger as long as he's in it, until...well, worst case, it could swallow the entire store. Bigger, meaner bugs are on their way, so the plan is to get Bubby out and close it before they get here. Got it?"

I stared at her. Bigger? Meaner? Blink. Blink. Um, holy shit? The shot of fortitude my Tristan anger had given me had worn off, revealing the quivering fear jelly inside of me. I held the sword in both hands, but I was damn near sure I wasn't rocking it like DeeDee. I was pretty sure I looked like a super sad, super geeky LARPer playing dress-up at the park. Gulp.

DeeDee grabbed a fistful of my shirt, pulled me close, and looked me square in the eyes. "Lloyd." Her face was hard. "It's time to kick some serious ass. Are you ready?"

CHAPTER 17

So there I was, trying not to get sucked into the hell gate, holding a heavy but not-flaming sword, staring down a suffering giant blue centipede. I was so terrified, my bones felt like cooked spaghetti. There was nary a spine nor a rigid surface inside me. I wanted to turn tail and run, but dude. No one wants to be that guy, right? The one who ran away and didn't even try to stop the world from ending?

The coward in every movie who has multiple chances to do the right thing and never does? Who sides with the bad guy then dies a horrible death? Nope. No way. If it was all over, I might as well be brave. Fake it 'til you make it, Lloyd. Fake it hard. At least then, there was a *chance* we wouldn't die. *Right?*

DeeDee was on the other side of Bubby, using that golden knife to saw away at the stringy goo holding him in place. Bubby howled like a wounded animal.

Okay. Okay. Focus. Step one: Get Bubby out of the gate. I took a whack at one of the goo strings with the sword, but it didn't even make a dent. I shook the sword. "How do I get this thing to light?"

"Press the button!" DeeDee said.

"What button?"

"You ever have a toy lightsaber?"

I nodded. Duh. Who hadn't?

"Just like that. Press the button!"

I looked at the hilt. Sure enough, there was a tiny round black button just like a toy lightsaber. I pressed it, and flames tickled up and around the blade. Fucking A! Now this was awesome. I touched the tip to one of the strings tethering Bubby. It cut loose, whipping back like a rubber band that had been stretched to the max. Oh yeah. That felt good!

Bubby was scared of the sword. Terrified, all four eyes wide and staring at it, pulling away from me, quivering. Oh, right. This thing had made the one-eyed halo of tentacle dude explode and rain down goop all over the store. Chances are, it could do that to Bubby. "I'll try to be careful."

But the strings were so tight around him, it was hard to find a place to cut that wouldn't hurt him, so it was slow going. But, once we'd cut away a few more strings, Bubby was able to move a couple of his claw arms, and was trying on his own to free himself, but he was still good and stuck.

Click. Slurp. Click. Slurp. Slurp. Click. Slurp.

"Uh. What's that noise?"

"Cut faster, Lloyd," DeeDee said.

Click. Slurp. Click. Slurp. Slurp. Click. Slurp.

I cut another string. It fwapped. DeeDee ducked. It hit an end cap near aisle three, knocking the rack over and sending canned chili and bottled nacho cheese sauce splattering to the floor. Man. Whatever this goo was, it was strong.

Click. Slurp. Click. Slurp. Slurp. Click. Slurp.

The sound was getting louder now. Closer. I looked around, trying to figure out where it was coming from. Morty was sitting on the hot dog island, legs crossed, chomping on Twizzlers and dill pickle potato chips like he was at the movies. "Can you give us a hand here?" I yelled. "We could use a little help."

"Sorry man," he said. "This is priceless."

Gah! Jerk! Why did I have to pay for Kevin's snark?

DeeDee and I kept working. Another string broke. And another. We had to duck every single time, because each one was an elastic band fwapping and flicking around, knocking things over, hitting fast and hard. Bubby wriggled, trying to break the half dozen remaining tethers on his own. They pulled and stretched, but didn't break.

"Keep going, Lloyd. Don't stop!" DeeDee said. "We need to close the gate. NOW!"

Click. Slurp. Click. Slurp. Slurp. Click. Slurp.

It was loud now. Right on us. "What is that?"

DeeDee screamed. "Lloyd, run!"

Too late. Something hit my arm, hard, knocking the flaming sword clean out of my hand. The flames fizzled out as it flew through the air, cracked to the floor and slid away, out of sight, into one of the aisles. Before I could even think about what to do next, something smacked me square in the gut really really hard, and sent me flying through the air. I slammed right into the hot dog stand, shoulder first. Eeow! Stabbing pain. It hurt so bad, saliva pooled in my mouth, and I was sure I was going to barf.

Morty looked down at me from his perch by the hot dog/ bun warmer combo. "When this is over, I'd like to file a complaint. The hot dogs are cold. Pretty sure that's a health code violation." He took a bite out of a footlong smothered in relish. I noticed his teeth were pointy and ragged like fangs and his skin had turned a little red. Gulp. Was that what he really looked like?

"Get going and fight already." He kicked me in the shoulder.

OW!

"Wrap it up," he said. "My desperate housewives aren't gonna wait forever."

Click. Slurp. Click. Slurp. Slurp. Click. Slurp.

Oh, no. The noise.

Suddenly, my shirt felt like it was on fire. There was a hot burning pinprick on my chest, followed by the smell of burning plastic. *Sssssssss.* My name tag was sizzling! Smoke rolled off of it. Just like Carl's name tag, the night...Gulp. Now I knew what the noise was. Not what, who.

Bubby howled. A half dozen green tentacles snaked out of the gate, wrapping around Bubby, using him for leverage. Green tentacles with barbed spikes at the end. A single yellow eye emerged from the swirling blue cloud. Great. This asshole again.

Bizowhatshisname. Bizosoth? Bizoshoggoth? Whatever. The one-eyed dickhead halo of tentacles, herald of hungry fish dude, was back for more. He looked me straight in the eyes, and the spot where his one eyebrow should be was raised and cocky. As if to say "Yeah. That's right. Me again. Ha!"

It was clear one-eye dude recognized me and wasn't too happy about our last meeting. He thwapped the floor with his tentacles, punching holes in the linoleum. *Crack. Crack. Crack.* Then, s*lurp slurp* as he pulled his body out of the gate, across the floor, leaving a trail of oozing green slug-slime on the tile.

I'd like to say that at this point, I had the Schwarzenegger swagger, and I was brimming with a "bring it, asshole, I got this" vibe, but no. I would have screamed like a toddler and run away, except that I was too scared to do either. I tried. No sound came out. No muscles moved. My heart was about to palpitate out of my chest. And my palms were so sweaty I kept slipping on the floor when I tried to get up and run away.

Morty pulled me up by the collar. "I think your sword landed in the candy aisle, kid. Grab me a pack of boner pills while you're over there because this whole scene here is making me limp." He pushed me, trying to give me a running start, but instead, I fell flat on my face.

"Move it, kid." Morty tapped his watch. "I've got a date."

"Fine." I stayed low, as best as I could, to stay out of Bizo guy's sight. The farther I got from tentacle dude, the cooler my name tag became. It was still hot, don't get me wrong, but it wasn't burning "Hello

My Name Is" into my chest hairs anymore.

When I looked back, Bizo's tentacles were waving in the air and cracking down, crunching in the floor, and I could hear him slupping as he pulled himself through the store, probably looking for me so he could flatten me into a Lloyd-flavored meat-fruit roll-up.

The chip aisle was completely overturned. I was ankle-deep in bags —Doritos, Conn's and Utz—crunch crunching as I duck walked as stealthily as possible behind the toppled racks, across the store, looking for the sword. When DeeDee stabbed him with it last time, he'd exploded. Clearly, it didn't kill him, just got rid of him for a while, sent him somewhere else. Until Tristan brought him back. Gah. Hipsters!

Man. My thigh muscles were On. Fire. Note to self: If I lived through this, I wasn't gonna skimp on the squats. Dammit. Where was that sword?

Crinkle. Crinkle. Crinkle.

Crap. What was that?

Crinkle. Crinkle.

The noise was close. Really close. The chips bags between my feet rustled and undulated as if something was slithering under them. Oh God. A hell snake. Snake dude was back! He wasn't in the picture with all the other creatures. Crap!

Something black and shiny emerged from underneath a Tostitos bag. Where was that Michael Bolton CD when you needed it? I laced my fingers together to make one big super fist and readied myself to rain down the hardest hit possible on the hell viper. I lifted my arms, ready to strike. Then I saw a number eight emerging from between the chip bags. Phew. It was just my stupid angel! The eight ball rolled around, clearing itself a spot, then landed triangle side up, of course. Always an opinion. "Desperate love will breach the gate..."

"No shit, man."

The triangle turned, gearing up for the next comment.

"No time for chitchat." I was not in the mood. I picked the ball up and threw it. It hit the front window with a chink then dropped behind the counter. Good. He could keep Tristan the hipster company. Those two jerks deserved each other. Unfortunately, Bizowhatzit must have heard the noise because I could hear him slurping in my direction now.

Crack. Crack. Slurp. Slurp.

Shit. I'd led him right to Tristan, fish guy's sacrificial midnight snack.

Okay, so I had to give up the duck walk in the interest of speed now because I was seriously out of shape and there was an angry halo of spiky tentacles on my tail. So I crawled like a terrified mouse through the chip bags.

The shelves of the first two aisles were completely overturned, thanks to the shaking ground and Bizo's angry thwaps. The rubble of chips and Top Ramen was a foot-deep all around. The candy aisle, other than Morty's Twizzler raid, was unmolested. The sword wasn't there. Only that stupid purple pumpkin. No DeeDee either. I scuttled, like a cockroach—speaking of, where was Kevin?—past aisle four. Nope. No sword there. Then to aisle five, which I had always gone out of my way to avoid ever since the Demon Caroline incident. But, sure enough, the sword was there under some toppled bottles of drain opener. DeeDee was hunkered down at the other end of the aisle.

"Lloyd, get over here." DeeDee waved me over.

I grabbed the sword and crawled to her. She was using the electrical tape in the hardware section to strap her knife to one of the dart-thingies that shoot out of the chanting taser. "I'll distract Bizosoth. You cut Bubby free. Close the gate before anything else gets through. Then, we'll send Bizo back."

Flap. Crunch. Flap. Flap. Crunch.

"What's that noise?" DeeDee asked.

"I don't know."

"Well, can you check?"

Oh, hell no I can't! But I didn't say that out loud. Instead, I swallowed my fear and stood up, slowly, slowly and peeked over the racks. A neon orange swarm of flying Flamin' Hot Crunchy Cheetos had coagulated into a dozen hell gnats. They surrounded Morty, swirling and diving around him. He was throwing tidbits of something at them, and they were swooping down to eat. He was feeding them like effing seagulls. Why weren't they attacking him? Why did he get a pass? Oh yeah, because he's from hell.

"The gnats are back," I whispered.

Flap. Crunch. Flap. Flap. Crunch. Morty was laughing now, enjoying his new pets, like he was feeding ducks at the park.

"Free Bubby, and he'll eat them. They're his favorite snack. Oh, no." She tugged on my leg. "We're too late. They're here."

"Who's here?" I shouldn't have asked.

Something large and dark passed over my head and touched down a few feet away from me. It was hairy and black, as long as a UPS truck, bent in the middle, and about as thick as a skinny tree trunk. The tip of it thumped down hard on the floor. Then another passed over me. And another. Then another one. Long, black, hairy trunks in a formation around aisles four, five, and six. The light from the fluorescent strips on the ceiling above me went dim. Something was blocking the light. My eyes followed the black hairy trunks up.

Dear, God. They weren't trunks. They're legs. Pressed against the ceiling right above me was a hairy black body. A black body with two segments. I'd seen bodies like that before. Tiny ones. Tiny, terrifying ones, lying in wait in their webs. I pressed the button and my sword lit up like a gas burner. My guts froze in fear, and not a normal winter freeze, an outer reaches of the solar system, rings of Saturn level cold, as a head turned down to look at me. The face had at least a hundred icy eyes and a dozen curved silvery-blue fangs. *A spider. Why did it have to be a spider?*

CHAPTER 18

"New plan," DeeDee said. "You free Bubby. I'll distract the huge, terrifying spider."

I nodded like it was all good, and I was totally down with the plan, but dude. I had to seriously fake the brave. I mean, I was quaking out of my underpants in terror, every hair in every pore on my body stood up stick straight. My muscles were noodles. I could barely keep a grip on the sword.

Let me add that when you're face to face with death, in the form of your worst nightmare—a spider big enough to eat you—your life really does flash before your eyes. Everything becomes crystal clear. No denying it. I was Lloyd Wallace, twenty-one-year-old loser. I had a list of failures three miles long, and my list of successes was empty, a blank page. Did you get that? No wins. Zero. What was the chance I could win when the fate of the entire world was counting on me? You do the math. I had to face it. I was about to die in a "Who Farted?" T-shirt.

Jesus, if you're listening. If you get me through this, I promise I will get my life together. I'll do whatever you ask, whatever it takes. Pinkie swear.

The massive hell spider eyeballed me with its emotionless eyes, then clicked its fangs together. I swear it was licking its lips. I mean, do spiders have lips? Don't answer that. I'm not getting close enough to that mouth to find out.

"Lloyd, duck!" DeeDee whispered.

I did because I was too scared to think for myself. I dropped to the floor, the sword skittered away, and I rolled up into a ball. Full fetal position, because I really wanted to *la la la la nothing to see here, not happening* this whole situation away. DeeDee must have dialed up the taser because I could hear low voices chanting.

The taser lines shot out, sinking deep into the spider belly above me. It reared up off its front legs and thrashed its head back and forth, punching out ceiling tiles as it writhed, angry and in pain.

Boom. Boom. Boom. Boom. The room rattled. The spider was on the move, its long hairy black legs spread over three aisles, bent at the joints, stomping, turning its body in different directions. DeeDee was gone. It was stalking her. *Phew.*

Yes, okay, I felt guilty that I was relieved. Because I hated that DeeDee was in danger, but at the same time, hello, I was cripplingly terrified of spiders and now it wasn't standing over me looking at me like a jalapeno popper. DeeDee was a cool cucumber in a crisis. She could handle it. In the meantime, I had to do my number one job: Free Bubby.

My name tag sizzled. *Oh, man. Really?* I looked up. Scratch that. Number two job: Free Bubby. Number one job: Stab Bizowhatsit and send him back into the void where he belonged, stat. Because I only had about ten seconds to figure out how to grab the sword, switch it on, and get the best of halo of tentacles dude, who was standing at the end of aisle five giving me the stink eye with his one mean red pupil.

So I did what any reasonable man would do: I jumped up, dusted myself off and did my best Fortnite Electro Shuffle. Yeah. You heard me right. Bizo's eye widened as he watched my fists pump and my Pumas squeak as I shuffled across the linoleum. He seemed totally confused. Ha! That's right. *Watch me dance, sucker.* I'd seen Guardians of the Galaxy. Dance off distraction!

I certainly didn't make it look as good as a pumped-up Chris Pratt. My gut bounced and my cargo shorts slid down, letting some arctic air tickle the top of my butt crack. But Bam. It worked! I shuffled, scooted and fist-pumped right on over to the not-currently flaming sword, popped down and grabbed it before Bizo was any wiser. "Aha!" I yelled, and I hopped up, sword in hand.

I didn't break eye contact with Bizo as I gripped the sword and fumbled around, searching for the on button. Dude. Where was that stupid button? Why was it so small? He realized he'd been played and made it clear by his anger-squint that he was not amused. Then he— smiled? Wait. Why was he so happy?

Something cold and slimy wrapped around my middle. (I'd say abs, but let's be honest here.) I looked down. Bizo had wrapped me up in one of his tentacle arms. Oh. Crap. I hadn't seen that coming. His tentacle was looped up and over the shelf and had come out behind me. I felt like the game hunter guy in the first Jurassic Park movie. He thought he had the upper hand on the velociraptor until he got sideswiped.

Bizo squeezed me so hard I felt like my eyeballs were gonna pop out. He yanked me down the aisle toward him. My feet fumbled, unable to get any sort of grip on the polished linoleum. I held tight to the sword, but oh my God, he was squeezing. So. Hard. *Come on, button. Where are you? Light you stupid sword, light!*

No time. He pulled me closer, faster, right at his big naked, mean yellow eye, covering twenty feet so quickly it might as well have been an inch. I put the sword straight out in front of me, the metal tip aimed right at the goo-body center where all of his tentacles met. I fumbled for the button, but too late. Out of time. We were eyes to eye. His body shook and grumbled. He squeezed me tight. Suddenly, something slimy pressed down on my arms, and my fingers felt like they were trapped in coagulating glue. So gross.

Bizo's grip loosened. The tentacle around my middle let go and slurped away. His creepy red pupil looked down. So did I. I was elbow deep in his slime gut, still holding on to the sword. Oh, my God. Ew. His body had swallowed my arms. I'd pushed right into him just as easily as I could stick my fingers into a cup of pudding. I could see my arms and the sword in his lime-green translucent body.

I'll let you in on a little secret. When you're suddenly elbow-deep in the slimy gut of a one-eyed, bloodthirsty hell beast, you can't help but stop and ask yourself some questions. Like, how did I get here? Or, how did my life slide so far off the rails? And, how the hell did I get this job in the first place? Who was dumb enough to think I was qualified to battle a horde of monsters and stave off the apocalypse?

Oh, right. I remember. Student loan debt and the devil.

Oh well. No time to get philosophical now. The sword was in him, so all I had to do was wait for him to pop or explode, right? Okay. Wait for it. Wait for it...Hmm. Why wasn't he exploding? Any time now. He'd been stabbed with a supernatural sword. How long could it take?

I knew I was in trouble when he looked more annoyed than hurt. When he saw the sword inside his body, he rolled his eye. Well, that wasn't good. He wasn't gonna pop, was he? Maybe it had to be lit to work.

He grabbed me by the waistband of my Hanes and yanked. Ugh. Epic wedgie! My arms slurped out of him—without the sword—then I was flying up up through the air, over the counter and face-first into the front window. *Chink. Ow. My brain.* I slid, like a bug against a windshield, down the glass and onto the floor, and lay there unmoving for a good long time, until the dizzy wore off and the pain simmered down to a low rolling boil.

I must have blacked out for a second because the next thing I remember was Kevin on my face, punching me in the cheek, yelling, "Wake up, kid. Wake up!"

"Wha?" Ow. My head throbbed like someone was hitting it with bricks.

"Hurrrr. Hurrrr. Ha-hurrrp."

Great. Tristan was curled up on the floor next to me, still sobbing, rocking back and forth like a baby, completely unaware of the literal hell he'd unleashed on earth.

"Get moving, kid." Kevin pointed up. "The shit's really hitting the fan. Look!"

I moved slowly—ouch my brain—just high enough to see over the counter. The swirling blue vortex had expanded. Almost three-quarters of the back wall of the store was now an open gate to hell. I watched the spider stomping around, looking for DeeDee, dripping blue blood from a deep gash where her rigged-up taser knife must have stuck it. It was yanking fluorescent light fixtures out by the roots as its body scraped against the ceiling, plunging sections of the store into electrical sparks and darkness.

Bubby howled, fighting against the goo holding him in the portal. The spider didn't like the noise. After each howl, it reared its head as if it'd been stabbed in the ears. Finally, it turned its butt toward Bubby and shot a bunch of webs at him. They splattered across him, holding him in place like superglue, and across his mouth, muffling his cries. Oh, God. The goo. It was spider webbing. From hell spiders. Oh, good Lord in Heaven. Why spiders?

Morty was cruising the overturned chip bags, nonplussed, choosing his next snack. The Flamin' Hot Crunchy Cheetos gnats were swooping and flying through the store. But they were acting strange this time. They weren't interested in attacking. They were moving erratically, not as a group, hitting the broken ceiling tiles, then the wall corners. Then, they suddenly made a break for the front door, slamming into it, over and over. *Chink. Chink. Chink.* They were taking out little bits of glass with every hit. They were trying to get out.

A second later, I figured out why. Even though the store was nearly pitch black, thanks to the spider ripping out the lights, I could see why the gnats were so desperate. Something new was emerging from the blue swirl. A beak. Fat and hard. Something poured out of the gate around it, so quickly and smoothly it moved like liquid. And another thing, and again. The store shook. Tiles fell out of the ceiling, crashing down in bits. Bubby squirmed desperately. The beak moved farther out, revealing a bulbous soft head and rows of deep black eyes, hundreds of them. It reminded me of an ...octopus? Only maxed out, with lots of extra tentacles and eyeballs. And, you know, absolutely huge. Its arms poured into the store and down the aisles like water, filling every row with fat oozing tentacles pocked with suction cups.

Its eyes slowly scanned the room, intelligent, focused, as if it was looking for something. I doubted it was boner pills or microwave mac 'n' cheese.

"I gotta get out of here. I gotta get out of here!" Tristan squealed He looked up and around, watching the ceiling crumble, holding on to the shelves of rocks and weird stuff as the store shook. "I'm too young to die!"

And in a flash, he bounded up and over the counter.

"Dude. No!" I called out after him, but it was too late.

Let's just say he did not exit quietly. He screamed in a long, steady uninterrupted frequency so high-pitched every dog in a three-mile radius was probably like "What da fu...?"

All the hell creatures zeroed in on his screams. He ran for the door, disbursing the Flamin' Hot Crunchy Cheetos gnats. He pushed it open and stumbled across the parking lot. His high-pitched wail turned to shouts of "Earthquake! Help! Earthquake!"

He was halfway across the lot when a watery octopus tentacle crashed through the door, sending glass raining down. The tentacle shot out, lightning-quick, and grabbed Tristan by the ankle. He fwapped face-first into the asphalt, and lay there, squirming, clawing at the ground, screaming. "Earthquake. Help!"

The octopus held him in place, tentacle wrapped around his hipster boot, ever so slowly reeling him back in.

Gulp. Now I knew what the octopus was looking for: Fish guy's sacrifice. The creatures responded to the catch. They started to move, carefully, deliberately and no longer concerned with me or DeeDee. They moved as if they were in a trance, guided by some higher power. The spider crouched down below Bubby's television, butt facing the swirling gate. Bizo migrated to the slushy station next to the front door. Octopus guy pulled himself all the way out of the gate and over to the corner at the end of the counter. His zillion eyes were maybe fifteen feet away from me. Counting Bubby, there was now one monster in each corner. The gate responded. It changed. The swirling glowing blue stopped moving. The arctic freezing air suddenly went tropical swamp hot. The gate burned angry fire red.

"That can't be good," Kevin said. He was on my arm. "Kid. You still got that paper with the poem on it?"

I nodded.

"Well, let's see it," he said.

I took the crumpled page out of my pocket and smoothed it out. Kevin looked it over. He sighed. "Well, this is it. Apocalypse pending." He pointed to the creatures in the painting. They've lined up for the ceremony to help the devourer cross over. One at each point on the compass."

"Devourer?" I didn't like the sound of that.

"The fish dude eats Loverboy, then he gets to eat the world. Human civilization ends, then fish guy remakes it into a steaming hot Eden for giant bugs and fishes, a steaming primordial sea of nightmares. My guess is fish man's on his way, and octopus guy's gonna slingshot Loverboy right into its mouth. Then, that's it. Game over, man. Game. Over."

"What do we do?"

"Desperate times, desperate measures, kid," he said. "I'll distract them. You free Bubby and close the gate before fish guy shows up. If you can't close the gate, get the critters out of alignment. Got it?"

"But...how?"

Kevin didn't answer. He crawled down my leg, up the counter, into the doughnut case and right up onto a devil's food doughnut with chocolate frosting.

"What are you doing?"

"Taking a chance, kid," Kevin said. "Look. I'm a roach. Even if these dicks destroy the human world, I'll survive. My life already sucks. If these guys take over, it'll suck even harder. Trust me. That's saying something."

Kevin chomped down into the doughnut. "Mmm. This is pretty good." He took another bite. "Holy cow. This is amazing." He turned back to me, his mouth circled in chocolate frosting and said, "If I don't make it, tell my roommates they're total dickheads, I hate them, and I hope they all die horrible deaths."

With that, he dug in. As in devoured that doughnut in record time. His body vibrated. "Oof. Here we go. Hold on to your butt, kid."

He convulsed and writhed and shook, and...grew? He doubled in size. He vibrated and shook and doubled again. Then tripled. He looked like a roach-shaped party balloon being inflated by a helium tank. Soon, he was as long as I was tall. "This is awesome!" He swiveled his roach head back toward me and said, "Press play, then kick some ass."

He swallowed two more devil's food chocolate frosted doughnuts whole, opened his wings, and fluttered over the counter. A shiver ran over me. Roaches can fly? *Blech.*

By the time Kevin reached the open jagged hole of glass that used to be the front door, he was about two stories tall, his body smooth, flat and wide. He stuck his roach butt into the broken shell of the doorway and entirely sealed it off, just in time to stop the Flamin' Hot Crunchy Cheetos gnats from escaping. Tristan was still face down on the asphalt in the parking lot, writhing against the tentacle holding him in place.

"All right, boys," Kevin announced. He slid into his best Mortal

Kombat Johnny Cage stance, with some extra arms, but still. Kevin was ready to rumble. The hell beasts looked at him. "Which one of your asses am I gonna kick first?"

CHAPTER 19

Free Bubby, close the gate. Okay. Okay. I had to stick to the plan.

Kevin was in attack mode, butt firmly blocking the door, legs punching and karate-kicking Bizo, who refused to move out of his corner. The other monsters watched, but they didn't move from their spots, either. Huh. Kevin said they were in some sort of ceremonial configuration, just like in the picture, aligned to open the gate and let the hungry fish cross over. That wasn't good, but maybe that meant they wouldn't chase me if I tucked and rolled over to the beer cave to help Bubby.

Bizo seemed glued to his spot, no matter how hard Kevin punched him. Bubby struggled, still strapped in the corner. The octopus didn't move, just held tight to Tristan, the midnight snack who was outside the store, pressed against Kevin's butt. The spider was the only one active. He was shooting a web into the vortex like he was sending a rope into the gate.

Uh. Oh. Unless you're the fat guy in gym class, a rope can be climbed. Gulp. Or he's fishing. What if it was fishing line?

I heard a scream. "Aaaaaaaaaaaaahhhh!"

No. A battle cry.

DeeDee ran right at the spider's butt. The red light from the gate reflected off something metal in her hand. A sword? *That's right, girl. Cut the line!* She jumped in the air, put the thing to her mouth and a sad little honk fizzled out of it. Wait, that wasn't a sword. It was one of those weird little trumpets we had lying around everywhere. She blew it again. *Honk. Honk. Honk.*

It sounded like the squeeze horn I had on my bike when I was nine. Octopus guy began to ripple and writhe. The spider rolled its head and Bizo wrapped two tentacles around where his ears probably would be if he had a normal head. That tinny little honk seemed to really bother them. DeeDee kept honking, and the monsters recoiled.

This was it. This was my chance. I crawled over the counter and ran as fast as my beer gut and Pumas would carry me, sweating like I was an inch from the sun the entire way. Jesus, it was boiling in here! When I got to Bubby, he was wilting in the heat, whimpering in pain. "Hang in there, man."

I grabbed a huge pair of heavy iron scissors out of the weapons cabinet and started cutting away at them. Webs slingshotted off but not nearly enough and not nearly fast enough.

Suddenly the room lit up. Some sort of bright green laser beam connected all the monsters, crisscrossing to make some sort of huge magical symbol that looped around them. One part of it shot straight into the center of the gate. Well, that wasn't good.

A big oval thing, glowing mean and yellow, like a lure bobbing on a line, emerged from the swirl of red. The octopus wriggled, its slimy tentacles slapping up and down, stretching down and out every aisle toward the gate, covering the floor. Tristan yelped and Kevin screamed "Hurry up!" as the octopus tried harder to pull Tristan inside.

"Cut Bubby loose, kid!" Kevin yelled, holding onto the door frame for dear life, holding his roach butt as hard as he could into the opening to keep Tristan out, as octopus guy tried to reel him in. The Flamin' Hot Crunchy Cheetos gnats thumped against Kevin's belly, desperate to escape.

"I'm trying!" I yelled.

A cavernous mouth lined with spiky fangs emerged from the angry red gate. It chomped up and down, breaking the spider web that had guided him out. Gulp. Fish guy. That yellow thing was his angler fish lure. And he was ready for lunch. The first thing he did was eat most of the aisle four end cap in one munch, crushing Honey Buns, oatmeal crème pies, and steel shelving like it was cooked spaghetti.

A gigantic icy white fish eye appeared next to me. Woah boy. Was it too late to run?

I'd never seen anything so horrifying and disgusting. Its scaly body was lined with sacs of milky liquid. Black dots moved inside of them. *Oh, Jesus. Babies. It brought babies.* Fish dude was a fish chick, ready to populate the world with more monster fish. *Nope. I'm not gonna run. This is my last chance to do right. I have to try.* I gulped hard and focused on Bubby, yanking, and cutting and loosening.

The gate opened far enough to knock Bubby's TV off one hinge. It dangled there in the corner, hanging on for dear life, just above the spider, and sparked on. Bubby's wrestling DVD must have been playing this whole time, because a guy had just stepped into the ring and said something about shamrocks and gold dust?

Bubby turned toward the screen. He couldn't see it. Fish chick's head was in the way. Bubby's expression changed, from sadness to resolve. Bubby pulled so hard against his bindings, they started to break. They cut into him, drawing blue gooey-blood, and he yelped in pain, but one popped, then another and another. *Holy shit.* Bubby wanted to see wrestling so badly he was freeing himself!

"Keep it up, Bubby!" I chopped at the webs, but I didn't need to.

Bubby writhed and pulled until he broke free and lurched forward. The green laser light linking all the creatures fizzled and went out. Bubby clawed away the webs on his mouth and howled. The Flamin' Hot Crunchy Cheetos gnats stopped thumping Kevin, took one look at Bubby's now-open saw mouth and scattered in all directions. That didn't save them. A few seconds later, Bubby was sucking them in, eviscerating them into mustard pus guts. Well, snap. Bubby was powering up with a late-night snack. When he'd finished them all off, his razor saw mouth was coated in bright orange Cheetos dust. He howled like a werewolf on the full moon.

The other monsters recoiled at the sound. Boy, they really hated noise. A moment later, Bubby was completely out of the gate, limping through what used to be the chip aisle. He grabbed a bag of Smart Pop and flipped the spider the bird.

"Hit the switch!" DeeDee yelled. She was crouched below the TV. The spider looked down at her, and she honked the tinny trumpet at it.

I flipped the manual override switch. The red vortex went still, sparked, then starting swirling in the other direction. It was still angry and red, but the edges began to recede. Yes! Yes! Yes!

Bubby, now furious and armed with a half dozen bags of Smart Pop, arched his back, opened his pincers wide and unleashed some sort of angry low-pitched lion's roar at the spider. Then, he punched a spider leg out of the way so he could see the television. The magical green laser fizzled out because Bubby was out of formation.

The vortex was shrinking quickly. It had closed in around fish chick, squeezing her tight. Her mouth had stopped chomping and her eye had receded. The gate was squeezing her back in.

Yes. Take that! Ha!

The Spider was stomping, angry, its head going up and down, eyeballing the edges of the closing gate. That's when Kevin screamed. "Grab him, kid! Or we're toast!"

I turned back to see Tristan flying through the air, straight at fish chick's mouth. *No!*

As Tristan tumbled through the air right at those giant dagger teeth, time slowed to the speed of oozing molasses. I reached out for Tristan. I ran toward him, but my legs were lead weights, fighting against the cosmic heaviness of watching the world end. Tristan flew toward that fish like he was on a greasy Slip 'n' Slide leading straight into her belly. He was only a few yards away from doom, still totally unaware of what was really happening, when something red shot up out of where the candy aisle once stood. The red thing arced through the air. It was a blood-red creature with wings and long, pointy ears. Wearing a blue cop uniform? Chewing on a Twizzler?

No way. In its monstrous features, I could just make out the faint hint of Morty's face. He was full-on red now, his human disguise fallen away and his demon incubus nature revealed. He flew right at Tristan, arms out, and caught him just as his tragically hip boot was snapped up by a fish incisor. The fish reared up and opened wide, swallowing the shoe. Then it looked a little confused, kinda how I'd feel if a pizza roll was snatched right out of the air the second before it landed in my mouth.

Morty flew Tristan, sacrificial snack, up up and straight through the front window, shattering the glass. They flew across the parking lot and right in through the front door of the Sinbad's gentleman's club.

I hate you, Tristan. You open the gate to hell, then get to look at naked titties while I'm left behind to battle all of your angry hell beasts. Dude. Life really isn't fair, is it?

The hell gate was still closing. Its edges were crunching in hard around the fish, cutting at him. Uh, her? She was straining, trying to keep it open, but wasn't winning. It was pushing her back in. *Yes!*

The other monsters didn't like this one bit. They writhed and slapped and punched against the walls, breaking out chunks of concrete blocks. Bizo was so mad one of his fwapping angry tentacles busted a hole through the ceiling and right on up out of the roof above him. The creatures seemed hell-bent on tearing the store apart.

Ha. Too late, suckers. The world's not going to end tonight! All that was left of fish chick was one eye, half a mouth, and her creepy glowing lure. *Yes! We've won. Take that!*

Bubby had gone full-on Charles Bronson. He was stabbing spider bits with the sharp-tipped ends of his legs, shooting that watery poison goop at it, and as you can guess, the spider was not happy about it. It clicked its fangs and prepared to fight.

"We've got to send them all back, so they can't make the formation again. It's the only way!" DeeDee had slunk away from the spider, rolled past the fish, and was running toward me.

Then Bubby howled, a sound so deep and long and pained, it shattered every remaining bottle of beer or barbecue sauce in the store. DeeDee and I looked up just in time to watch the angry spider spear

Bubby through the gut with one leg, skewering him like a big blue kabob. He cried. His blue goo blood was everywhere.

"No!!!!" DeeDee screamed and tried to run for him. "Bubby!"

I grabbed her. "We can help him some other way."

I pointed at the counter. Still untouched, still standing, stocked with rocks and weird shit we might be able to use. We had to regroup. Dude. Anyone who'd ever played Halo or The Walking Dead game knew you had to regroup every once in a while.

Of course, getting to the counter was a different story. The floor was completely covered in writhing octopus tentacles. DeeDee hopped up on one and sprinted off, straight at the counter, hopscotching around suction cups like she was on the playground. I watched DeeDee jump up off a tentacle, do a somersault right over the counter, then disappear behind the register.

Oh well, if she can do it. I swallowed hard. It was now or never. The universe didn't give second chances. I stepped onto an octopus leg and started running. Okay, more like Fred Flintstone-ing, my feet shuffling and slipping across slime. It wasn't fast, and it wasn't pretty. My shoes were soaking wet and covered in octopus goo, but I eventually made it to the counter. I jumped. I tucked. I rolled and landed gut first right into the hard edge of the counter. Again. Ow.

I struggled to lift one leg then the other up onto the counter where I lay for a second, beached like a whale, before mustering the ab strength to roll over onto the floor next to DeeDee. Don't let anyone lie to you. I don't care how much adrenaline you've got, you don't magically turn into Superman in a crisis.

"This isn't going so great." I panted, way out of breath. Dude. I couldn't remember the last time I'd worked out that hard. Oh wait, now I remember: Never.

"Are you kidding? We've got them right where we want them." She smiled, but it was a 'yep, we're doomed' smile. For the first time ever, she looked scared. And sad. She looked at me for a few minutes, like she wanted to say something heavy, but she backtracked at the last minute. "Is the sword still inside of Bizosoth?"

"Yeah. I couldn't light it," I said. "I'm sorry."

"It's okay. All we have to do right now is send them back, one by one, so they can't open the gate again. That's it," she said. "Are you ready, Lloyd? The world's counting on us."

I said nothing. She gave me a quick kiss on the cheek. She grabbed a pack of cigarettes off the floor, stood up and pressed no sale on the register. The drawer slid open. She grabbed a gold coin and looked back at me. "Don't be scared, Lloyd. If we die, I'll find you. I know where the gate to heaven is. I'll get us there."

She hopped over the counter, and she was gone.

If we die? Hold up a minute. She had a plan for that? Jesus. No wonder she was so cazh! She had a post-death Plan B! Something hit my foot. The angel eight ball. It hit me again. "Not now," I said, pushing it away.

It pushed back. "Shut up and listen, punk," the triangle said. "Desperate love will breach the gate."

"Yeah. I know. That's already happened!"

"Remember Henrietta's prophecy."

Henrietta? The old lady who gave me the stupid angel eight ball? "She's just a crazy old lady!"

"No, dumbass She's an oracle. She was giving you tools. Now use them!"

The ball rolled, and the triangle turned again. "In darkness, three rocks might save you."

"What?"

"It's dark, so use the rocks," triangle said.

"What?"

"Oh my God, I really do have to spell it out for you, don't I? Press play, dumbass!"

Press play? That's what Kevin said. Rocks. The stereo. The music! Okay. I deserved that. Duh. If a tinny honk from a half-assed trumpet could upset these epic hell beasts, if a snake monster could be subdued by a Michael Bolton CD, what would Ronnie James Dio do? Oh Kevin. You just might be a genius.

I hopped up. Wow. Shit was really going downhill in here. Bubby lay limp, bleeding and speared by a giant spider leg, whimpering as the beast webbed him back into his corner. Yep. It was gonna try to open the gate again. Poor Bubby. His eyes flickered as if he was moving in and out of consciousness. At least he was alive.

Once Bubby was secured, the spider retreated back into its corner, into formation. The magical green beam buzzed back to life, wrapping around all the monsters. It dialed up to full power, and the end shooting into the vortex now looked like a big fish hook. The bits that were left of fish chick—basically just a mouth—chomped down on it.

DeeDee was tiptoeing across angry, writhing octopus tentacles over to Kevin and Bizo, who were wrapped around each other in a jumble of swinging roach legs and barbed tentacles. Kevin was trying to pull Bizo out of formation, but Bizo was fighting hard to stay in. They were toppling slushy machines and punching chunks out of the walls, rattling the store as they fought.

Another huge chunk of the ceiling above Bizo crumbled in, opening up to the clear, black October night. I could see stars. Another fwap, and Bizo had knocked down part of the wall between the front of the store and the employee lounge, leaving Chef standing there in the gap, in his dark shades and chef's hat, stone still and silent like he didn't know what the hell just happened.

"Chef!" I yelled. "Get out of the way!"

His head turned like he heard me, but if the scene unfolding in front of him bothered him, he didn't let on. He just stood there, sniffing the air.

But the jerk halo of tentacles didn't move, even as an avalanche of concrete blocks tumbled over him. None of the beasts did. They were still synced up, the green laser held steady, slowly but surely holding the demon angler fish out of the gate.

Okay, Lloyd. Focus! The music. That'll slow them down. Kevin's Zune was covered in chunks of broken glass, but the two stones were still wrapped in copper wire, hooked into the speakers. I brushed the glass off of the Zune and stood there for a hot minute, trying to figure out how to work the stupid thing. Jesus, Kevin. Why didn't you at least buy an iPod?

A flash of movement outside caught my eye. I looked out through the jagged remains of the front window. Tristan was running straight at the store, full speed. *Oh. My. God. Did he want to get eaten?*

Morty, once again in human form, was chasing him. He struggled to catch up without the use of his now-hidden wings. I glanced back at the gate. Fish guy—uh, girl—still had enough mouth out of the gate to eat a balled-up Tristan like he was a honey barbecue boneless chicken wing if she wanted to badly enough.

"Kevin! Loverboy's coming back!"

Kevin's roach head swiveled back to look at me. "You're kidding."

"I'm serious!"

Kevin let go of Bizo and moved toward the door, ready to block it with his butt like he had before, but he was too late. Tristan slid right back in through the front door like a bacon-wrapped scallop served on a silver tray at a fancy cocktail party.

Morty ran in soon after, leaning on the door frame, panting. "Sorry y'all. I tried. But this one's real stupid."

"I am not stupid! I'm saving my one true love from an earthquake!" Tristan grabbed DeeDee, who was tiptoeing up to Bizo, unnoticed until now.

"You seemed to forget all about her when you were up to your eyeballs in titties," Morty said.

"Yeah, well, then I saw a pair that looked like hers," Tristan said.

Gah! I hated him!

Bizo's face went all smug. He shot octopus guy a look and pumped one tentacle up and down as if to say "Oh yeah. Back in business!"

While Bizo was distracted, DeeDee pushed Tristan aside, then sunk her hand right into Bizo's lime Jello gut. After some serious yanking, she managed to get her arm back out. It was dark, so it was hard to see, but I swear I saw a pack of Pyramid 20s and something yellow next to the sword in his gut. DeeDee straightened her name tag and said, "Have a nice day." Then she backed away from him, nervously looking up at the hole in the ceiling.

Tristan whirled around and tried to grab DeeDee again. "Come on, honey. It's not safe here."

"Trist. Run," she said.

The floor was undulating. The octopus was closing in on Tristan. She pushed him toward the exit. "I'll be right behind you. Go. Go!"

"Okay, babe." Smugly confident, he took a step toward the door, but it was too late. A tentacle wound around his leg and whipped him up through the air. He screamed. "Aaaaaaaahhhhh! Another tremor! Aftershocks! Aaaaaaaahhhhh!"

Lagopex turned to face the tragically hip, screaming morsel careening toward her mouth. Her teeth parted, just enough, straining against the gate.

"If he'd stayed at the titty bar this never would have happened," Morty snapped. "I'm out. I'm getting my three-way before all the hot human broads are gone forever."

With that, Morty stomped next door to the Temptations Tavern.

CHAPTER 20

All right. So where were we? Oh yes, Morty went next door to get laid before the hell beasts destroyed the world as we know it and all the hot chicks in it. Chef was standing in the rubble, either totally unbothered or so afraid he couldn't move. Bubby was fading in and out of consciousness. He'd been webbed back into his magical corner, which had flipped on the green laser light of doom, which held the angler fish chick from beyond just far enough out of the gate to eat Tristan. Tristan was hurtling toward her like the world's dumbest, yet most fashionable, chicken nugget. The spider guy ran a couple of legs along the wall, looking for the manual override switch that would reopen the gate. And DeeDee and Kevin were staring nervously up through the hole in the roof over Bizo.

Uh, wasn't anyone going to try to stop Tristan from getting eaten and sealing the deal on the end of the world? Anyone? No? Just me? I had to do something. I went after him, but in full-on Lloyd loser mode, took two steps then tripped over the stupid eight ball. "Duck," it said. "Now!"

Whoop. Whoop. Whoop.

Huh. What was that noise? I didn't like it, not one bit. Even the hell beasts stopped what they were doing and looked around.

Whoop. Whoop. Whoop.

The air vibrated. I ducked down behind the counter, but not so far that I couldn't keep my eye on the action. Two thin, craggy shadows, darker than night and blacker than the gothest goth girl's wardrobe, shot straight down out of the hole in the roof and sunk into Bizo's single yellow eye. He wailed, so loud and high I thought my eardrums would explode. He thrashed. DeeDee and Kevin tucked and rolled out of there, dodging barbed tentacles as Bizo punctured the slushy machines, splurping icy frozen syrupy goodness all over the floor.

Whoop. Whoop. Whoop.

Bizo lifted off the floor. The dark things that came in through the

179

ceiling came into focus. They were talons, and they were attached to the giant demon bird with the gold eye who ate robbers like crackers. The cigarettes. The gold coin. The 'stolen' sword in Bizo's belly. DeeDee was officially a genius. She'd conned a hell beast into ridding us of another hell beast! Boss fight. Pro move. Level up.

The demon bird pulled Bizo up and out of the hole in the roof. It cawed.

Whoop. Whoop. Whoop.

Then *Crash. Clunk. Thump. Thump. Crack.* They were fighting up there, on the roof. A green barbed tentacle crashed back down through the hole. *Oh no. Birdman lost!* The tentacle landed in the puddle of spent. melting slushy on the floor, completely detached from a body. The magical green laser beam flickered.

"Aaaaaaaahhhhh!" Tristan screamed.

Lagopex opened her mouth. Then the green light went dead. Completely dead. In the exact moment when Tristan was about to hit fish chick's pointy incisor, a voice boomed from Bubby's television.

"Can you smell what The Rock is cooking?"

Tristan and fish chick made contact. Fish chicks mouth dropped down, and Tristan skidded over the top of her slimy head. He careened right into a stack of hip, locally brewed artisan-flavored hard seltzer stacked against the freezing steel wall of the beer cave.

Bubby stood in front of his television, covered in broken webs, watching Dwayne Johnson smack talk some bald buff guy I later found out was Stone Cold Steve Austin. I had to hand it to Bubby. He was a real fan. He loved Dwayne Johnson so much, he'd freed himself again, despite being badly wounded. With that move, he'd closed the gate completely, slicing fish chick in half. Her detached head fell dead to the floor the second Tristan should have been lunch.

Bizo was gone, carried off, out of alignment. The spell was broken. The gate was closed. Hell. Yeah.

Kevin and DeeDee high fived. I had the satisfaction of watching Tristan get knocked out cold, then get bopped in the face as loose beer cans cascaded out of their boxes and right onto his head. That was gonna leave a mark. Ha!

The eight ball hit my foot again. "Press play, remember?"

"What? It's over. We won!"

"Really? Because I still see two very angry monsters, and you've got no gate to send them through."

Oh, crap. The spider, no longer constrained by his ceremonial spot, was stalking toward DeeDee and Kevin. The octopus guy gave me a thousand nasty side-eyes as he wrapped one tentacle around an unconscious Tristan, and the other plucked one of fish chick's unholy eggs sacs off of her corpse.

"Guys! I don't think they're giving up!" I yelled.

But they seemed to know that. Kevin cracked several sets of knuckles and shook out his arms and legs, gearing up for another fight. Chef had wandered into the middle of the store and was digging through the upturned candy aisle looking for something. He was right in the line of fire.

"Chef! Move!" He tilted his head in my direction but kept digging. Was he deaf?

DeeDee ran straight at the spider, hopping over octopus tentacles and melting slushy sugar like she did this kind of thing for fun every damn day. "Press PLAY!" she screamed.

"Do it now, or I'm never talking to you again." Angel eight ball said from the floor.

"Okay, okay!" I picked up one of the speakers and pressed it against the store intercom, turned that on, and then pressed play on Kevin's Zune.

"Ye-aaaaaaaw!" It was DeeDee's battle cry. I turned to look. She was jumping up at the spider. It reared back, opened its fangs and prepared to eat her, to plunge venom and death and awfulness right into her. It went at her fast and hard. She was a goner.

"DeeDee no!" I jumped over the counter and landed right on one of its legs. "Die!"

I opened wide and bit right into his disgusting arachnid leg. Oh, my God. So disgusting. But no one was going to eat the love of my life without a fight!

Suddenly, music crackled across the intercom. The guitar pulsed, the drums kicked, synthesizers synthed as Dio's "Rock 'N' Roll Children" ripped across every speaker that hadn't been torn out of the wall.

The fangs made contact with DeeDee's body.

"Noooo!" I screamed.

But the fangs bounced right off of her. Wait. What?

She smiled. "It's the music, Lloyd. Kevin's rocks. They're a protection spell. Just like the bullet! Now's our chance!"

Wait. So these guys couldn't hurt us as long as the music was on? No way.

Kevin was karate chopping octopus tentacles, but that slippery leviathan of doom was hard to stop. He was a multi-tasker. He had Tristan in one tentacle, an egg sac in another, and had just thwapped Bubby against the wall, knocking him unconscious, with yet another tentacle. Bubby lay motionless in octopus guy's grip.

DeeDee, clearly emboldened and feeling indestructible, was on the spider's back, riding it like a rodeo bull, hanging onto its hair for dear life as it tried to buck her off. She was stabbing it with something. It started spinning in circles, trying to fling her off. She held on, but I couldn't. I lost my grip and flew off, through the air and right into the stereo. Ow.

The music flicked off for a second. I must have accidentally hit shuffle, and it was searching for another song. Spider landed a hit on DeeDee, and she went flying. That's when spider dude got smart about the music and set its sights on the speakers.

Shit. Weren't the rocks supposed to save us? Why are the monsters still here?

Angel eight ball rolled right on up next to me. "Henrietta said three rocks, not two!"

There were only two rocks hooked up to the stereo. I didn't have long before spider dude nabbed me, so I grabbed a thin whitish rock off the rack, and started twining the copper around it fast and tight, linking it to the other rocks. "Henrietta didn't say which three rocks, did she? Eight ball?" I looked around. Where was he? Priceless. The one time I actually need an opinion, he was a ghost.

The Zune finished shuffling, and "Rainbow in the Dark" crackled across the speakers. The store lit up bright as daylight for a split second. It was so fast, my brain didn't really have time to register what happened, but I swear I saw colored lights. Blue, orange, red, and yellow slice down next to Bubby, cutting a few fat octopus tentacles right in half.

"Did you guys see that? Tell me you guys saw that! I knew it!" Kevin screamed and pumped a couple of legs up and down. "That's what I'm talking about. Dio forever, man. Rock on, Ronnie!"

The Octopus screeched, waving its bleeding stumps.

The spider reared up, aimed its front legs at the stereo, and stomped down. It didn't hit me. It couldn't, at least not while the music was playing, but that didn't mean it couldn't do any damage. I fell to the floor. The register and the doughnut case landed on top of me. I was pinned.

Angel eight ball rolled up next to me.

"Why didn't that work?" I yelled.

"She said three rocks *might* save you. Might!"

"*Might* isn't very helpful then, is it?"

"It did cut the octopus, so that's a win."

"Not good enough!"

That's when the spider used another leg to pull the speaker wires clean out of the electrical outlet. The music fizzled off. The spider angled itself over me, moving in for the kill. Well, this was it. I was doomed. Eaten by a giant spider. Figures. It's always the stuff you're afraid of the most that gets you in the end. It clicked its fangs and came for me.

"Remember, true victory will be sweet!" Angel eight ball's triangle flashed in front of my face. It had somehow become airborne, flying like a fast-pitch baseball, right at the spider. Angel eight ball squirted a short strong burst of red liquid into the spider's eyes. It tried to roll for cover, but was quickly scooped up in the spider's fangs, shoveled directly into its mouth, and swallowed.

Holy shit. That spider just ate my guardian angel!

Then it came for me. I wriggled but was trapped. The register was heavy, and the doughnut case even heavier. I struggled to breathe. Well, this was it then. Goodbye world. I closed my eyes. I didn't need a close-up view of the mouth that was about to eat me. I held my breath.

And nothing happened. *Come on, spider. Get it over with. Why aren't you eating me already?* I could feel the cold emanating off of its big hell body, feel it quivering above me. Great. He was a sadistic hell spider who liked to drag it out, make his lunch suffer. Just my luck.

I opened one eye. The spider's eyes were wide open, two inches from my face, staring...blankly? I mean, spider eyes aren't exactly emotive, but this one was zoned out like he was high as a kite. I knew stoned eyes when I saw them. What the hell?

Huh. His fangs were right above my heart. He'd tried to eat me, for sure. But his fangs had pierced the doughnut case and were stuck inside of it. He had one glazed doughnut with frosted pink icing and sprinkles speared on each fang, and he was lapping the other ones up, shoveling them into his mouth full speed. His spider mouth was ringed with pink frosting. A handful of sprinkles clung for dear life to his, uh, let's just say lips. When it'd eaten all the pink-frosted doughnuts in the case, it sucked the doughnut off of one fang, then the other. And groaned. "Aaaahh."

Seriously, it made the same noise a fat dude makes after devouring a whole pie at Thanksgiving dinner. I should know, I've made that sound.

Then, its spaced-out eyes rolled back in their sockets. Its body began to shake.

Crunch. Crack. Crunch. Crack.

Holy. Crap. Its body snapped violently in half, right in the middle. The creature gyrated and rattled as a tiny weird yellow circle opened in the air above us, no bigger than a quarter. The tiny thing was a vortex, kinda like the one Kevin's roommate's arm was always coming out of. The spider's body and legs, chunk by chunk, bent and broke and cracked at unholy angles, then was quickly, painfully sucked into the tiny vortex. That teensy yellow hole crunched that spider down like it was a bag of potato chips in a garbage truck compactor. And it didn't even fight back.

Man. As much as I wanted this awful thing to die, this was hard to watch. It squealed. Bits exploded, raining down blue blood and bile all over me. (Note to self. Always keep your mouth closed when hell beasts hover over you.) Until the vortex had crunched and crunched, and the final tip of the final leg disappeared into that yellow vortex. Then the yellow thing spun, zipped closed, and disappeared, dropping something small and hard onto the floor next to me. *Chink.*

I managed to push the register over, off of my chest, just enough to squeeze out from under it. The empty doughnut case clunked to the floor. True defeat will be sweet, indeed. Wait. Henrietta was a genius. True defeat *is* literally sweet. The pink doughnuts! I stumbled up to warn the others. Here I go, Lloyd's totes gonna save the day! I knew how to kill the monsters. Hazzah!

But my joy was short-lived. The scene before me didn't scream "Hey, we've got this!" I was too late.

Octopus guy was in the middle of the store, tentacles splayed in all directions. He had DeeDee wrapped up in one tentacle, an unconscious Bubby in another. Kevin was suction cupped to the wall. Tristan dangled upside down by one leg. The octopus was peeling open fish chick's egg sac. And, poor Chef. He was all wrapped up in tentacle, an inch from the octopus' open, hungry beak. Chef held tight to that weird purple gourd, even though he was about to be chomped by a nihilistic cephalopod.

"Chef!" I screamed. "Fight him off!"

Chef didn't respond. He didn't seem ruffled or concerned at all. He didn't speak, didn't scream. Just stood there silently, sniffing the air, holding onto his pumpkin as cazh as if he were serving our dinner. He didn't look like a man about to be eaten. He was staring certain death straight in the beak and didn't give two fucks.

I couldn't just stand there and let him get eaten. His steaks were perfect! And no one deserved to end up in the gut of giant mean-spirited hell octopus. There was still one pink frosted doughnut left, behind the emergency glass in the weapons safe. I looked at Chef, at the beak about to crunch him in half like a gummy bear, and made a mad dash for that last precious doughnut. Across slimy tentacle-covered floors, melted slushy sugary syrup, oozing spider blood, and the upturned remains of every neatly stacked rack and every glass reach-in beer cooler door.

I could make it. Yes. I crunched. I jumped. I panted. A. Lot. Because I was out of shape. There, I said it. Happy now? If I lived through this, I was definitely doing more cardio. I swear!

I was knee-deep in Doritos, halfway there, when octopus dude snuck up on me. He grabbed me by the leg, lifted me up, and smacked me face-first into the linoleum. *Eo. Ow.* Next thing I knew, the room was upside down and spinning, going out of focus.

Had. To. Get. Pink. Doughnut.

The octopus opened wide and stuffed Chef right into his beak. It snapped closed, bending Chef in half. Backward. *Crunch. Gulp.* And just like that, he'd eaten Chef.

"Noooooooo!!!!!!" I screamed. The octopus raised me higher, then thwacked me down hard against the floor. The room went black.

CHAPTER 21

Blurple. Blup. Ppppsssslurp. Blurple. Blup. Pppssssslurp.

The noise sounded like a vat of hot boiling pus.

Blurple. Blup. Ppppsssslurp. Blurple. Blup. Pppssssslurp.

Huh. So this was what it sounded like to be digested. I must be in the octopus' gut. That's why it was warm, and holy cow did it stink. Like festering dog turds doused in skunk juice and chili sauce, but on fire.

Eo-owch. My head throbbed. My muscles burned. Every bit of me was riddled with sharp, shooting pain. Boy, that octopus was a jerk. Why didn't he chew me up first and put me out of my misery? He had to be an asshole and eat me alive, whole, Sarlacc-pit style? At least Chef went quick, in a snap. Literally. Man. Poor Chef. No one deserved to die like that. Or like this.

Something jabbed me in the ribs. Welp, here we go. I was about to be broken down into bits like a fast-food burger, absorbed into the intestinal tract of hell, and pooped out like so much nothing. The irony.

Ow! The rib-jabbing continued. Seriously, ouch.

I opened my eyes. Kevin's giant roach face lingered above me.

"He ate you, too?" I asked.

"See? I told you we could summon Ronnie James Dio if we got those rocks wired up right. Did you see him? In that rainbow? I guess he wasn't kidding about a 'Rainbow in the Dark' was he? Man, he chopped up octopus tentacles like he was a rock n roll Ginsu knife."

Kevin was awfully cheery for having been eaten by a hell octopus.

"Get up, kid. We've got work to do." Kevin kicked me in the ribs. Again.

"Ow!" Dude. What was the rush? I mean, an octopus ate us. We were toast. What more was there to do?

I rolled to the side and came face to face with four sad white eyes. Bubby. His pincers opened up, revealing a circular razor mouth curled down into the equivalent of a frown. He whimpered in pain. "Hey, Bubby. I'm sorry you got eaten, too. I tried, dude."

Blurple. Blup. Ppppssssslurp. Blurple. Blup. Pppsssssslurp. Blurple. Blup. Ppppssssslurp. Blurple. Blup. Pppsssssslurp.

Ugh. I hoped this Sarlacc Pit business didn't last a thousand years because that noise was unbearably creepy. Did I really need to be reminded that I was being actively digested? That was a whole other level of jacked up.

I sat up. Slowly. Very slowly, because it felt like someone was scrambling my brain with a stick. "Holy crap!" I scooted back in terror. Ee-ouch. Again.

Octopus guy's cold, glassy black eyes stared me down, less than ten feet away. It took me a second to register that the head around them was mostly gone. The eyes were part of a big raw chunk of meat that appeared to be...melting?

Blurple. Blup. Ppppssssslurp. Blurple. Blup. Pppsssssslurp.

Holy crap. I really was in an octopus' guts all right, but the octopus had been turned inside out like a gym sock. All the guts were on the outside. The entire store was at least a foot deep in steaming, bubbling purple and black ooze. Guts and suction cups and tentacles blurped and sizzled. It looked like the octopus had split open and started disintegrating. "Hell yeah, I'm alive!"

"Well, duh. Don't just sit there, kid. Give me a hand." Kevin grabbed Bubby under his first row of arms and started to pull him across the floor.

I didn't know how long I was out, but it was long enough for someone to have cleared a path through the toppled shelving and scattered potato chip bags straight to the room with the green door where I'd taken that magic healing shower after Demon Caroline had flattened my face.

Bubby howled each time Kevin tugged. He was bleeding, oozing cool Kool-Aid blue blood that steamed when it hit the humid, warm air. (Apparently, the insides of hell octopi were boiling hot and could really dial up the thermostat.) Kevin was still gigantic by roach standards, but I could see the chocolate doughnuts were wearing off. He'd shrunk down to about half his biggest size already. Kevin was still a big boy, but Bubby was twice as long.

Kevin dragged the limp and badly injured Bubby in short bursts, struggling and panting. "Help me, kid. I can't move this fatass all by myself."

I got up, very very slowly because I felt like an eighty-year-old man who'd just joined a CrossFit gym and did a dozen back-to-back workouts on his first day. While getting hit in the head with mallets. Everything hurt. Bad. I grabbed onto Bubby's middle and lugged. Next thing I knew,

DeeDee was across from me, lifting Bubby's other side.

"You're finally awake. My hero!" She winked. At me?

I blushed. Hero? She didn't mean me, did she?

DeeDee was covered head to toe in slime, but still drop-dead gorgeous. I did a quick assessment. I was coated in slime, too. So. Gross. But it could have been much worse. We were beaten up, bruised and slimy, but we were okay. We were alive.

The store didn't fare as well. Everywhere I looked there were steaming guts, holes in the floor from spider stomps and barbed tentacles. The place was completely wrecked. I could see twinkling stars and night sky in the chunks missing from the roof. The wall between the store and the employee lounge was nothing but crumbled concrete block. The storefront was mostly shattered glass where windows and doors were supposed to be. The face of the beer cave had been ripped off, leaving only the backside of a steel cooler exposed, filled with toppled cases and broken bottles. We were slip-sliding in the guts of a giant rotten octopus. My brain couldn't process this—and frankly, didn't want to. Because, come on, WTF?

We pulled Bubby to the green door, and Kevin said, "I'll take it from here."

As soon as Kevin and Bubby disappeared into the bathroom, I asked DeeDee what had happened. The last thing I remembered, I was toast. Okay, the avocado on an octopus' toast. Death was certain.

All she said was, "We did it, Lloyd. It's over. We won."

I heard the water flip on in the magic shower, and Kevin cursing as he tried to stuff a two-story-tall centipede into a space meant for a human. "DeeDee, is there a control panel for this thing? We need it to go up a size or two!"

"On the wall by the towel heater," she yelled through the door.

"Yeah. Yeah. I see it," Kevin said.

"How did we win?"

"I'm not sure exactly. I'm pretty sure it was Chef. Plus, Bubby managed to get out of the gate on his own, so that helped. He sure does love the rock."

"What rock?"

"You know, Dwayne Johnson. *The* Rock."

Huh. Henrietta's words bounced around in my head. *Desperate love will breach the gate.* Tristan, check. *In darkness, three rocks might save you.* Three rocks. Did Dwayne "The Rock" Johnson count? Or was it the three rocks on the stereo? Or did Ronnie James Dio really swoop down out of a rainbow and kick octopus ass like Kevin said? Which rocks? Man. Oracles. If they expected to be taken seriously, they needed to issue easier-to-follow, step-by-step instructions. They were too vague.

I was about to ask if DeeDee had seen Dio, too, when she hugged me, squeezing me tight for a good long time. Kevin, unaware that we were sharing a tender moment and that he should shut up already, was still yelling through the door at us, making conversation.

"Make a wish, kids, because we're definitely getting a fat bonus for this! I want a big ole TV, and I'm not letting my dick hole roommates anywhere near it," he said. "I'm done watching those awful garage band videos my roommate posts online."

"Okay, Kevin," DeeDee said. "We get it."

Spell broken. She let go of me. Okay, more like peeled herself off of me because we were both coated in guts, and guts were really sticky.

"What does he mean 'make a wish'?" I asked.

"He's talking about hazard pay, but don't worry about it," DeeDee said. "Faust is pretty tuned in to what we all truly desire. We don't have to wish. Faust is like the ultimate Santa. He always shows up with the perfect gift."

"Bubby, is he—?"

"He'll be fine. I think." She sounded unsure. "Anyway, when he's finished, we'll get you in the shower. You look pretty beat up. And, well, slimy. Either way, we can't go out in public like this. Biohazard and all. We don't want to give the containment guys any excuse to come down here. Trust me. They're super creepy."

Containment? Biohazard? Creepy? I suddenly felt more grossed out, which was saying something when you were already coated head to toe with the innards of hell beasts.

DeeDee picked a chunk of octopus intestine out of my hair and looked up at me. Her tough eyes went soft like she was about to say something heartfelt and epic. "Lloyd..."

So of course, that's when Morty strutted through the opening that was once the front door, zipped up his pants, and rolled right on up to us. "Didn't need these after all." He threw a blister pack of Hammer All Night boner pills at me. "I still got it. Sorry I broke the rules and all, but you gotta strike while the iron is hard."

He pointed at his penis, waiting for us to get the joke. Ahem. Yeah, we got it bub. Not in the mood. We were in the middle of some heartfelt relationship stuff. Read the room.

"It's all right, Morty. I'll let it slide this time." DeeDee's vulnerable face was gone. She was cool, all business. "Thanks for the assist, by the way. I didn't know you were such a softy."

"Zip it, hot stuff. I've got a reputation." His eyes darted around like a dude in a foil hat looking for surveillance cameras. His voice went low.

"I had to step in. Did you see that fish chick? I am not gonna dip this majestic pecker into one of those for the rest of eternity. No way. I prefer the supple bodies of human ladies. They appreciate the goods, ya feel me? Oh shit. Wait a minute. What's that stuff you've got all over you?"

He glanced at the slime on our clothes, then around at the bubbling guts, as if noticing the eviscerated octopus for the first time. "How'd a bunch of scrawny rejects like you pull this off?"

Kevin stepped out of the magic bathroom. He'd shrunk again. He was a little taller than me now. "Remember that purple pumpkin? I told you not to eat it. You eat it, then it eats you."

"Wait. That little thing did *this*?"

We all looked around. Okay, yeah. I didn't know about these guys, but if a dusty purple gourd could do this, I was never eating any type of squash or pumpkin ever again. I was eighty-sixing all cucurbits.

"Okay, that's messed up. You need to label your crap. I was about to eat that thing! Guess I owe you one, Kev." Morty's nose crinkled up in disgust. He scanned the toppled racks, the busted out beer coolers, the guts, the holes in the ceiling. "Good luck cleaning this up. Looks like I better find another gate."

"You do not need another gate, demon," said a low, forceful voice with a vaguely Caribbean accent. "You stay where you belong, or you pay the price."

Pawnshop Doc was on his knees in the beer cave, eyeing Morty suspiciously. His incredibly buff body loomed over an unconscious Tristan. Tristan had symbols drawn all over him with colored sand. It didn't look like the kind of stuff that could be dry-cleaned out of ridiculously complicated cardigan smoking jackets. (Haha. Take that, hipster!) A handful of black pillar candles were set up around him, burning hot and bright, quickly melting down to stubs. "Now go home hellspawn," Doc snipped. "I must concentrate."

Doc held his hands over Tristan and began chanting. A translucent black fog kicked up around his body.

What the? Wait. Scratch that. Not gonna ask. Didn't want to know.

"Fine." Morty shrugged. "Do me a solid, would ya? Make me a gate out of here?"

Doc glared at Morty and snapped his fingers. Morty stepped over an unconscious Tristan, past a pile of toppled, guts-coated Red Stripe ponies, and right through a Morty-sized blue gate that zipped up tight behind him.

"Oh. Before I forget. Check this out." DeeDee pulled something small and shiny out of her pocket.

It looked like one of those fancy antique pins classy rich ladies wore back when photos only came in black and white. It was a silver spider, clustered in gemstones. It had eight ice-blue jewels for eyes, and its legs were studded with sparkling black diamonds. "Our little friend looks much prettier like this, doesn't he?"

"Little friend?"

"Who would have thought that horrible creature could turn into something so beautiful?"

It took a minute for her meaning to sink in. "That's the spider? *The* spider? But, how?"

"Now we know why we aren't supposed to eat the doughnuts." She winked.

"The doughnuts?" I couldn't even straighten out the thoughts enough to make a sentence.

"I said it before, and I'll say it again," DeeDee said. "The things you accomplish around here with food are absolutely amazing."

Yep. You heard that right. She was saying the glazed doughnuts with the pink frosting and sprinkles did this to the spider. The yellow vortex. The crunching. Okay, then. It's official. I was never eating a doughnut—any doughnut—ever again. Or any suspect gourds or pumpkins. But kudos to Henrietta. True defeat was sweet indeed.

DeeDee turned to Doc. "He's all yours. Catch."

She threw the spider pin through the air, and Doc caught it in one hand without looking up, without so much as a flinch, like he was a movie wizard. "Do not be so careless, woman. Cages are easy to escape. The creature is not vanquished, only trapped."

This guy had a way with big words, didn't he?

"You must manage your creatures, or we all pay." He looked at me, then at DeeDee. "Your spurned lover will survive. If he awakens in a familiar bed, he will never know the evening's true events, so make haste, woman."

Doc stood up. The black fog around him dissipated into nothing. The candles went out. Doc stepped over Tristan and walked right through the busted-out front door without another word, gemstone-encrusted spider in pocket.

That was the moment my survival mode snapped off, and my muddled thoughts became clear. Holy shit. We had used a cursed doughnut to trap a gigantic hell spider in a piece of magical jewelry. If we hadn't, it would have eaten us and destroyed the entire world. I couldn't deny it any longer. Magic was real. Hell was real. (And filled with spiders. Of course. It's hell, right?) Demons. Monsters. All of it was real.

I couldn't handle it. Being safe at home, in my room, playing Xbox, eating my Mom's home-cooked food. Free laundry and groceries. That I could handle. Battling hellspawn with cursed magical doughnuts? Nope. I'm outta here. I didn't care about the debt. No amount of money was worth this. I'd flip burgers for minimum wage forever if I had to. I'd let the creeps at Bloods R Us drain me dry. But this? I couldn't. I quit. I couldn't ever look at this store again. Although it was so destroyed I might never have to.

"My favorite employees have clearly had an eventful night."

I recognized his posh voice immediately. Asmodius Faust, proprietor of the 24/7 Demon Mart, and *a* devil, not *the* devil, according to DeeDee, stepped through the jagged glass remains of the front door. He was dressed to the nines, tailored designer suit and polished designer shoes, head to toe in black, naturally. He glided over to us, disinterested in the pulsing hot guts around us.

"You have proven your worth a hundredfold. I was right about you, young Mr. Wallace." He clapped me on the shoulder, unfazed by my slimy coating. "A pure heart, through and through. I knew you would achieve great things if given the chance. You and Ms. DeeDee are a formidable pairing. Finally, I have assembled the optimal team."

Did he say optimal team? We weren't the Avengers, dude. This team member was done. Finito. I was vamoose, out of here. I was not the right guy for this job. Being on the dream team was a nightmare.

Faust didn't notice my newfound resolve, because all of his attention was on DeeDee. "I heard about your scorned lover. How unfortunate," he said.

Gah. I wished everyone would stop referring to Tristan as a lover. I didn't need the visual. And he was such a jerk!

"But we both know love is a tricky, dangerous business," Faust said. "As they say, the sight of lovers feedeth those in love."

"Or feedeth Lagopex the Devourer, if they aren't careful," DeeDee said. "I'm sorry, sir. I try to keep my personal life separate from the store."

Faust tenderly lifted her chin and gazed into her eyes. "It is not your fault. Your beauty starts at the skin but goes deep down to bone and soul. Luring fools to love is your burden. You're a siren. Too beautiful a song and too bright a light to pass by. You'll leave many hearts in pieces on the rocks before true love moves you."

She blushed. Holy shit, this dude was smooth!

He sunk his hand into his suit jacket and pulled out two thick red envelopes. "Now. Let's take care of business, shall we?" He handed one to me, and one to DeeDee. "A small token of my gratitude for the ingenuity and gallantry you displayed this evening. The world is indebted to you. The city slept soundly and safely. The sun will rise again this morning because of you. Now, I must speak with Kevin."

Kevin was looming over Tristan, scratching his head. Kevin had shrunk even more. He was about half my height now. Faust glided over to him, and I swear I saw him pull a small television, about the size of a computer monitor, out of the flat fold of his tailored blazer. Kevin danced a jig when he saw it. "Yes! Can you put it in my room for me? I'm gonna be too small to handle it. Plus, I don't want my roommates to see it. You know how they are."

"Certainly. I anticipated that request." Faust snapped his fingers and a man-sized green vortex opened up. He stepped through it, then he and the vortex disappeared.

Of course, it was a vortex. And of course, he used it like a doorway. What did it say about me that I didn't even flinch this time? It had become normal. I ran my fingers across the envelope Faust had given me. It was heavy and thick, the paper blood red and expensive, smooth like velvet. It was sealed with wax, the symbol on Faust's ring pressed into it. I was about to open it when a muffled groaning sound came from nearby.

Uuuuuuhhhhhh. Uuuuuuuhhhhhh.

"What's that?" I immediately flipped into panic mode. I shoved the envelope deep in my pocket. No time now. This wasn't over.

"I don't know," DeeDee whispered. She pulled that golden knife out of her boot, and yeah, it still had streaks of spider blood all over it. "Stay close."

Uuuhhh. Uuuuuuhhh. Uuuuuhhhh. Uuuuuuuhhhh.

We tiptoed around until we pinpointed the noise. It was coming from under a pile of dissolving octopus eyes in the middle of the store.

"Step back."

My heart jumped as Faust materialized in front of us, fresh out of the vortex, with a cane in his hand. He moved entrails and eyeballs aside until we could see what was moaning underneath.

It was Chef! His body was bent backward, his ankles touching the back of his head. The poor guy had literally been snapped in half. He looked like a crumpled up Ken doll owned by a sadistic four-year-old. I didn't know how he was still alive or still moving. His feet schlepped up and down like he was trying to walk. His hands reached out and around, trying to find something to grab on to.

Uuuuuuhhhhh. Uuuuuuuhhhhhh. Uuuuuuhhhhhh. Uuuuuuuhhhhhh.

Chef moaned. My heart kickstarted up to a thousand beats a minute.

"Oh, my God! Call an ambulance!" I screamed. "Call 911! What are you waiting for?"

DeeDee looked at me, her eyebrows wrinkled together, confused. Faust poked Chef with his cane.

"Oh dear." Faust surveyed the suffering Chef. "I think we might need a replacement."

"What are you waiting for?" I said. "Look at him. He needs help! What's wrong with you?"

How could Faust be so cold? Oh right. He's the DEVIL. Chef grabbed and clawed at the cradle of slippery guts all around him, accidentally knocking off his sunglasses.

Chef looked at me. I looked at him. His eyes. They were...He was... Gulp. The ice-cold fingers of No. Fucking. Way. skipped down my spine. "JESUS CHRIST!"

Yep. I screamed, and Chef responded by trying to pull himself closer to me. He came up with a fistful of monster guts instead. He sniffed them, then took a big bite. He chewed and grunted like octopus guts were the best burger he'd ever eaten.

My knees got weak. My head spun. "Chef. He's a..." I backed away.

Faust reached out for me, but DeeDee stopped him. "Give him a few minutes to process this. I don't think he knew."

I stumbled out the front door onto the sidewalk, where I immediately bent over and straight-up hot vomited right into the handicapped parking spot. I steadied myself, hands on my knees. I took some deep breaths and told myself to stay calm. Eventually, my saliva glands dialed down from full-on barf mode to something close to normal. I sat down on the curb and looked up at the sky as I tried to wrap my head around it all. "This can't be happening."

Something bumped into my thigh. It was angel eight ball. He was covered in slime, and a chunk of his plastic eight was missing. "I need to take my brain out and give it a shower," angel eight ball said. "Once you've been in the gut of a hell spider, there's no going back. You can't unsee that."

"Tell me about it," I said.

He sat there next to me for a few minutes, silent, as we both came to grips with the night. We watched the sky lighten from pure black to royal blue as dawn approached.

"Thanks for trying to save me." His anemic red squirt wasn't particularly effective, but I appreciated the effort.

"Just doing my job." The triangle turned. "When I met you, I never dreamed you'd live up to your gaming handle. AwesomeDemonButtKicker98? Ha. No way, I said. But now you can wear that name with pride. You sure showed me. Good work. Which reminds me, what'd you get for it?"

"What?"

His triangle turned. "Your bonus. You know, hazard pay? What did Faust give you?"

"Oh." I pulled the fancy red envelope out of my pocket. It was bent and damp, but otherwise fine. I broke the wax seal. "Looks like a bunch of papers."

"Well? Come on," angel eight ball said. "Don't leave me hanging."

I opened the papers and smoothed them out. They were...bills? My student loan statement. A printout of my bursar's account at community college. "Wait, what?"

I looked at the papers, the balances, over and over, because I didn't believe what I was seeing. Faust had paid off all of my debts. Every single one. Student loans? Gone. There was even a money order for my Mom, for the full cost of the semester of community college I'd messed up. There was a Venmo receipt for the two grand in back rent I owed Simone. He'd also paid my car insurance for two full years. There was the two grand in cash I'd left in my (presumably destroyed) locker earlier tonight. Then, an iPhone slid out of the envelope. There was a receipt taped to the back. He'd paid for the phone and three years of service.

I closed my eyes and projectile cried for a minute. Seriously. Tears shot straight out of my eyeballs at ninety-degree angles. This wasn't a cheek-dribbling whimper. These were straight-up bullet tears. I was debt free. I had a working, insured car. I had money and a phone. I was FREEEEEEEEEE!

A warm feeling simmered up and filled me. For the first time in a long time, I felt relieved, like my life was finally on an upswing. I'd made it. I did it! Everything was going to be okay for once. I had a clean slate. I could start making a life. I could only go up from here.

"I'm so happy," I whimpered. It wasn't particularly manly, but dude, debt free! "No more Demon Mart, no more gate, no more giant spiders. I'm outta here. I quit!"

Eight ball's triangle turned. "Uh, you can't quit."

"Oh yes, I can, and I am. Effective right now."

"Nope. Sorry," eight ball said. "You made a deal with God."

"What?"

"You said, and I quote: 'Jesus, if you're listening. If you get me through this, I promise I will get my life together. I'll do whatever you ask, whatever it takes. Pinkie swear.'"

"Yeah? So?"

"Well, the G-man was listening, and he says he wants you to keep working here. That's what he's asking you to do. I thought you knew. You didn't get His text? I can forward you my copy if you want."

"What? Hell no! I'm out. I quit. It's over."

"No, it isn't. God answered the prayer, now you have to pay up. That's how it works."

"No, it doesn't. Prayers are wishes, not legally binding contracts. Everyone knows that."

"Uh, no. They're binding agreements. Trust me," eight ball said. "And you pinkie swore. That's serious business."

"You're full of crap. That's not true." I admit I was whine-arguing, my frustration amplified by emotional rawness and sheer exhaustion. And, you know, I didn't want a kids' toy to steal this moment of unfettered joy from me. I didn't get a lot of joy, overall.

"Which one of us works in heaven? Oh, yeah. That would be me," angel eight ball said. "Deal's a deal. He could have let the spider eat you, you know."

"Shut up," I said.

"I don't make the rules. But trust me, you better keep your promise," he said. "Nothing good happens to people who renege on deals with God. Or the devil, just FYI. And don't forget you promised you'd do cardio, too."

I was contemplating kicking the angel eight ball clean across the parking lot when Kevin, now about the size of a house cat, scrambled outside. "Heads up, kid. The cleaning crew's here, so you need to skedaddle. You don't want to be anywhere near 'em when they're eating. They're like sharks. They kick into full feeding frenzy mode real fast. Plus, as fat and juicy as you are, you sticking around would be like waving prime rib in front of a camp of rabid hobos."

"What?" My head was still reeling from the stupid eight ball, so nothing Kevin said really computed. "Cleaning crew? Eating?"

"Aw, crap. Here they come." Kevin pointed out at the lot. "Head home now, kid."

A small crowd had gathered under the neon sign. Not a crowd so much as a group. A dozen men in matching tan coveralls, wearing the same weird dog collar and dark sunglasses that Chef always wore, were ambling slowly toward the front door. They moved together like a poorly managed herd. Some shuffled. Others had their arms out, reaching. Every one of them moaned.

Uuuuuuhhhhhh. Uuuuuuuhhhh. Aaaaaaaaaaaahh. Uuuuuuuhhhhhh. Aaaaaaaaaaaaaahh.

This was the cleaning crew? Why was Kevin so worried about what they were going to eat?

Don't answer that. Deep down, I already knew. I just didn't like the answer. The moans. The slow, stiff walk. *No. No way.* This couldn't be happening. The sublime joy of being debt free dissipated. My legs turned to jelly. My mind reeled.

"They're—? And, Chef. He's a—"

No, they couldn't be. They didn't exist. They weren't real. That was fiction, all made up.

"Yeah. Yeah. They're all zombies, kid." Kevin shrugged. "You still haven't read your employee manual, have you?"

The End

Thank you so so much for reading 24/7 Demon Mart.
If you liked this book, check out the rest of the series.
Monster Burger: 24/7 Demon Mart 2
Hell for the Holidays: The Christmas Special

Visit www.dmguay.com or follow me on Bookbub if you'd like to be alerted when new books in this series are released!

BOOK SAUSAGE

Here we are again at the end of another book, and finally, the fun part. It's book sausage time! This is where I pull back the curtain so you can see how I killed, chopped, molded, and stuffed all of my embarrassing/ funny/ sad/ romantic/ <insert chosen emotion here> life tidbits into the proverbial sausage casing to make the book you hold in your hands right now.

So let's pull this Band-Aid off, shall we?

Cue the misty smoke and the soft-focus lens while I flashback to the summer of 1981. My sister and I had just watched the Salem's Lot television miniseries with our mom. I was six years old, and yes, probably too young to handle reruns of a legit scary vampire television series. The sun had just set. My sister turned out the light. Our bedroom plunged into darkness. Suddenly, we hear a noise. Something is scratching at the window. Then, we hear a voice. A whisper. "Open the window." Scratch. Scratch. "Open the window."

My sister hops into my bed. We hold on to each other, terrified. Scratch. Scratch. "Open the window."

I'm nearly pooping my pants at this point because this had totally just happened in Salem's Lot. You know that scene when Mark Petrie's best friend Danny Glick, who'd been murdered in the woods, returned from the dead as a vampire and wanted to eat him? A face comes into view in the darkness. My sister and I scream. "AAAAAAHHH!"

That's when the vampire outside our window began to laugh hysterically. It was my Mom. Scaring us out of our minds, because she thought it was hilarious. (She still does, FYI.)

And that, my friends, is the moment I understood the power of horror fiction, and I became a true fan. Now, before you dis my Mom, please know that she is the sweetest lady on two legs, a mild-mannered (now retired) Catholic school teacher who spends her days playing pickleball and bringing meals to friends with cancer. She also happens to be the person who took me to the movies to see The Thing, Fright Night, Creepshow, Poltergeist, Pet Sematary, Return of the Living Dead, The Fog, Nightmare on Elm Street, Halloween...The list goes on. In true 1970s parent style, she didn't think twice about watching R-rated horror movies with her kids, because that's what she liked, and you share what you like with your children. (Thankfully, I was too young for the theater when The Exorcist came out. My sister's still traumatized.)

Without my Mom, this book wouldn't exist because the 24/7 Demon Mart series is an homage to my lifelong love of horror movies and novels. (Stephen King was the only fiction on the bookshelf at our house in the 1980s. Thanks, Mom.) This book, in particular, is inspired by one of my family's all-time favorites: Evil Dead 2. Like DeeDee, I have watched that movie at least a hundred times, and was totally amped when Ash Vs Evil Dead hit Starz. Yes, I DO believe Bruce Campbell is a national treasure!

Evil Dead fans probably noticed the tributes to the series included in this book. Henrietta Getley, the elderly oracle, is named after Henrietta, the basement hag in Evil Dead 2. Her last name is stolen from Ed Getley, who is the blond guy with the epic mullet (and Annie's boyfriend) in that same film. He becomes a hair-eating deadite. Of course, DeeDee's "Hail to the carbs" salute is a nod to Bruce Campbell's epic line in Army of Darkness. Do I even have to say it? Yes, I do. "Hail to the king, baby."

Okay, before you think this is all one hundred percent Evil Dead, don't forget there are plenty of Lovecraftian hell beasties trying to take over the world here. And this book is definitely inspired by all of those Lovecraft critters I have encountered on the written page and on screens large and small. In obvious places (Yes, I tried to play the Call of Cthulhu video game. Dude. What was up with that?) like from Lovecraft novels directly, and honestly, from the many B-grade movies, including Stuart Gordon movies Reanimator and From Beyond. (I met Gordon once when he was a guest at a 24-hour horror movie marathon in Columbus, Ohio. My movie marathon buddy Brian's claim to fame was that he stood next to Gordon as they both peed in their respective urinals in the men's room. Just putting that out there.)

Now you're probably asking, "Okay, I get the horror part,

but why a convenience store? Why the beer cave?"

Because it's hilarious. Duh. And because I'm an alcoholic who buys a lot of beer at corner stores. Just kidding. (Okay. Busted. I'm *kind of* kidding.) The truth is that I worked the graveyard shift at a convenience store in Portland, Oregon, for six months in the mid-1990s. That experience was ripe for storytelling. The truth of that job was almost as strange as the fiction.

I was young and very very broke, and naive enough to think nothing bad could possibly happen to a 19-year-old girl working alone all night in a corner store filled with beer, smokes and cash. When I took the job, my district manager—who looked, no coincidence, like Ricky the day manager, who yes, if you must know, is the spitting image of Ricky Smith in Better Off Dead—said flat out: "Are you sure you want to do this? Everything bad you've ever heard about working in a convenience store is true."

Um. Yeah. And I still took the job. Maybe it was the extra 25 cents an hour over minimum wage the company gave me as "hazard pay." Oh, I remember. I took the job because I was so so so so broke.

While no actual demons, succubus, or hell beasts ever did step out of my beer cave, something about the store, glowing neon in the night, lured in an odd assortment of humans. Some odd in a delightful way, others, not so much.

Bob the Doughnut Guy was one of the good ones, and yes he was a real guy. Named Bob, with the same physical description. He delivered doughnuts to my store every morning around five a.m. He always stayed to chat, and he became my first friend in Oregon. He was like a dad to me, inviting me over for cookouts with his family and helping me fix my car, at a time when I was young, broke and very far from home. I don't know if he's still alive, but if you're out there dude, thanks a lot.

Lottery Larry, who I will manage to sneak into this series at some point, came in every night as well. He was a shy, middle-aged hermit who'd come in for an hour every evening to chat while he blew through about fifty bucks in scratch-off lottery tickets. I think he hung around for the company because he sure wasn't winning all of his money back. I'm pretty sure I was the only other human he saw regularly.

I met some nice people at that job, but don't be fooled. It wasn't all Top Ramen and roses. Yes, I was robbed at gunpoint. But I have to give my robber some props: He had good manners.

As I emptied the register, he said, "I'm sorry about this. I'm having a rough time." Sure, he was pointing a gun at me, but that guy still should win the award for most polite armed robber. (Note to all you robbers out there: The employee manual—yes, I did read mine—says we have to give you the money if you ask for it, so you don't need the gun. Leave the weapon at home and save us all some stress, okay?) Interesting tidbit: I've only had a gun pulled on me twice in my life, and strangely, both times, the perp apologized. Weird, right?

Another one of my regulars was a gruff elderly man with nipple-high polyester pants, orthopedic shoes and a cane who came in around midnight every night to peruse the rack of porno mags. Unfortunately for me, our rack was located behind the counter, so I had to stand there and hand the magazines to customers. This guy, well, he magically always wanted one off the bottom shelf, so I had to bend over to get them. Ahem. Yeah. You see where I'm going with this, right? He bought a magazine every fourth night, maybe, but he sure did make me bend over a lot. He always wanted the ones on the bottom, you feel me? That man, with his three-inch-thick coke-bottle glasses, didn't even try to hide his prurient interest. He looked at my thighs like they were Slim Jims, and he hadn't eaten for a week. Leg Show was his favorite, by the way. I'm five feet nine. Maybe I was his own, personal free-of-charge leg-show.

He wasn't the only customer who viewed me as a corner store sex goddess, guardian of the Natural Lite beer cases, waiting in the glow of the fluorescent-white lights for the right knight to ravage me.

One night, I was slipping the 40s into the chutes, loading up the reach-in beer cooler, when the phone rang. I answered. The man on the other end was a regular customer. He sounded desperate and being naive and young, I was worried about him. We had what seemed to be a normal conversation—until he told me he had been masturbating the entire time we'd been on the phone. Sigh. I hung up on him, spurning his advances. Duh. Come on, boys, this is not how you woo a lady. Read the room. He started coming by the shop, "hanging out" when I was alone in the middle of the night. He asked me out, many times. I told him no. The situation dialed up to eleven when his mother found out. Her intervention didn't quite go the way any of us expected. She started coming into the store every night during my shift to berate me loudly in front of customers, yelling that I "must be a lesbian because I wouldn't date her son." Her son the phone masturbator. Her son the stalker. Who somehow thought he had a romantic claim on me because he'd come in to buy Olde English 40s three times a week. Neither of them would stop. They did this to me every single night until I quit and moved nearly three thousand miles away to New Orleans. And why yes, if you must know I actually attended the sold-out WWF show in New Orleans in March of 1999. I was ringside, and rumor is you can see me and my "Hey Rock, Cook This" (with an arrow pointing at me) sign in the broadcast.

But, by far the most intense interaction was a man who came in late one night saying he wanted to kill himself, and that I needed to talk him out of it. He was hysterical, clearly having some sort of manic episode. I honestly didn't know what to do. He was visibly unstable, acting erratically, and I was alone with him. The street and sidewalk outside were empty, deserted. It was three a.m. I called my manager; he called the police. When the cruiser pulled up in the parking lot, the guy grabbed a spork out of the relish dish by the hot dog station, put it to his wrist and threatened to kill himself, right then, with a spork. The police calmed him down and drove him home. The next night, those same cops came in for sodas and told me it wasn't the first time they'd intervened. Apparently, he'd once been found in public in only his undies, with a suicide note pinned to the front of his briefs. Dude. Poor guy! If he's still out there, I hope he got the help he needed.

What's my point? Who knows? Maybe the actual humans low-paid service workers deal with at three a.m. are just as off-putting as mystery demons with ostrich legs, snake dudes in trench coats or Morty the smarmy succubus. Maybe, sometimes, you are so broke and so desperate that you're willing to guard a hell gate. I know the $4.50 an hour I made was SO TOTALLY worth putting up with all of this. I was a valued, highly trained professional earning big bucks to man the phone sex line, the suicide prevention hotline, and restock the beer all at once. (Ha.)

Seriously. This is why I'm always nice to people working retail and in restaurants, even if they're grumpy. Because until you've been in the trenches, you have NO IDEA what kind of crazy they've dealt with before you even stepped in the door.

So this is where I will leave you this time. Thank you so much for reading. More books in the 24/7 Demon Mart series are coming, including Monster Burger, which will be an homage to all the zombie fiction I have known and loved. (Shaun of the Dead, anyone? Anyone?)

But my one final gift for you is this: My Mom's, aka Lloyd's Mom's, cheesy potato recipe. Now, bear I mind it's my great grandma's recipe, ergo it's slim on particulars. Back in the day, people knew how to cook so they didn't feel the need to write every single little thing down. But, give it a try. It really is Midwestern Mom five-star cuisine!

Epic Cheesy Potatoes Recipe

Peel potatoes and slice very thinly.
(We use the slicing side of a grater.)
In a shallow baking dish, place one layer of potatoes.
Cover with sliced onion, American cheese slices, salt and pepper.
Repeat layers of potatoes, onion, and cheese, until the dish is
nearly filled.
Add milk, filling this dish to about ¼ inch deep.
Microwave, uncovered, until finished cheese is melted and potatoes are cooked through. (This takes a while. I usually cook in five minute increments. Check doneness, and then cook more if needed.)

WHO THE HECK IS DM GUAY?

   D. M. Guay writes about the intersection of real life with the supernatural. She's an award-winning journalist living in Ohio, a hobby urban farmer (you can't beat her beets!), a painter, and a retired roller derby player. Her favorite things—besides books— are tiki bars, liquid eyeliner, the 1968 Camaro, 24-hour horror movie festivals, art by Picasso, rock concerts, and most of all, people who make art, despite adversity, no matter what life throws at them.

Half the profits from her annual book sales go to research for kidney cancer treatments and cures. She has stage 4 kidney cancer and is still alive and kicking eighteen months *after* her oncologist said she would be dead. Thanks for reading. Visit her at www.dmguay.com, follow her on Bookbub, or visit her at twitter.com/dmguay.

Made in the USA
Monee, IL
23 January 2022

89686434R00125